D1014364

Praise for *Jesusgate*...

"Take modern criminal investigators, send them back in time to Jesus'
day, have them investigate the death of Jesus — and you have a pretty
good idea how interesting *Jesusgate* by Grayson Warren Brown can be.
It is a fascinating and exciting way to retell the account of Jesus' last
days. I know the readers will enjoy it. Well done!"

—JOSEPH GIRZONE, author of the *Joshua* books

"The Jesus in this book is not the Jesus of dull Sunday homilies or dry
theological tracts, but a vital, real, and very powerful presence.'

—ANDREW M. GREELEY, author of *White Smoke*

JESUSGATE

JESUSGATE

GRAYSON WARREN BROWN

Candleflame
An Imprint of OCP Publications
Portland, Oregon

Dedicated to
Pauline Brown
1913-1996

ISBN 1-57992-037-3

© 1997 Grayson Warren Brown
Candleflame
An Imprint of OCP Publications
5536 N.E. Hassalo
Portland, OR 97213
Phone: 800-LITURGY (548-8749)
Email: liturgy@ocp.org
Web site: www.ocp.org

All rights reserved
Printed in the United States of America

Library of Congress Cataloging-in-Publication Data

Brown, Grayson Warren.
    Jesusgate / Grayson Warren Brown.
        p. cm.
    ISBN 1-57992-037-3 (pbk.)
        1. Jesus Christ—Crucifixion—Fiction. 2. Bible. N.T. Gospels—History of
Biblical events—Fiction. 3. Television broadcasting of news—Fiction. I. Title.

PS3552.R685517 J4 2000
813'.54—dc21   00-044461

Cover design: Lundgren Graphics, Ltd. / Cover art: Larry Lurin, Inc.

– PREFACE –

Jesusgate is a modern fable centering on the crucifixion of Jesus and the people involved in sorting out how and why it happened. In the story two periods of time coexist in one dimension.

In this imaginary world, there are modern inventions such as jet planes and television as well as Roman soldiers who carry swords and ride on horseback. Hopefully, part of the enjoyment in reading this book will be the constant travel between the world we know and the world of antiquity.

The book has three main characters, two fictional and one from history. One of the fictional characters is Marcus, a Roman soldier. The Roman army in this story has been made over to somewhat resemble a modern police force. This portrayal is not without some foundation: Rome, after all, did in part play the role of a police force in the Middle East during the time of Jesus. Still, readers will notice somewhat modern investigation techniques and fictional departments such as the "investigations unit" that would have been unheard of during the time of Christ. The second fictional character is a woman reporter named Gerry Simmons. She is a compilation of many sharp and gutsy investigative reporters I have read about or seen on TV over the years. Lucius Sejanus, the third main character, did in fact exist during the time of Christ and was head of the heralded Praetorian Guard. Everything I read about him suggested that he was indeed a man to be reckoned with; I have, however, elevated his legendary demeanor even a step higher and given him an almost "Darth Vader–like" quality. I might add that his relationship in this novel to the infamous governor of Judea is based on historical fact.

I should note that my research revealed an unexpected bit of information centering on a possible "political affiliation" of Judas. This historical hypothesis came from several historians whose work I studied. However, the conclusions drawn from this possible association in the story are entirely my own.

This is a story not about the life and ministry of Jesus per se but rather about how people, both then and now, might find themselves suddenly and quite unexpectedly caught up in events surrounding the life and death of a highly charismatic and controversial figure. It is important to remember that people in Jesus' day saw him in different ways: some believed him to be merely a good rabbi; others believed he was a rabble-rouser and troublemaker; still others believed he was the "one who was to come," the savior of the world. Even the Gospels clearly state that people had at times quite varying opinions about who Jesus was during his life on this earth (Matthew 16). Given these historical complexities, I felt it was essential to go beyond simply villainizing those characters in scripture who in some way played a role in the ultimate demise of Jesus. I have tried instead to reveal what might have been their motives and points of view. That is not to suggest in any way that what they ultimately did was right, but it is important for us to see that given certain circumstances, almost anyone, if not careful, can find themselves caught up in a series of events that can produce disastrous results. Not all heinous social acts, after all, are caused by people who set out to do public harm; many such acts are caused by people who believe they are acting for the public good.

When most people study the events surrounding the crucifixion of Jesus, they are amazed to discover just how familiar the arguments for his death still sound today. The politics and the apprehension about the message as well as the messenger all ring a strangely familiar bell. This happens because the ingredients that are needed to build a case against men and women like Jesus are the same today as they were then, and people of Jesus' persuasion often find themselves up on crosses or on gallows or at the end of an assassin's bullet. Perhaps it is because men and women like Jesus often show the world by their very presence just how selfish and intolerant the world can be. They present a challenge that forces us to either change our lives or silence the one who would seek our repentance.

I wish to acknowledge and sincerely thank by good friend Dr. Margaret Ann Roman, professor of English Literature at the College of St. Elizabeth in Morristown, New Jersey, for her help in editing this project.

– CHAPTER ONE –

Geraldine Simmons had finally come back home to New York after ten years as a Middle East correspondent for a local TV network. She had covered everything from local wars to Passover festivals. She had come to know priests, politicians, revolutionaries, and prophets, and she had been intimidated by none of them.

Geraldine, or Gerry as everyone called her, had been the youngest female correspondent ever assigned to the Middle East. Tall, athletic, and strikingly beautiful, she had worked hard in her early days to overcome her good looks that, back then, she considered more of a hindrance to being taken seriously as a newswoman. She would often wear her hair in a loose, unglamorous way and would never put on any more makeup than required by the camera. Still it made little difference: her dark brown eyes and tall slender figure often broke through all attempts at disguise. She knew early on that the only way she would ever live down her beauty was to become one hell of a reporter. Now at age forty-seven, and with a whole slew of journalistic awards to her credit, she felt much more comfortable with herself and, in fact, was even a bit pleased that she could still, without even trying, make men twenty years her junior look twice in her direction. When she was first given the assignment, few in the news bureau thought she would last. The Middle East, they had said, often within earshot of her, was no place for such a young, inexperienced reporter, especially a woman. But Gerry never doubted for a moment that the Middle East was one of the hotbeds of controversies in the world, and she wanted from her first days at the news station to go there.

This had nothing to do with wanting to be the first woman reporter in the region. Gerry Simmons was used to firsts and therefore received little gratification these days from being called a pioneer. She had been, after all, first in her class all through college, graduating with a degree in both journalism and political science. She was the youngest woman ever to land a position as a TV news reporter. (She also was doubtless the only person ever to turn down a chance to work at a major network right out of college, preferring instead to work for a more independent cable news organization.) She was also the first woman to report from the front line of a battlefield. And the biggest "first" — of which she was reminded constantly in the early days — was that she was the first black American woman to accomplish all of these things. No, her desire to go to the Middle East was not sparked by any craving to be the "first" anything there; it was because she wanted to work as a reporter in what she believed was one of the last places on earth that was still filled with intrigue, not just politics.

At this moment, however, she was staring at the ceiling of her New York apartment, still trying to adjust to being back on daylight savings time. She found herself feeling a little sorry for herself being back in the city. It was hard after ten years to get the taste of the Middle East out of her mouth. Some of her colleagues had trouble understanding her apparent lack of joy over finally coming home. "That's because they've gone soft and don't understand what real action-reporting is all about," she thought.

She believed few people outside the Middle East had any idea of how complicated and, from her point of view, how wonderful the region was. It had amazed her that the place, with all of its complicated diversities, simply never blew itself to pieces. Yet it didn't. Instead it seemed to survive despite itself. She gave much of the credit for this to the presence of the Roman armies stationed throughout the Middle East. "Say what you will about the empire," she thought, "if it weren't for it, the Middle East would have self-destructed years ago."

Of course, she had learned never to say that around the countless friends she had made while living in Judea. Whenever that thought did accidentally slip from her mouth, she was passionately reminded that the "God of Israel" had kept the Jews alive thousands of years before Rome had ever known Israel existed. Often they would spit on the floor after saying the word "Rome" and follow with the words, "May God curse the day they stole our land!" Or something along those lines. The only people who did not vehemently protest Rome's presence, at first much to her surprise, were members of the high priesthood. Oh they too would protest Rome's presence in public, but whenever you got to know a member of the priesthood well enough to gain his trust, he would rarely ever criticize Rome's presence in private. She thought of herself as liberal-minded and philosophically disapproved of the idea of totalitarian dictatorships, but she was still convinced that Rome was the glue that kept the people of the area from destroying themselves.

"So many factions," she thought. "Scribes and Pharisees, Samaritans and Sadducees; Essenes and Zealots and the high priesthood; the Herodians, the Romans...And everybody believes that they are the ones with the only true answers to Israel's survival. And the best part of all is that everyone says he's speaking for God. Everyone that is except the Romans. They say flatly and without reservation that they are speaking for Rome. My God," she said out loud, "what a country." Then she said, "Look at me, I've been home for three days, and already I miss it so much I'm talking to myself. Palestine is a reporter's dream. In comparison, New York looks like a retirement village."

She was about to get up when the phone rang. "Gerry?" a voice said on the other end. She recognized the voice right away; it was Jim Pratt, the news director. "Hi, Jim," she said, a little surprised at hearing his voice so early in the morning.

"Gerry, I want you to get down here right away. And you'd better pack a bag just in case; I may be sending you off on an emergency assignment for a week or two."

"An assignment, where? Just in case what?" Gerry said as she sat up in her bed.

"Just in case the rumors we are hearing coming out of Jerusalem are true," said the voice on the other end of the line.

"What rumors?" Gerry said. "What's going on?"

"Gerry, as fast as you can."

Gerry heard the "click" on the other end. After staring at the receiver, she jumped to her feet and grabbed one of the suitcases she hadn't yet unpacked. Her mind was racing, retracing Jim Pratt's words and the sense of urgency in his voice. She ran downstairs, grabbed a cab, and within minutes was rushing into the TV newsroom. She dashed into Pratt's office. It was empty.

"Where's Jim?" she asked a young man standing nearby.

"He's down in the conference room."

Gerry ran down the stairs to the conference room where she saw Jim, along with the station vice-president, the station manager, and the station attorney.

"Hi, Gerry, come in and have a seat," said Jim Pratt, who then turned and finished saying something to the attorney. He turned back toward Gerry. "Gerry, you're not going to believe the bizarre story coming out of Jerusalem this morning."

"Jim," Gerry replied, "I lived there ten years, remember? Nothing is going to surprise me. Just tell me what happened."

"We just got a report that Jesus was arrested late Thursday night by members of the temple security forces, on orders from either the High Priest Caiaphas or King Herod."

Jim waited to see her reaction.

"That doesn't surprise me all that much," answered Gerry. "Jesus and the Jewish religious establishment never saw eye to eye. It was only a matter of time before they hauled him in before the Sanhedrin. I can't imagine much can come from it, however. I've seen Jesus on several occasions. He's pretty smart. I don't believe there is a scribe living that can successfully prosecute him, at least not using the Torah. Besides, even if they do put him in jail, he would become such a martyr living in a jail cell that they would have to let him out, just to keep his fame from getting any wider than it already is. In fact, I got the impression just before I left Judea that his mission, or whatever it is, was beginning to wane a bit in popularity, despite his charisma. Jesus didn't pan out to be the type of messiah many of those folks had been looking for, so putting him in prison could be a boost for his appeal. Strange they would pull this stunt during their Passover holidays. Do we have any more information, such as where he is being held, or what the official charges are?"

"We haven't been able to get any more information officially. The governor's office, the king's representatives, the temple's people are all acting as though they know nothing about it. Everyone we have spoken to so far has referred us to somebody else. That tells you right away that something's going on. Any time folks over there start acting as though they have no idea what's going on, something big is going on. But some of the unofficial stuff is getting pretty intense, including one rumor that he was killed in an armed scuffle with the security force. That rumor is very sketchy, however, and we haven't been able to confirm any of this. We do know a man was injured at the site of the arrest, but he hasn't been I.D.'d and we have no further details. We need some answers, Gerry, and even though you're over here now, it would seem to us that you might be the best person to coordinate, and if necessary, cover this story."

Gerry looked up with surprise. "Me?" she said. "I just got back. Don't get me wrong, Jim, you know how much I love the place and would jump at a chance to go back and cover this. But what about Bob Smith? He's bureau chief over there. Can't he handle this? Where's Mary Beth? I thought she was scheduled to take my place already? She's the best Middle Eastern correspondent you have; that is, of course, next to me," she added with a grin. "She could handle the ins and outs of whatever breaks over there."

Jim answered with just the slightest hint of impatience in his voice: "Smitty left Wednesday morning for vacation. He's on some kind of expedition in the Himalayas or something, and Beth is in Egypt covering the conference between Rome and the Arab kings. She and I talked this morning, and we both agreed that if this story pans out in the direction it might be headed, it would be better for her to stay there and monitor the reactions of the conference participants, and for us to send you to Judea. I mean, next to Smitty, you have more experience in the region than anyone. I'm sure by now you know who to call over there to get some straight answers. Remember, there's an outside chance that Jesus may have bought the farm over there. If that's the case, we need to get on top of this fast."

"You mean Jesus might actually be dead, and nobody has made any statements to the press? Nobody?"

"So far, Gerry, you know as much as we know. Now personally, I don't believe he's dead. Maybe the reason for the silent treatment is because one of the guards reportedly did get a little rough when they arrested him. Perhaps he was injured, and nobody wants to admit they bungled the arrest. Maybe it was some sort of assassination plot that got botched. Nevertheless, I want you to get on the phone and start calling your old contacts in Judea. By now the networks are probably getting wind of the story as well, so we better get on the stick. Sorry you didn't quite get your well-deserved time off, but we need you, and I knew you wouldn't have wanted to miss any of this."

"I'll get right on it, Jim. And by the way, I agree with you. They wouldn't be dumb enough to assassinate Jesus, particularly at this time of year. I'll make some phone calls and see what I can find out." Gerry got up from the table and started toward the conference room door.

"By the way," said Jim, "I took the liberty of making a reservation for you. Like I said, just in case. The flight's the 11:26 from JFK."

Gerry smiled and headed for the door when the phone in the conference room rang. Jim put up his hand signaling for Gerry to wait a minute while he spoke on the phone.

"What!" he said into the phone. "What! They did what?" Without being asked, Gerry came back into the room and sat down. "Has this been verified?" he asked. Then Jim listened for a long time as though someone was telling him a lot of information. He began taking notes on a notepad near by. "I'll be damned," she heard Jim say. "OK, I'm going to send Gerry Simmons over there right away. I want her on top of this from the beginning. In the meantime, verify as much as possible, and get ready to make preparations to break into programming. Find out if there are local representatives of any of these factions stationed here in New York, and get me the name of the Roman ambassador. I'll be up in a minute. Oh, Ted, pull up the obit files of Jesus and have them updated, ASAP."

Jim hung up the phone. He turned to Gerry and said, "The news is even more bizarre than we imagined. Jesus is in fact dead. But he wasn't assassinated. He was executed by the Roman government. He was arrested late last night; he was tried last night by the Sanhedrin; and somehow he was subsequently tried by the Roman authorities as well, convicted, sentenced, and crucified all in a matter of hours. He died three o'clock Judea time, around eight in the morning our time."

Gerry's first reaction was anger, not at Jesus' death as much as at the absurdity of such a story being true. "Jim," she said with great restraint, "are you sure of your sources? Because, frankly, this seems impossible to me."

"Gerry, it's coming over the wires now. Rome released an official statement two minutes ago." Jim handed her the notepad. On it were written the words: "Jesus of Nazareth was tried and convicted of sedition against the state and was executed in accordance with Roman law. The charges were brought against him by the Sanhedrin and other members of the Jewish state."

"But that's impossible," Gerry said. "First of all, if this happened the way you said it did, then it would have been completely illegal. Even if the Sanhedrin wanted to get Rome to somehow carry out a capital execution, it's illegal for someone to be charged and tried on a capital offense at night, according to Jewish law. Second, what could they charge him with? It would have had to be something religious. The most serious charge they could have leveled at him was perhaps blasphemy, but they could never make that stick with a folk hero like Jesus. Not and get away with it. I'm telling you, this guy knew the ins and outs of Jewish law better than anybody I ever saw, including the priests. Besides, even if they did get him on a blasphemy charge, Rome would never execute him on a Jewish religious matter.

You know as well as I do, Rome could care less about any of that stuff. I know the new governor over there is not the most stable person on the planet, but he would never let himself get caught up in doing the dirty work for the Sanhedrin."

"Gerry, didn't you read what I wrote? He was charged with sedition, you know, trying to overthrow the government of Rome. You say you've heard him speak. Did he ever openly preach revolution?"

"Never. The only idea that could be possibly stretched into revolutionary talk was this whole business about one's ultimate patriotic loyalty being to the kingdom of God and not the kingdom of Rome or Herod. But that whole concept comes right out of their religious culture. Everybody over there in one way or another has this kingdom stuff drilled into them from the day they are born, and Jesus was always very cagey on the subject. If the Sanhedrin charged everybody who believed in the kingdom of God in one form or another with sedition, everyone over there would end up in prison, including most of their long dead prophets. No," Gerry said shaking her head, "this isn't right. There's a lot more to this than this official nonsense is telling us."

Gerry looked up and saw the look of impatience on Jim's face. Gerry laughed, got up, and headed for the door. "I know, I know," she said, "so what the hell am I sitting here yappin' at you for? I'll make some phone calls and then get ready and make my flight. If I hear anything more before I leave for Judea, I'll let you know."

As Gerry headed for the stairs, she suddenly realized she didn't even have a desk to sit at in the reporters' area. When she got to the top of the stairs, she was met by a young man who informed her that Mr. Pratt just phoned him with instructions. "Ms. Simmons? Please follow me." He was obviously excited and spoke again: "Boy, that's some story about Jesus. Will you be going over there to cover it, Ms. Simmons?"

"Yes, I'll be leaving in a few hours, and please call me Gerry."

He led Gerry to an empty desk and pulled out the chair for her. She gave him a perfunctory smile and went to work: she called her old friend David Ben Leven, editor of the local Judean newspaper, the *Judean Daily*. A woman answered the phone.

"Mr. Leven, please." Gerry said, "This is Gerry Simmons calling."

"Yes, Ms. Simmons, Mr. Leven is expecting your call."

Gerry chewed the end of a pen, waiting, impatient. After a short while, David Leven picked up the phone.

"Gerry, he said with a mock sound of surprise, how are you? Are you enjoying your home back in New York? Tell me, have you seen any new plays on Broadway? How's the weather back there?"

"All right David, cut the crap. What the hell is going on back there? Have the Romans gone nuts or something? Who's behind this madness? Why, on earth, if the priesthood wanted to get rid of Jesus, would they have him crucified in broad daylight?"

"Gerry, I wonder how you could have lived with us for so long and still not know us. Obviously whoever was behind this, and you used the right word when you called it madness, not only wanted him dead but wanted him discredited as well. If he were murdered in his sleep, who knows what kind of martyr he might have ended up? Who knows who might have been blamed? Whoever engineered this wanted Jesus killed as a common criminal by Rome — enemies of the Jewish people anyway — turning the whole matter into a sticky PR problem, but one that will eventually go away. The real question seems to be: Who was behind this, and how did they get Rome to play into their hands? Central Rome is not going to like this. The empire is going to have a hard time explaining how they became the instrument of Jesus' death."

"Has any more news come either out of Roman circles or from the priesthood?" Gerry asked.

"Well, there were reports that Jesus was not only crucified but suffered from an unusual amount of brutality at the hands of the Roman police. The Romans would want to distance themselves from any sort of scandal like that right away. A news conference has been scheduled for tomorrow morning at the Roman police headquarters for the province of Judea, where, I would venture to guess, they will deny everything and once again tell everyone how professionally they all acted. I'm sure you can guess who will be doing that."

"Marcus?" asked Gerry.

"Of course," said David. "Marcus is the brightest, most articulate commander they have over here. Who else could they give this to, a creature like Vergas? The funny thing about it, though, is that Marcus wasn't even here at the time. He was in Jericho on leave."

"I'll bet they called him back in record time," said Gerry. "I'm sure he'll do a good job. There's nobody who can tiptoe around the truth as nimbly as Marcus."

"I'll bet this sort of makes you miss the old place doesn't it? Too bad you're not over here to cover one of the biggest stories to hit Judea in years. I guess you'll just have to read about it in your local news."

Gerry thought, "At last I finally got one over on my old pal. Won't he be surprised when I show up in Judea." "David," Gerry said, but she was surprised to hear the voice of David's secretary on the other end of the phone. "Mr. Leven wanted me to ask you how many nights you would be staying at the Judea Inn, and if you will be coming in on the 11:26 flight from New York, or the 1:15 from Newark?"

Gerry laughed and shook her head. "I knew he had great intuitive insight as a journalist," she thought, "but how on earth did he ever figure I would be the one coming over to cover this, having just left the place a few days ago? I guess he put two and two together and as usual came up with an answer no one else would have suspected." It would be days before David admitted to her that he had just happened to call Jim Pratt looking for her the moment she'd left the conference room. Jim of course had told him of her impending arrival. "It never hurts to keep your reputation as a genius alive and well," David chuckled to himself.

"Tell Mr. Leven I'll be arriving on the 11:26, and ask him if he would be so kind as to book me for five nights at the hotel. Tell him I would be most honored if he might find it in his heart to meet me at the airport. And tell him also to have a full report ready for me when I arrive." The woman on the other end laughed and assured Gerry that Mr. Leven would be there as the plane arrived and then wished her shalom.

Gerry looked up from the desk in time to see the young man who had met her at the top of the stairs coming toward her.

"Excuse me, Ms. Simmons, but Mr. Pratt asked me to give you these." The young man handed Gerry an envelope containing one open round-trip ticket to Judea, along with some expense vouchers and petty cash. "Please sign this before you go so that Mr. Pratt knows that I didn't pocket the money myself," the young man said with a smile. "Mr. Pratt also said, and I quote, 'Get going,' unquote."

Gerry thanked the young man and headed toward the elevators. She knew for sure that by the time she reached Judea much more of the story would have unfolded. She knew that the news conference with the police would be the first of many. What would the governor's office have to say? They would have to explain why they crucified Jesus. And how about the Sanhedrin? Would one of the scribes be willing to talk on camera as to why they charged Jesus with a crime like sedition against the empire? Since when did they care about the overthrow of Roman authority? Would any of Jesus' fellow "revolutionaries" be holding news conferences as well? She suddenly began once again to feel that Middle Eastern tension surging through her.

Gerry pushed the elevator button and looked at her watch for the time. "Got about two and a half hours," she said. "That's not a lot of time." While waiting for the elevator, she suddenly found herself feeling a touch of sadness. For the first time she seemed to realize that a man she had come to admire for his outspoken philosophies on matters of justice for the little guy, and love for all, including his enemies, was actually dead. "They all end up this way, don't they?" she said to herself. "All the Martins and Malcolms and Gandhis; all the wild-eyed idealists who try to change an unchanging world. *Les Miserables* once again. This time in Judea." But just at that moment she heard the elevator door open up, and in a flash she was back to her old self. "Here we go," she said as she hailed a taxi, and sped off to Judea.

The normally half-empty 11:26 flight from New York to Judea was packed, mostly with reporters from New York. A short while ago Gerry lay pining away on her bed, thinking about how much she was going to miss the Middle East, and a few hours later here she was on a plane heading toward Judea. She had to fight a wicked temptation to thank the Sanhedrin for their apparent lack of sanity. Through most of the flight, Gerry was kept awake by the reporters' chatter; occasionally she fell asleep, only to be awakened in a half-dream state to hear the words "Jesus," "Rome," and "dead" hanging in the air. Gerry spoke to many of her colleagues, but if anyone knew any more than she did, no one was volunteering any new information.

When they reached Jerusalem at 5:46 A.M., she got off the plane with her hand-held luggage, walked through the front doors of the airport into the street, and saw David Ben Leven, the crusty, legendary editor in chief of the *Judean Daily*, sitting on his small, crumpled car reading a newspaper, the sun just coming up behind him. David was a small, portly grandfather figure who looked at first glance as if he would be more suited to cobbling shoes than being a newsman. With his horn-rimmed glasses that always looked as though they needed cleaning, to his rumpled shirt and tie, David looked at times almost docile. It was a look he cultivated quite carefully, because underneath that rumpled exterior was one of the keenest journalistic minds in all of the Middle East.

Gerry had met David when she first arrived in the Middle East. The bureau chief who was stationed there at the time had called David and asked him if he would join them for an introductory lunch and perhaps make an assessment of this "young girl reporter" with whom New York was saddling him. They talked at lunch for hours, and when it was over, David turned to the chief and in front of Gerry said, "Bob, I wouldn't worry about being stuck with this kid if I were you. Instead, I would worry about holding on to my job. Because she's going to do great over here. In fact, she might even become bureau chief herself in a year or two. And you know what that would mean: you might have to go out and get a real job."

They had all laughed and gotten up from the table, but Gerry never forgot the way David had looked at her that day at the conclusion of the meal. It was as though he said with just a look, "Don't worry. Trust your instincts. If you do that, you'll make a hell of a reporter."

"David," Gerry called out. David waved, got up from his car, and walked briskly over to Gerry. They embraced, and then, as a father would his daughter, David kissed her on both sides of her face. He was careful not to show that kind of fatherly affection too often. He knew she enjoyed the affection, but also sensed she resented these fatherly expressions because she was always striving to be his equal as a reporter and didn't want to feel even the least bit subordinate.

"How are you, Gerry? Welcome home."

"I'm exhausted, and I've got jet lag and don't understand what the sun's doing up, but it's good to be home," said Gerry. "How are Miriam and the kids?"

"They're fine," said David, "and already they miss your visits. Sarah has gotten engaged since you left. A fine boy too. You'll have to come by and eat as soon as there's time."

"That's wonderful news. I'm glad to hear something positive has happened since my absence," said Gerry. "So tell me, what has developed since we last spoke?"

As David and Gerry sped along the narrow streets toward the Judea Inn, David proceeded to tell Gerry all he had been able to find out. It seemed that the Sanhedrin had held some sort of impromptu trial, and the chief priest himself may have acted as the principal protagonist in Jesus' conviction. David said he already had a line on someone who was at the trial and who would be willing to relay the accounts of what took place.

"Will he do it on camera?" Gerry asked.

"I don't know," David said. "He might."

Gerry asked about the twelve men who acted as Jesus' advisers and cominsters. "It seems," said David, "as though they have all gone into hiding, except for two of them."

"Which two?" asked Gerry.

"Simon the Zealot was seen heading toward the Parthian border while Judas was seen in the city at different locations. I would guess that once Simon reaches the safety of the Parthian border, we might hear some sort of political statement come from him about how oppressive regimes such as Rome always destroy the legitimate leaders of the masses. He might even call for the people to revolt. You know those folks from the Zealot party never really believed in this passive messiah-type message. It was always a mystery how someone like Simon ended up with Jesus anyway, but I would think there's a good chance he must be extremely disenchanted with the way things turned out. But then there's another school of thought that suggests that Simon could not have been more pleased."

"Why would you say that?" asked Gerry.

"Because maybe this proves once and for all that the Jesus-type of message is simply too unreal in an occupied land like Judea, or, for that matter, anywhere else in this violent world. Who knows, but if Simon was genuine, I would think he would have a hard time getting any other real revolutionaries to ever follow nonviolent, peaceful solutions again."

Gerry took a moment to ponder all she had just heard, then turned to David and asked, "Why do you think Judas didn't go into hiding with the rest of the members of Jesus' band?"

"Well, that's the funny thing," answered David. "There's a rumor going around that Jesus was turned in somehow by one of his own people. And the word on the streets is that it was Judas."

Gerry looked startled. "Judas? Why Judas? Or for that matter, why any of the men who worked so closely with him?"

"That, my friend, is what we need to find out. Who knows, this could be a rumor started by the Sanhedrin to somehow suggest that Jesus wasn't as loved as everyone thought he was."

"How has the city reacted to the news of Jesus' death? Have there been any outbreaks of violence?"

"No, not really. You know, as long as I live, I will never understand people. You know when Herod jailed John the Baptist, I expected there would be one hell of a riot in this town. So did Herod from what I understand. In fact, the only reason he didn't put him to death right away was because he was afraid of what the people would do if they found out that this man, who was supposed to mean so much to his followers, was murdered. Then when Herod got tricked into it by that little temptress Salome, he got all nervous and doubled the guard. But do you think anybody did anything? People griped, and people moaned, but when the smoke cleared, and the dust settled, they did absolutely nothing. If I had been an adviser to Herod, I would have told him not to worry; nobody cares what happens to really good people in this world. When Herod saw how easy it was to kill John, he was almost ready to get Jesus himself. In fact, he would have if Jesus hadn't gotten word and hightailed it out of Galilee.

"And now," continued David, "Jesus is dead. Murdered as sure as if someone walked up to him from behind and stuck a knife in his back. And you and me and one thousand other reporters will spend the next few days running around taking pictures and interviewing everyone we can find, and all kinds of people will talk about law and order, and either how good he was or how bad he was. But when all is said and done, Jesus will be dead; you'll be back in New York covering subway murders and parades; I'll be here writing about all the people God has appointed as spokespersons of the month; it'll be back to business as usual. People just don't care about real prophets anymore. Now, go to the temple tomorrow and tell all the men then that they should no longer wear their hats, or that the Torah should be on the left side of the room, as opposed to the front, and, I guarantee you, you'll have a riot like you've never seen. But kill a man who stands for something other than our most primal, evil, greedy instincts, and we'll all hang our heads for a while and then go on as before."

Gerry had often heard this speech before, only in different variations. Yet this time it seemed to hold more value than it had in the past. She thought she must be tired from the plane ride and knew that she wouldn't be getting any sleep before Marcus's news conference.

"David, you're getting more and more cynical in your old age. It must come from working on a newspaper for so long instead of on TV where you can get out more and see the beauty of the world."

"Yeah, right," David said with a grin. "It's always better to televise misery than just to write about it." They pulled up in front of the hotel. "By the way, your boss told me to tell you that a camera and sound crew will meet you at the hotel at eight o'clock, which is about an hour and a half from now. Why don't you go get an hour's sleep?"

"Thanks, David, but I slept on the plane, and I'm young, remember? Are you going to be able to stay awake until the news conference?"

"I'll be there. Why not? I always get joy out of seeing Commander Marcus do his act. I'll bet with all this press, he'll be magnificent."

"Now come on, David, I like Marcus," she said. "Remember, according to your own words, he's the brightest, most articulate Roman soldier over here."

"I know," said David. "That just goes to show you how bad the rest of them are."

Gerry laughed and shook her head as she got out of the car. She looked back through the window and said, "Go to bed and get some sleep. You're getting too old to be functioning on less than twelve hours."

"I'm getting too old for all of this stuff," said David as he drove away through the early morning streets.

Gerry sat in her room drinking coffee and reviewing what she'd learned from David. There was a knock on the door. "Strange," she thought, "I wasn't expecting my camera crew for another half-hour." When she opened the door, she was surprised to see David.

"Good morning," she said. "I thought you were going to take a nap?"

"I went to the office and thought I'd stop by and share some news."

"What's up?"

"Well, it seems as though this morning everybody is suddenly ready to talk. Everyone except the governor. He might have one of his flunkies read a prepared statement later on today, but everyone else seems ready to spill their guts."

"Like who?" asked Gerry.

"Well, a representative of the Pharisee council of Judea is ready to speak. Someone from the high priesthood is supposedly getting ready to make a statement. Even King Herod seems ready to speak. This could be a busy day, my friend, so drink all the coffee you can now."

Just then another knock on the door, and this time it was the camera crew. She recognized the pair as members of a local freelance video outfit that the station used on most occasions. "Hi guys," Gerry said, putting out her hand.

"Shalom, Gerry, welcome back. Kind of a short trip wasn't it?"

"It sure was. Do you guys have wheels?"

"Yes, ma'am."

"OK, let's roll."

David said he had to make a stop first and would see them at the news conference.

Gerry was one of the first to arrive at the headquarters for the Roman police force for the province of Judea. But before long the room was crowded with reporters, and someone shouted that the officers were on their way. Gerry smiled to herself and turned to David, who had just joined her in the room. "Here comes the first of many interesting pieces to the puzzle," she said.

"Yeah," said David, "and probably the first of many lies."

The official purpose of the press conference was to deal with the role the Roman army had played in the execution of Jesus. Already rumors about the so-called inappropriate behavior of some of the members of the execution detail, resulting in what some had called an unusual amount of cruelty in the execution of Jesus, had begun to surface. Perhaps of even greater interest to the public were the even more recent rumors about certain "unnatural phenomenon" at the exact moment of Jesus' death. Rumors suggesting bizarre movements in the heavens or strange earthquakes around the Jewish temple had been circulating around Judea hot and heavy.

A Roman officer with the approximate rank of a police deputy inspector entered the room. His name was Vitellius Marcus. He was accompanied by Captain Vergas, the commander in charge of all executions in the district. Three or four other soldiers of lesser rank trailed behind him. The commander sat at a table at the front of the room while the other officers stood behind him. Most of the soldiers looked somewhat annoyed at what they perceived as a lot to do about nothing, all of it brought about by the press and politics. The commander, however, appeared calm and relaxed amid the flashing cameras and pushing reporters.

Marcus looked to be only in his early forties, yet his hair was already graying. He had startlingly clear eyes that revealed intelligence and ruthlessness. His uniform was extremely neat. The other officers in the room, particularly the lower-ranking ones, looked as if their uniforms hadn't been cleaned in weeks. Most of these men were mercenaries, hired to serve in the Roman army by the Roman governor. To them, the uniform was only a set of clothes that they had to wear every day; the uniforms were just part of the job. Marcus, in contrast, was a genuine and ambitious Roman officer who had learned the importance of appearance.

While still claiming to be "just a soldier," Commander Marcus had ambitions toward higher office. And while he hated being stationed in the province of Judea, he had begun to think at long last that he was truly in the right place at the right time. He believed that the present governor was neither smart nor shrewd enough to stay in power very long. And now with this Jesus mess, he thought, perhaps the right opportunities were approaching.

He believed that if Pilate was removed, the next governor, although he would undoubtedly be picked from the ranks of the Roman politicians who clung around Caesar like leeches, would be almost forced to pick an executive staff from among the politicians and soldiers already serving in this God-forsaken place. That, he figured, would be his ticket up. With the reputation he was fast obtaining as a tough, yet smart, commander, he felt assured that under a new administration, he would soon be promoted to district commander, maybe with the rank of general. Later, he could become secretary to the governor for internal security, and finally lieutenant governor. From there, a governorship of his own was sure to follow. He only hoped it wouldn't be back in Judea.

This was by no means Marcus's first press conference. He knew some of the local newspeople quite well, but because of the international ramifications of this situation, press from all over the world were here. He made sure he knew as many reporters' names as he could. Depending on how he handled this, he might gain the attention of the higher-ups in Rome and get moved up the ladder even faster than he had dreamed. He could not believe Pilate was stupid enough to get tricked by the Jews into executing Jesus of Nazareth on trumped up charges of sedition. Did Pilate really believe that Jesus could become a threat to Rome? After all, Tiberius Caesar could have cared less whether some "half-baked prophet," as Caesar had once called Jesus, was running around proclaiming himself to be a god. Messiahs were a dime a dozen in Judea. And while this one was surely the best of the bunch as far as Marcus was concerned, in the end, even with his national fame, he was surely no real threat to the empire. No, this was a Jewish matter, Marcus thought, and should have been left to the Jews to deal with. Besides, he mused, you didn't have to be a genius to see what had happened. The jealousy between the local Jewish establishment and Jesus had been building to a head for years. And with that half-crazed crackpot Herod running around believing every day that someone was out to steal his kingdom (while at the same time being too stupid to see that Rome already had it), charging everyone with conspiracy, it was obvious that a clash and violence were approaching. But Jesus ending up dead, and at the hands of the Romans, that was a surprise.

As Marcus became aware of what he was thinking, he decided that he had better make sure his personal feelings in this matter did not come to the surface during the press conference. Especially his feelings for Herod. Marcus hated King Herod Antipas. In fact, he hated the whole Herod clan, the Herodians. He had a very personal reason for his lack of affection for the Herodians. He had lost a nephew in a senseless family scrap between Herod and the Arabian king Aretas. Herod's half-nice, Herodias, hadn't liked being married to her step-uncle, poor old Phillip, who had never gotten a kingdom of his own when the old man Herod the Great passed away. Herodias had decided to ditch Phillip and set her sights on her other step uncle, Herod Antipas. The only thing standing in her way was the daughter of King Aretas, whom Herod had just married.

Marcus never knew exactly just how she managed to pull it off, but before long Herod was divorcing the daughter of the Arab king and marrying his former sister-in-law and half-niece, Herodias. When the Arab king found out Herod had divorced his daughter, he took it very personally and sent an army to destroy Herod.

If Rome hadn't been sent in to restore order, Aretas would have taken over Herod's whole kingdom. Restoring order had been easy because they all feared the power of Rome, but in the brief police action it took to get things back in order, Michael, Marcus's nephew, was killed. It had been Michael's first action, which made it all the worse for Marcus. Michael would have become an excellent soldier, young and brave. No soldier minds dying in battle with honor, Marcus thought, but to die over the incestuous goings on of the Herods was another matter.

Still, Marcus thought as the room began to quiet down, no matter what his personal feelings were about Herod or Jesus or anyone else, he had better make sure his part in this little drama came across as both clearly nonpolitical and purely professional. He believed he had to at once distance himself from the mistakes of Pilate, while at the same time appearing loyal to both his governor and Rome. He had decided that Pilate had missed a great opportunity to show these Jews what power was really all about.

Why did he appear to waffle on his judgment and then give in under pressure? If Pilate really believed that Jesus wasn't guilty, Marcus thought, all he had to do was tell the Jews that he would not execute him and that his decision was final. Then, when Herod's stooges started stirring up the crowd, Pilate should have moved in the police and arrested them. Finally, when they threatened to go to Rome, he should have said, "Go ahead. Do you honestly believe that anyone in Rome cares what you Jews think?"

Some problem with the sound system arose, and then it turned out there weren't enough chairs for the reporters. Soldiers rushed about while Marcus continued to smile at the reporters and think through all that had happened.

Marcus had never held Pilate in great esteem. Pilate, a political appointee who got his position based more on who he knew than on what kind of leader he was, was indecisive, his policies swaying from week to week. Some believed Pilate had gotten his position simply by marrying into the royal family. His wife was the granddaughter of the late emperor Augustus, and many believed, the illegitimate daughter of Claudia, third wife of the present emperor, Tiberius. Yet those in the inner circle of power knew the real source of Pilate's ascendancy and power was his mentor, the most powerful and awesomely feared man in all of Rome, a man even the emperor held in awe. He was Lucius Aelius Sejanus, leader of the Praetorian Guard, the regiment of soldiers that guarded Rome itself.

The mere mention of the name Sejanus made soldiers stand at attention. As long as Pilate did what was right for Rome, no one in the entire empire would dare mutter a word against him. But if Pilate began to do things considered not in the best interest of Rome, Sejanus would let him swing in the wind.

Marcus remembered that Pilate had come into power with a flourish. While former governors made their headquarters at Caesarea, some fifty miles northwest on the Samaritan coast, Pilate stationed troops in the capital city of Jerusalem itself. He marched in with great fanfare ready to show the Jews the very face of Roman authority. Unfortunately, that face was the emperor's, on every banner and every Roman uniform. When the Jews saw this, they almost began a riot. Pilate had underestimated the Jews' passion in matters of religion. It seemed they really believed all these pictures of the emperor violated their commandment against idolatry. When it appeared that a revolt was about to take place, Pilate backed down. He ordered the removal of every banner with the emperor's picture on it. The army was ready to step in and crush the insurrection, but no, Pilate ordered the removal of the banners. So much for fanfare.

Pilate's explanation of his actions to his superiors did, however, make a certain amount of sense, at least to politicians and soldiers. It had to do with the dreaded Parthians. Every Roman soldier Pilate knew remembered the dark days of the Roman-Parthian wars. The Kingdom of Parthia, just east of Judea, was Rome's most deadly enemy. And every Roman soldier both feared and respected Parthia's ferocity. By now the history and tactics of the Roman-Parthian battle were taught at the academy as the worst military defeat in Roman history, even though it took place over fifty years earlier. Seven full Roman legions were destroyed by the Parthians in that war. And the Parthians remained the only people Rome had not dominated. Everyone, including the Parthians, believed that one day Rome would avenge that famous loss, but only when the time was right.

Pilate, as a newly appointed governor, believed that if the Jews revolted on religious grounds (the only grounds that could fully fire their passion), then they might become desperate enough to call in their neighbors, the Parthians. With the people of Judea on their side, Parthia might decide to strike first and end the possibility of the often-talked-about Roman revenge. Pilate, in his first major assignment, had not wanted to be responsible for possibly losing Judea a few weeks after arriving, so he had decided it was better to make the smart "political" choice.

The soldiers had finished moving in the extra chairs, but they were still trying to get the deafening static out of the sound system. Everyone but Marcus was showing signs of impatience, making sarcastic cracks about Roman efficiency and about being able to build roads but not fix a microphone. Marcus continued reviewing what happened.

While Marcus did not like to admit it, Pilate's reasoning in removing the public images of Caesar had made some sense. But then, not long after that incident, a rather large group of Galileans became disorderly at one of their religious festivals during Passover, and Pilate called in the army and ordered them dispersed. When they refused, Pilate gave orders for the whole mob to be attacked. It would seem, Marcus thought, that this could have incited the city to take up arms with the Parthians just as quickly, yet, Pilate seemed to have cared less. In the incident over the images of Caesar, Pilate had acquiesced to the will of local authorities, fearing they might turn to the Parthians; in the incident with the Galileans he seemed not to give a damn about the local authorities or their possible ties to the Parthians. This type of inconsistency made it hard for soldiers like Marcus to know just what kind of policy they would be asked to enforce from one day to the next. That above all else made Pilate a much less than ideal commander in Marcus's eyes. "Pilate is not the kind of governor I will one day become," thought Marcus.

Marcus had been away on vacation when he received the call from the district general in charge of the entire region. He was informed of the news regarding Jesus' death and was told that since this all took place in his command area, he should expect to hold a press conference within the next twenty-four hours. "Just handle questions dealing with the execution detail and convey the general notion that everything was done according to regulations. Don't try and speak for the emperor or the governor, or anyone else. Let them hold their own news conferences," he was told. "A more thorough investigation into everything that happened will take place later in the week, but for now, just handle the press regarding your men and the execution."

Marcus believed this press conference would be easy to maneuver through. The only thing bothering him as he carefully unfolded his prepared statement was the reported reaction of that one young rookie soldier. Even though he was very young, this was not his first execution. What had frightened him so? None of the veteran soldiers seemed particularly bothered by this crucifixion. What made this young man suddenly cower and cry when Jesus died? "No matter," Marcus thought. "We have him under raps. Perhaps he just wasn't cut out to be an executioner." At last the sound system was working, and

Marcus walked to the podium: "Ladies and gentlemen of the press, good morning. My name is Commander Marcus. I am the deputy minister of justice in charge of local security for the province of Judea. On my left is Captain Antonio, in charge of capital enforcement, and behind him is Captain Vergas, in charge of prisons.

"First let me state that I am not here to comment in any way on any official government policy regarding Rome's involvement in this case. Nor am I in a position to comment on any particulars surrounding the trial of Jesus or on the role of the governor or the Herodian kingdom in this whole affair. I am sure that information will be coming from sources much more knowledgeable about these things than myself. I am sure that Governor Pilate will be making a statement to the press, as well as King Herod. I know how anxious you all are to get the story, and I am sure with a little patience, you will have answers to all of your questions.

"I have called this news conference because it has come to our attention that certain allegations regarding the conduct of my officers during the crucifixion of Jesus the Nazarene have been leaked to you members of the press. I wish to state here and now that this office has conducted a thorough investigation of any and all charges pertaining to this matter and has found that our officers acted in a totally professional manner. I have here a chronological list of events leading up to the actual execution of Jesus, which Captain Vergas will read to you at this time. After that I will be glad to answer any questions you might have."

Captain Vergas—a man of about two hundred and eighty pounds, dark hair, bushy eyebrows, a cruel, slightly twisted mouth — began to read from a carefully prepared list. No one thought for a second that this chronology of events came from the brain of this slow-moving hulk. In many aspects he was reminiscent of the character Lukea Brazzi in Mario Puzo's *The Godfather.*

"At 6:56 A.M., Jesus was handed over to the Roman authorities by members of the Jewish temple authority forces. He was held in confinement in a holding cell until called for by his excellency Pontius Pilate. His excellency held a preliminary hearing where he heard testimony in the presence of the prisoner. The prisoner was then returned to his cell while the governor considered his case. At 10:32 A.M., the prisoner was called again before the governor, and more testimony was heard. He was then returned to his cell where he awaited his sentence. At 11:36 A.M., we received word that the prisoner was pronounced guilty and was sentenced to immediate execution in accordance with the laws of the Roman Empire. At 12:02 P.M., he, along with two other prisoners convicted of capital offenses, was bound in the prescribed manner and taken to the place of execution where he was then put to death. At approximately 3:02 P.M., he was pronounced dead, and the body was taken down and handed over to members of the immediate family."

Vergas folded his paper in half and handed it across the table to Marcus. For a fraction of a second there was silence in the room, as if in respect for the death of Jesus. Then suddenly the room burst into a clamor of voices shouting questions. Marcus, slowly and deliberately, began to take reporters' questions.

"Let me start on this side of the room. Susan?"

"Commander Marcus, there have been reports from people who supposedly saw Jesus on his death march that he looked as though he had been beaten and brutalized and, in fact, was quite bloody. Can you comment on that?"

"Jesus did sustain some injuries during his capture when a brief struggle broke out, and one temple guard was reportedly injured by one of Jesus' bodyguards. There also may have been some injuries sustained while in the presence of the temple guards, but we would have had nothing to do with any of that. Yes, over here."

"Sir, is it true that Jesus was flogged by members of the prison staff while at the same time they hurled racial slurs at him, such as 'Jew king,' and mockingly called him messiah?"

"We did receive an order from the governor to administer corporal punishment in an effort to obtain the truth from the prisoner. However, it was by no means overly severe, and at no time did any of the officers use any racial or prejudicial language toward the prisoner."

Marcus thought, "That was your first stupid answer. How does a man get flogged with a whip made of leather with bits of rock and bone in it and not have the results be too severe? And what is this business about 'racial or prejudicial'? That doesn't make much sense." He smiled to himself and thought, "Thou dost protest a bit too much on that one. You'll be guarding crucifixion sites in Judea the rest of your life if you give too many more answers like that."

"Sir, if I could ask a follow-up question, can you tell us why Jesus was ordered beaten by the governor? Was this done to elicit some kind of confession out of him, and if he had confessed, would he have possibly been spared the death penalty? Or was this done as a part of the overall punishment that Rome gives all prisoners found guilty of capital offenses? In other words, when someone is found guilty of whatever it was Jesus was presumably found guilty of, is the sentence flogging, followed by death, or was the beating done for some other purpose?"

"Well, I'm afraid here you are getting into areas I can't really comment on. Questions regarding why Jesus was handed whatever punishment he received will have to be raised with the persons authorized to hand out such sentences. This department only carries out the penalties; we have nothing to do with the legal process involved."

"Yes, Carlos."

"Marcus, we received reports that someone was pulled out of the crowd by Captain Vergas and made to carry the rather heavy cross beam that Jesus had been forced to carry. I have two questions about the incident: (1) Is that a common procedure in these sorts of matters? And (2) Was there any reason for choosing a dark-skinned Libyan to carry the cross?"

Marcus paused for a second and smiled briefly, recalling the conversation he had had with Captain Vergas a few hours earlier. "I hear you 'volunteered' somebody to help Jesus carry the crossbar. Why did you do that? Don't tell me you're getting a little compassion in your old age?" Vergas had replied, matter of factly, that he had decided that the way this Jew was falling and stumbling all over the place, it would be three o'clock before they ever got up the hill. "Why did you pick that fellow from Cyrene?" Marcus had asked him. "Because he was big," Vergas had said. "Besides, them people are all animals anyway." This conversation with Vergas had reminded Marcus of something he learned in his days as a cadet. He remembered a Roman senator giving a lecture at the Roman military academy on the importance of power. "Power," the senator said, "is the ability to create truth. If one hundred people with rocks say today is Tuesday, and one thousand people with swords say it is Wednesday, it doesn't matter in the end what day it is, you with the swords can make it whatever day you want, especially for the people who only have rocks." There had been a chuckle in the room from the other cadets, but Marcus remembered thinking, "What drivel. No one can change truth."

In the same way, the senator had continued, "If you take a people who have lived free all of their lives and tell them that from now on, the truth is they are not free but slaves who will give their lives over to the power and glory of Rome, if your swords are big enough, that too will become truth for those people. They were born free; they were meant to live as free men and women; they can point to philosophical and religious mandates regarding how they should live as free people. But the fact is, you have created a new truth about their lives, and that truth is that now they are slaves to the empire. And eventually they will live out their lives that way."

Again, Marcus had believed this was nothing but political hot air. But after years of watching Rome devour whole countries and seeing people who swore, by all that was "truth," that they would never live under Roman domination eventually succumb and even accept the rule of Rome, he began to accept this business about power and truth.

Marcus reflected that in many ways Captain Vergas believed in this "power to make truth" theory. He wasn't interested in some other culture's notion of truth or justice. To him truth resided in power, in the sword. So when Vergas said, for example, that Libyans were animals, it was not that he disliked Libyans based on his having taken time to know them. He felt he didn't have to know the "truth" about them. Why bother? When you have your own opinion, backed by the biggest sword, what you think becomes truth. And everyone else's "truth" is irrelevant.

Marcus suddenly realized his mind had wandered a bit and jumped back into the business at hand: "Carlos, in answer to your question, it is not uncommon for a prisoner to become so weak from either fear or some other physical problem that he simply becomes unable to carry the large beam used as a part of his execution. In those cases, oftentimes people are pressed into service on behalf of the prisoner. I mean, let's face it, if a prisoner refuses to carry the cross beam, there isn't a great deal anyone can do. After all, the prisoner knows he will be dead soon regardless of what he does or does not do.

"It was determined that Jesus simply could not, or would not, as the case may be, carry the cross beam any farther; thus a man from the crowd was asked to carry it for him. As to the race or color of the man having any significance in his being chosen to assist, there is no evidence of such distinctions being employed. The gentleman in the back. Yes, sir, you."

"I would like to follow up on that question posed by Carlos because I too heard that there were racial remarks used when the man from Cyrene was either asked, as you said, or forced, as some others suggest, to carry Jesus' cross. Perhaps since Captain Vergas was in charge of the detail, he can comment on just what happened."

For a moment, all eyes turn to Vergas, but he simply said to the crowd, "No comment. Please direct all questions to the commander."

Marcus could tell that the reporters wanted to press Vergas further but that they knew that they would get nothing more from him. They knew that from now on they would only get that somewhat blank stare, no matter how they pressed him for an answer. They decided to stick to Marcus.

"Sir, I can only give you the same answer I gave Carlos. At no time did the man's race come into the picture. The only consideration would have been that he appeared big enough to carry the cross beam without too much difficulty, and in fact, he carried it with no apparent problem."

Marcus turned to look for the next hand raised when he spotted Gerry Simmons in the crowd. Marcus liked Gerry, though they had talked only a few times. He not only liked her personally but also respected her as a reporter: she seemed to take pride in getting the facts before she let a story go out on the airwaves. When Marcus heard she was being transferred Stateside again, he had meant to get in touch with her and have a farewell drink. However, it seemed their schedules would not allow them that opportunity, and Gerry had departed without ever having had the chance to say goodbye.

"Gerry, welcome back to Judea."

"Thank you, Marcus. Perhaps one of the most disturbing reports we heard on our way over here today came from a woman who said she was at the actual execution site, and she says that the soldiers literally held some sort of dice game for the clothes of Jesus, even while he was dying on the cross. Is there any truth to this, and if not, why do you think someone would report such a story?"

Marcus had heard this had happened, and he himself was disturbed that Roman soldiers could have acted so unprofessionally during an official execution. If he had been captain of the guard and saw anyone in his squad acting so poorly, he would have severely disciplined him.

Marcus already knew the answer he was going to give. He came upon it quite accidentally some time ago, when he first developed a passing interest in the writings of the Jewish prophet Isaiah. His interest wasn't spurred by any religious motive but rather began when he was ordered to read all he could on Jewish messiahs. He was told to do so purely as a military matter. "These Jews," he was told, "are always putting their hope in a messiah who will come and wipe you filthy Romans off the face of the earth." He could still see his former commander laughing as he pointed to Marcus when he said the words "filthy Romans." The commander had gone on: "As long as you are in this hellhole, you might as well know what the natives are expecting from their messiahs."

Marcus recalled his former commander telling him that the main reason Marcus should familiarize himself with this liberation talk was so he would be able to fully understand what was being talked about when someone — whether in the streets or temple — began carrying on about a new kingdom. "Judea is full of preachers," the commander had said. "Some of them deliver a message of peace; you know the 'love thy neighbor' kind of thing. Some of the others, though, will preach slitting your throat, and they'll do that preaching right under your nose if you let them. If they talk love, repentance, and sin, fine. If one of them starts preaching that stuff about being the long-awaited liberator come to set them free and begins telling the crowds to follow him to the glorious gates of the new Jerusalem, find him, arrest him, and beat his brains out."

Marcus had read all the material he could lay his hands on and understood most of the writings to be basically Jewish myths and professions of faith. But he had been deeply struck by the writings of Isaiah. He believed Isaiah sounded more like a Greek poet than one of the fire and brimstone Jewish prophets he had read excerpts from. Isaiah wrote with such passion and beauty that Marcus often found himself rereading passages for his own enjoyment. He now sensed the irony of a Roman using knowledge of the Jewish Bible to answer a question about one who some believed was the very messiah Isaiah talked about.

"There is absolutely no truth to these allegations. We are Roman soldiers and as such are trained to do our jobs professionally and with dignity. However, in answer to the second part of your question, it is hard to know what is in some people's minds, but I can offer a theory.

"As you know, Israel is an occupied land, and even though Israel has benefited greatly from the services Rome has provided, there are some who feel that no matter how much Rome provides, they would rather be independent. The independence movement has long been alive in this part of the empire, and all men everywhere can understand why some people will always feel the need to try and force independence on everyone, no matter whether the general populace wants it or not.

"Well, many in this movement looked upon Jesus as a leader who might through revolutionary means or some other way lead Israel to independence. I might hasten to add that it is unclear whether or not

Jesus himself believed this, but nevertheless there is certainly evidence that many of his followers, including some in his own twelve, believed this. Now, people in this liberation movement believe that the so-called liberator would be one who in fact could only come from their God. And since there were supposedly certain events that historically were to take place during this liberator's life on earth, some people tried to interpret many things that Jesus did as signs that he was in fact the liberator and true king of Israel.

"Our reports indicate, however, that to the people pushing independence, and to the special-interest groups, Jesus apparently did not fulfill many of these expectations in life, and so there are some who will try and use this death as some sort of rallying cry for independence."

Marcus paused for an instant to give his audience a chance to digest what he'd said. He then went on: "Anyone who has ever read the writings of the Hebrew prophets knows that this liberator, if authentic, not only will have certain events take place during his life but supposedly will have certain things happen during his death as well. And one well-known quote is that this liberator will say that 'they,' presumably meaning whoever put him to death, will cast lots or gamble for his clothes. It doesn't take much to deduce that people aware of that type of writing are now trying to cash in on the unfortunate death of this man by adding fabrications to the actual events that took place during his death."

Marcus was just about to take a moment to congratulate himself on what he believed was a splendid answer when a soldier walked into the room and bent toward Marcus's ear. He began to whisper something. Marcus interrupted him, turned toward the crowd, and asked to be excused for a moment. He stood up and walked toward a corner of the room with the newly arrived soldier. They spoke for a moment and then Marcus returned to the table.

"I'm sorry for the interruption. If there are no more questions, I have some more news that has just come to my attention, and I have been given clearance to pass it along to you." But one more reporter had questions that couldn't wait.

"Yes, Thomas," said Marcus.

"Marcus, you obviously have all of our journalistic curiosities at a peak, but just before you tell us this latest piece of information, can you comment on any of the stories going around about the so-called unnatural phenomena that took place, such as storms occurring the moment that Jesus died, or the stories of earthquakes, and so on. Are these all just stories being spread by followers of Jesus in order to add to his mystique?"

"Absolutely. It rained at one point during the day, but that is not at all uncommon this time of year."

"Is it true about the soldier?"

Marcus thought that the old axiom about Judea was true: the best way to get the news around town about anything was to classify it a state secret. He also thought that if there was a God, he must be working for the Romans: the news he had just received, and which he was about to pass on to the press, could not have come at a more opportune moment, just before he had to explain something he had absolutely no explanation for.

"The story about the soldier is obviously all blown out of proportion. A soldier, for you ladies and gentlemen of the press who may not have heard, apparently was taken ill at the site of the execution. He is presently under a doctor's care and is doing fine. But once again, people who obviously have an interest in Jesus turning into a legend started spreading rumors that this soldier was affected in some supernatural way. I personally believe that he was affected by his tuna sandwich, which he had let sit in the sun too long. Anyway, I assure you the soldier is doing fine and to my knowledge has no plans to leave the army and become a follower of the dead man."

People in the room started to laugh, and before any more hands were raised, Marcus decided to tell them the latest piece of news.

"Ladies and gentlemen, the latest news I have to report to you is that at approximately 6 A.M. this morning a man tentatively identified as one Judas Iscariot was found dead of an apparent suicide. If his identity is verified, he would have been one . . . "

Marcus was interrupted by another soldier who walked over and whispered in his ear. Marcus turned back to the reporters: "Ladies and gentlemen, the body has been positively identified as that of Judas, who was one of the twelve disciples of Jesus."

The room exploded with questions. Reporters began to all shout at Marcus at once. Marcus remained cool as he began to take reporters' questions. This time Marcus didn't call out names; he simply identified the most common questions and answered them.

"I believe someone asked how he died. It appears he hanged himself."

"Who discovered the body?"

"It seems a shepherd while out walking early this morning came upon the body. He notified the police."

"Do we know for sure it's a suicide?"

"We don't know for sure at this time; it's being looked into. Since there were reportedly no external cuts or bruises on the body suggesting any other bodily harm, it appears to be suicide."

"Was there a note?"

"Not that we know of at this time."

"Who positively identified the body?"

"I don't have that information at this time."

"What time did he die?"

"We don't know for sure; however, it would appear to have been sometime during the last six to eight hours."

Marcus waved his arms before him, signaling an end to the session: "Ladies and gentlemen, I am being called away on other business. With all that has happened, I am sure you understand. I wish to thank you for coming, and if any further news develops, either I or someone from this department will be in touch to help answer your questions."

As Marcus walked toward the door, he simply ceased acknowledging any more questions. The other soldiers in the room suddenly rose as if someone had turned on a switch and began to surround Marcus as though he was a chief of state. As they left the room, Marcus had a funny feeling that this Judas thing might just be the first in a series of surprises that this execution might produce. He was, however, quite satisfied with his own performance at the news conference.

"No matter what happened," he thought, "no one can say we didn't handle the press." However, he felt suddenly consumed with a desire to find out what really happened — not just on the part of the police, but what really happened over the last three years that brought this man Jesus to his execution. Marcus thought, "Better get rid of this feeling, soldier. Remember, truth is whatever the guy with the biggest sword says it is." Somehow, though, despite everything he had heard himself say at the news conference, it all now sounded like dribble.

Marcus stopped at the door and yelled over to Gerry Simmons, "When did you get in?"

Gerry answered, "About two this morning."

"Call me at the barracks, before you go back to the States. Maybe we can have that glass of wine we never got around to having before you left."

"Great!" yelled Gerry, "let's do it."

– CHAPTER TWO –

MARCUS STARTED BACK toward the Roman barracks, but decided to return home first. He instructed the other soldiers to go on ahead as he turned down the side street leading to his small house.

As he approached his house, he suddenly felt uneasy. "I must have been more nervous than I thought," he said to himself as he walked through the front doors and went into the living quarters. The windows were mostly covered. "Strange," he thought, "who covered the windows this time of day? Surely my servant knows how much I like the rays of the sun streaming into this room." He became even more uneasy as he suddenly realized that he had not seen or heard his servant anywhere in the house when he entered. "Must be in the garden," he thought, even though by now he had a hard time convincing himself of that.

He walked over to a table, and even though he rarely drank while on duty, he poured himself a glass of red wine from the silver decanter. He was about to drink when he thought he saw someone move from the darkened corner of the room. In one swift motion, he pulled his sword from its sheath and pointed it toward the shadow.

"Who's there?" Marcus shouted in a loud voice. "Show yourself, or die where you stand!"

"Impressive," replied the figure hidden in the shadows.

The voice that came out of the corner was as cold and as sharp as Marcus's sword. It was a voice calm, yet filled with menace. Marcus had heard that voice before. It was the kind of voice that made even a simple "good morning" portend death.

"Good afternoon, commander," said the voice from the shadows. "I hope you did not mind my giving your servant the rest of the day off, but I believe that you and I should have a chance to speak to one another, without interruption."

Marcus felt suddenly sapped of will. He put his sword back into its sheath and waited for the figure to emerge from the shadows. His throat suddenly became dry, and the palms of his hands began sweating. By now there was no doubt who was standing in his living quarters. Marcus stood at attention, as he saw the most feared man in the entire empire emerge from the shadows. It was Lucius Aelius Sejanus.

"Sit down, Commander Marcus," said Sejanus.

Marcus tried to utter some sort of greeting of welcome, combined with a salutation, but it all came out jumbled and inane. He felt as though it would have been an insult to ask Sejanus what he was doing in his home, so he sat down as ordered and waited for whatever was going to come next. In all the battles he had fought, he had never felt as intimidated as he did at this moment. "What was it about Sejanus," he thought, "that could inspire such fear in men? Surely he was flesh and blood, just like everyone else." As a way of building courage for himself, he reflected, "If I were to run him through with my sword, he would simply die just like anyone else." Yet Marcus also felt that any mere mortal even daring to think of such a move toward Sejanus would somehow find himself quickly and inexplicably dead. He suddenly hoped Sejanus would not hold this slight trip of fantasy against him.

Staring up at this figure Marcus finally understood why Sejanus seemed so particularly menacing standing there alone in his living room. He realized that in the past whenever he had seen Sejanus he was always surrounded by the crack and deadly troops of the Praetorian Guard, and Marcus had always accredited Sejanus's menacing looks in part to the presence of the other soldiers. Now, with Sejanus standing here alone, without the guard, yet still looking as intimidating as ever, Marcus suddenly realized it was not the guard that gave Sejanus that look of menace; it was the presence of Sejanus that gave the look of menace to the guard. The thought brought a slight, wry smile to Marcus in the same way that someone about to be hanged might smile at a sign warning of danger posted on the gallows.

"Commander, I wish to give you an assignment of great importance to the empire. I want you to find out all you can about just what happened here and who pulled what strings in order to make these events unfold in the way they did. Question anyone you need to, but report back only to me. I want to know how the mightiest empire in the world could be manipulated into this position of embarrassment. I want to know if this is a conspiracy plotted by the Jews to make Rome look bad in the eyes of the world. It would not be beyond these people to sacrifice a man like Jesus in order to gain political leverage against the empire. In the same way I want to know more about this apparent suicide of Judas, as well as the whereabouts of the rest of Jesus' apostles. My sources tell me that Judas may not have been exactly what he appeared to be. I understand there is rumor that a suicide note will be delivered to members of the press within the hour. If this is true, I want to know who was responsible for the note getting to the press before it came to us. I want that person's name. Finally, I want to know about two of our soldiers involved in this matter. I want to know just what did happen to that young soldier you have conveniently hidden near your barracks, and also what happened to this man."

Sejanus handed Marcus a piece of parchment with the name of a Roman centurion on it. He recognized it immediately: Antoni Demetrius, Marcus's closest friend. Demetrius and Marcus had both graduated from the Roman military academy, although two years apart. Demetrius, his senior, was one of the bravest men he had ever known. He had distinguished himself in many battles over the last eighteen years as a Roman soldier and had risen to the rank of centurion. Marcus knew his whole family: his wife of fifteen years and his handsome young son, Tarius. He was there at the birth of their second child, a girl, who died shortly after birth.

As young men, he and Demetrius both talked of the day when they would serve in Rome as generals together. Demetrius had even once saved his life when a man crazed with the plague had rushed out of a doorway with a knife right at Marcus yelling, "Death to Rome!" Demetrius pushed Marcus aside with one hand, while with the other he plunged his sword into the man's heart. Marcus remembered how they both stood staring at the body lying in the street. Neither said much the rest of the day. It was the first time either of them had ever spilled blood. How very long ago that was. But why was his name on this parchment just handed to him by Sejanus?

"Sir," Marcus said. "I don't understand. Has something happened to Centurion Demetrius? Last I heard, he was serving in a unit in Capernaum. Is the centurion hurt?"

"Calm your fears, commander, the centurion is physically unharmed. What I wish to know is if he is still fit to serve in the Roman army and if he is still fit to command."

For the first time, Marcus found himself getting a little impatient. "Sir, I do not understand. Has the centurion committed some offense against the empire?"

Even as the words left his lips, Marcus felt certain Antoni Demetrius would never commit an offense against Rome. He was as patriotic as any man he had ever met. Marcus believed he himself was more capable of treason than Demetrius. He would even doubt Sejanus's loyalty above Demetrius's. Marcus caught himself, and once again hoped Sejanus could not read the expression on his face or the ideas that had passed through his mind in a moment of passion.

Sejanus began to speak, and this time there was just the slightest hint of irritation in his voice. Hearing it was enough to make Marcus anxious and fearful. Marcus could not help admiring Sejanus's skills at instilling fear in those he commanded. "If Sejanus ever screamed," he thought, "the entire Coliseum would collapse in fear."

"It seems the centurion met Jesus, and that meeting produced rather interesting results." As Sejanus said this, he kept his eyes fixed on Marcus, trying to pick out and interpret even the slightest reaction. "He claims his son was saved from a threatening illness by this man. If Jesus was either knowingly or unknowingly a part of a plot to embarrass the empire, thus weakening its internal security, then anyone claiming such phenomena as cures and miracles from this man immediately falls under my suspicion, especially if he works for us. I understand you and the centurion go back a long way together. I trust he will feel comfortable telling you exactly what happened. He will tell the truth to you, and you will tell the truth to me. The centurion is presently being confined to his quarters. However, he is being moved to a secret location within the hour so that no one from the press can speak to him before I know what has happened. You will find his location on that paper. No one will be allowed to talk with the centurion but you and me. No one."

Sejanus stepped a bit closer to Marcus and in a lower voice said, "These are dangerous times, commander. When the security of the empire is at risk, I put nothing past anyone. If the empire falls, as no doubt one day it will, I would hope it was because it was beaten by an enemy who simply developed the strength and the skills to defeat us. I would hate to believe it was because we grew so complacent that we could no longer see the enemy at our very throats."

Sejanus drew back a few feet and resumed his detached but menacing delivery: "Finally, I wish to impress upon you the importance of this assignment. I am entrusting you with a matter of great national security. I trust you will not let your friendship for the centurion, or your allegiance to your fellow soldiers, or any prejudices you might have stand in your way of getting at the truth in all of these matters. It disturbs me somewhat that you have already let your feelings for Herod impair your judgment thus far."

Marcus realized that he must have appeared startled at Sejanus's statement. He was about to speak when Sejanus held up his hand in such a way that Marcus felt his words lump up in his throat and nearly choke him.

"I know you lost a promising young nephew in the incident concerning Herod and Aretas. However, that has caused you to cloud your judgment in certain matters in the past. You no doubt believe Herod is behind this whole Jesus matter. You are wrong, commander. Herod is a fool. I suspect that if this is some sort of plot, the real brains behind this embarrassment to the empire is the high priest Caiaphas. If anyone in Judea can cause harm to us because of this Jesus problem, it is Caiaphas, who is far more dangerous than his famous father-in-law, the great Annas. Annas and the majority of the Jewish priesthood are driven by greed and use religion in order to line their pockets. To people like Annas, the empire, as long as it permits them to get rich on the backs of their poor, is really an ally. Whenever they need to they can preach about the infidels of Rome, while telling their people that until God sends the messiah, they must pay, and pray. But Caiaphas really believes in all that he preaches. He is willing to sacrifice anything for the survival of his temple and his God. He is not motivated by greed; thus he is harder to control. He, in all things happening in Jerusalem, is much more dangerous than Herod."

Sejanus looked sternly into Marcus's eyes and said, "Never let your own personal prejudices interfere with your responsibility to the security of the empire again. You are an ambitious man, commander, and I know you will go far if sponsored correctly. You handled what must be said to the press admirably. Now handle as well what you must do for the empire."

Sejanus headed for the door. He turned just as Marcus was springing to attention, reached into his vestplate, and pulled out a small ring bearing the insignia of the Emperor Tiberius. He handed it to Marcus. "This will give you the authority to question anyone in Judea. But remember, report your findings only to me."

He turned and continued toward the door. "Sir!" said Marcus. "How shall I find you in order to report my findings?"

"Do not worry, commander. When the time is right, I shall find you. Hail Tiberius Caesar, emperor of Rome!" Sejanus said, lifting his right hand toward the ceiling.

"Hail Caesar!" said Marcus, first hitting his chest with his fist, and then raising it in salute as well. And with that, Sejanus was gone.

Marcus sank back into a nearby low couch and began the process of sorting through his thoughts. "By the gods," he thought, "what is going on here?" From the moment he had received the news while on leave in Jericho, Marcus had known that the death of Jesus would create some controversy, but he never believed it would go so far as to draw this kind of attention from Sejanus. He believed that all parties involved would do as he had done with the police and crucifixion detail: simply stonewall everyone and wait for the storm to blow over.

But Marcus was troubled more than anything with one burning question: Why did Sejanus come to see him? A million possible answers ran through his mind, from the good to the frightening. What, in the first place, was Sejanus doing in the region? Was Marcus being set up for greatness at last, or as a fall guy? Did Sejanus believe Marcus would truly be able to sort out the answers in the Demetrius situation, or did he want him to provide evidence against his old and trusted friend? What better way to convict a man of Demetrius's stature than to have evidence brought against him by an old friend and fellow officer. Did Sejanus want him to investigate even Pilate (a proposition that in itself did not appear too comforting), or was the empire looking for a reason to come in and destroy both the Jewish kingdoms and the high priesthood all in one swift move? Were Sejanus and the other Roman officials hoping Marcus's investigation results could provide the impetus to do so?

"So many questions," Marcus thought. But then something quite suddenly came over him like a splash of cold water. He heard him-

self say out loud, "I'm a soldier. I have orders. I'll carry them out."
He stood up and moved toward the door. "First things first," he said.
"Let's look into this Judas business." And finding himself subcon-
sciously imitating Sejanus's movements, he pushed through his front
door and moved into the street.

– CHAPTER THREE –

BULLETIN:

We interrupt your regularly scheduled programming to bring you this WXOT special report. Live from our studios in New York, here is Gary Thomas.

"Good morning, ladies and gentlemen. This just in. Well-known evangelist, civil rights leader, and faith healer, Jesus of Nazareth, is dead. He died while in the hands of Roman authorities, who had placed him under arrest on charges of sedition against the Roman Empire. Jesus was thirty-three years of age. For more information we switch you now live to Mary Beth Livingston, in Egypt."

"Good morning, Gary, and good morning, ladies and gentlemen. News of the death of Jesus is just beginning to filter around the Middle East, even though he has apparently been dead several hours now. As you know, Gary, I am in Egypt covering the conference between, on one hand, Egyptian and Arab kings, and, on the other, General Augustus Magnus, the personal representative of Emperor Tiberius. Now when the news first began to filter out about Jesus' death, I had a chance to speak to General Magnus just as he was entering the meeting at the palace. This was his response."

A prerecorded clip came on the screen:

"General, could we have a word just before you go in? Could you give us a statement on the death of Jesus in Jerusalem?"

"Well, this is the first I've heard of it, and there isn't any comment I can make at this time, except to say that the Middle East is a dangerous part of the world, and any of us can meet death at any time in these parts."

"Sir, there was an initial unconfirmed report that said Jesus was actually executed by the Roman government and that the local governor in fact pronounced the sentence. Does that sound consistent with Roman rule in this part of the world?"

"I don't believe the report is true. But, obviously, I'm not in Judea, I am here, so it's hard for me to comment. I do believe, however, that if Rome had anything to do with the death of Jesus, something that none of us is aware of must have happened within the last several hours that would have drastically changed his status from that of a preacher to that of a criminal."

"Sir, what would be the type of change that would have Rome suddenly arrest him and put him to death?"

"Well, he would have had to begin preaching either a violent overthrow of the duly appointed government already in power or the overthrow of the empire itself. Other than that, unless he suddenly became some sort of outlaw, Rome would have had nothing to do with executing him."

"But you believe it's safe to say that if nothing had changed in Jesus' preaching or social behavior, then Rome would not have arrested him and executed him in Jerusalem?"

"Yes, I believe that is safe to say. Now again I must add that I cannot speak for the local authorities, but Rome is not in the habit of arresting and executing local preachers on any sort of religious charge. Please excuse me, I must get inside."

"Thank you, general."

"We are here back live again, and, Gary, that taping took place about an hour ago, and, as you can see, the emperor's personal representative here in Egypt seemed to rule out all possibilities that Rome would have had anything to do with the execution of Jesus. He made the statement that unless Jesus became some sort of 'outlaw,' and it seemed to me that the general was clearly suggesting that at least in his eyes, Jesus was not, then Rome would have had nothing to do with executing him. But as you now know, just ten minutes ago an official communique from the Roman governor's office in Judea confirmed that Jesus was in fact executed by Rome, and I quote, 'in accordance with Roman law,' on charges of sedition. He died at around 3:05 today. Gary?"

"Mary Beth, did you get the feeling that the general genuinely knew nothing about the death of Jesus and in fact was surprised to learn of his death?"

"Yes, Gary, I did. And I have to believe that the decision was appar-

ently a local one and was not made with the full knowledge of Rome.
Now I might hasten to add that the local governors in these areas do
have a lot of power to make decisions such as this on their own. It
would seem strange, however, that Rome would allow such a thing
to take place and have the blame put squarely on Rome's shoulders.
After all, this was a nationally known, well-respected preacher and
evangelist whose execution was sure to make international headlines."

"Mary Beth, we're going to ask you to stand by. I understand we
have the Roman ambassador in New York standing by. We switch you
now live to Bob Collins at the residence of the Roman ambassador
here in New York."

"Gary, as you can see, I am standing in front of the residence of
the Roman ambassador. As you can also see, the Roman ambassador
is not standing here with me. He had agreed over the phone to be
interviewed, but suddenly it seems he has changed his mind."

"Bob, what happened?"

"When our station manager called the Roman embassy with news
of Jesus' death and the possibility that Rome was involved, we were
told the ambassador would be holding a news conference at this hour.
When we, along with dozens of other reporters, arrived, we were told
the ambassador would meet with us shortly. Then just about three
minutes ago, we were suddenly told that the ambassador was now
unavailable for comment, due to some urgent imperial matters, and
that the ambassador, and I quote, 'or one of his official representatives,' would speak with us at another time. When we asked just what
had happened, we were given no answer, and a rather large centurion
politely but emphatically showed us the door. Gary?"

"Bob, I don't know if you could hear Mary Beth's report, but she
had earlier spoken to General Magnus in Egypt, who flat out said that
Rome would have had very little if anything to do with the death of
Jesus. However, not long after that interview was taped, the Roman
office in Judea sent word that they did in fact execute Jesus. Do you
get the feeling that Rome is genuinely at a loss as to what happened
and is even somewhat embarrassed by what has taken place?"

"That's the feeling I get, and that feeling seems to be shared by
most of the people I talk to, especially other members of the press. I
believe either the local governor made an independent decision on his
own to execute Jesus, or someone very carefully and skillfully managed
to weave Rome into an internal Jewish religious matter that resulted

in Jesus' death, and Rome's embarrassment. In any event, I know the empire will not like this sort of coverage at all."

"Thank you, Bob. Now, Mary Beth, in Egypt, I have a question for you. You have covered the goings and comings of the empire in that part of the world and should be as capable as anyone of answering it. It's this: If this was an independent decision on the part of the governor, and Rome does not agree and is in fact embarrassed by the decision, do you think the governor will be removed?"

"Absolutely not. With all of the publicity this might generate, Rome would never remove a local governor under pressure. You can expect Rome to back him to the hilt. An important point to remember about the empire is that it got where it is by being both militarily powerful and extremely cunning. And part of being cunning is learning how to use and manipulate time and when to act and when to be patient and let things blow over. Further, Rome, you can be sure, will never remove one of its procurators simply because some non-Romans are displeased with him. Rome would not want anyone to think that any outside force held in some way the power to persuade the empire. Instead, Rome would simply wait until everything blew over and then take action against one of its procurators. Now, if Jesus had been less of a national figure, Rome might act right away, but with the spotlight now on them, they will be sure to put up a united imperial front."

"But you do believe that Rome will investigate all of this internally?"

"Absolutely. It wouldn't surprise me if Rome is, so to speak, quite hot under the collar. The empire has always suffered from an image problem, and this episode cannot help it any. My guess is that there will be a lot of explaining going on over the next few days."

"Thank you, Mary Beth Livingston, in Egypt and Bob Collins at the Roman ambassador's residence. We'll be, of course, covering this story as it unfolds, and we'll bring you more information tonight on the five o'clock news. We understand that a news conference is about to take place regarding the actions of the local police in the arrest of Jesus, and our correspondent Gerry Simmons will be there to cover it live when it begins. WXOT will bring you that news conference live as soon as it begins, as well as keep you updated on any other events surrounding this story. For now this is Gary Thomas in the WXOT newsroom."

– CHAPTER FOUR –

A s MARCUS LEFT HIS HOME, he still felt the effects of having just spent a half-hour with Lucius Sejanus. He wasn't sure just what the Judas situation would produce, but he felt somehow that this assignment was much more to his liking than what was undoubtedly going to be next on his list: questioning his old friend Antoni Demetrius. What if Demetrius told him that the man Rome had just executed as a criminal in fact healed his only son? What if Demetrius said that he believed this man was some sort of god or a great and holy prophet? How would the empire take having one of its own soldiers professing faith in a man the empire accused of being a common criminal? Would Rome want to shut him up? If so, would they simply transfer him to some remote outpost and leave him there until he was too old to interest anyone? Or would Sejanus decide to shut him up in a more permanent way?

Marcus decided to push all of this to the back of his mind and made his way toward the barracks. He had not told the reporters at the press conference everything he knew about Judas, son of Simon. He had not told them, for instance, that the body was already at the barracks, in the basement in one of the cells. He wasn't sure just what he would find, but he believed that the first step would be to examine the body carefully and try to see if he could find out more about Judas dead than he knew about him when he was alive.

When Marcus reached the barracks, he noticed that the men seemed to jump to attention faster than usual. The men always stood up when a superior officer entered the room, but they usually did so grudgingly, slowly. They did it because it was regulation, and that was all. But this time there was something different in the attitude of the men. Even Vergas seemed to react differently than normal. Marcus waved his hand for the men to sit and then motioned to his aide to step outside with him.

"What's going on?" he asked the young officer.

The officer, whom Marcus had come to like a great deal, smiled and said: "Something unexpected, to say the least, happened a short time ago. We, the officers and soldiers, were just gathering to go over our orders and assignments for the day when the door to the barracks opened and in walked five members of the Praetorian Guard followed by none other than Lucius Sejanus. He looked at us, all of us standing stock still and in pure bewilderment, and said that you were as of now put in charge of a special assignment of great importance to the empire. He went on to say that everyone under your command had better do their jobs like their lives depended on it. He said: 'Do everything he says without the slightest hesitation, and with the utmost efficiency, or you will be sent to me.' Then he concluded in a voice that would freeze hell, and I quote: 'If that happens I can assure you that you will curse your mothers for ever having brought you into this world.' And before you knew it, he was gone. Marcus, what's this all about? What's going on? Does this have anything to do with this whole Jesus thing?"

"In due time, soldier," was Marcus's reply, "in due time."

Marcus and the young officer reentered the room. Marcus yelled "Sit" before they rose to their feet again. He wasn't quite sure he liked the idea of Sejanus speaking to his men in that manner. Like most officers, he was a bit protective of his command. He couldn't figure out why Sejanus would make his presence in Judea public, after just telling him to report back only to him. "Unless," Marcus thought, "he was somehow trying to imply, even to my own men, that I somehow had a bigger hand in this entire Jesus matter than I in fact had."

Marcus waved for Vergas to come over to where he was standing.

"Where is the body?" he said to Vergas.

"In the basement, commander, cell twenty-eight."

"Has anyone touched anything?"

"No, sir.'

Marcus went down the long flight of stairs to the prison and walked to the end of the hall to cell twenty-eight. The door was locked. A guard was standing nearby.

"Open it," he said to the sentry.

As the soldier unlocked the door, Marcus turned to him and said, "Allow no one to enter this cell as long as I'm in here."

"Yes, commander."

Marcus walked over to the body stretched out on the cell floor.

He had, of course, seen this man before. Marcus bent down to examine the body more closely. It appeared as though the neck was broken. Judas's clothes were dirty and torn, and his hair was mussed and stringy.

As he continued his examination, he noticed a small dagger in the dead man's belt. "Strange," he thought to himself, "I thought all of these people were against such things as knives." That was the second time that thought had occurred to him, the first when he heard about the reported scuffle between the man called Peter and one of the temple guards during the arrest of Jesus. As he examined the knife more closely, he noticed what appeared to be blood on the blade. There was something strangely familiar about this type of knife, but he couldn't put his finger on it. Something was out of place. That's what was making whatever was wrong hard to figure out. It was because something didn't fit.

"Sentry!" yelled Marcus at the door of the cell.

"Yes, commander," answered the soldier.

"Ask the investigations officer to come down here right away."

"Yes, sir."

As Marcus waited for the officer to arrive, he continued his examination of the body. It was then he noticed the finger missing from the left hand. The wound appeared to be at least a day old; still Marcus felt the need to look around the body, as if he might find the finger. He realized what he was doing and shook his head, slightly amused at what he had just caught himself doing. "I guess it would have been hard for you to cut off your finger after you had hanged yourself," he said to the body, "provided of course it was you who did this to yourself."

Marcus then began a thorough search of Judas's clothing and discovered a small number of silver coins in a small pouch pinned on the inside of a sleeve. The bag had Hebrew writing on it. Marcus read it and considered the implications of the words. He found nothing else of interest, so he rose and stepped away from the body and waited for the investigations officer to arrive.

Shortly, the door of the cell opened, and the officer entered. In most garrisons, the investigations officer was in charge of the unit responsible for covert operations, internal security investigations, and, in general, cases that needed a great deal of detective work. These men were usually very bright and often went on to become very high-ranking officers in the Roman army. The investigation officer in Marcus's command was considered one of the brightest in the area, and at age twenty-six he was also one of the youngest.

"You called for me, sir?"

"Yes, there are two items I want you to look at and tell me what they mean to you." Marcus first handed him the knife.

"It's an assassin's knife," the officer told Marcus. "The men who carry these usually either are religious fanatics who believe in a very extreme military interpretation of the messiah prophesies or are simply mercenary assassins."

"Is it possible that someone carrying one of these might simply have one for normal purposes?" Marcus asked.

"It is possible but highly unlikely, because anyone picked up with one of these on him would immediately come under intense suspicion. Where did you get it, commander?"

Marcus did not answer but instead handed him the pouch of silver. "What do you make of this?"

"A bag of silver apparently from the temple treasury."

"Thank you, officer," Marcus said, and then dismissed him.

As the man was walking toward the cell door, Marcus turned and called him back. "Take a look at the left hand of the body; tell me what it suggests to you." The officer returned, bent down toward the body, and investigated the left hand.

"Well, the wound looks fairly fresh, probably no more than a day or two old. Considering it doesn't look as though it has been tended to in any medical way, I would say this was done just around the time he took his own life."

"Does that suggest anything to you?" asked Marcus.

"A note," said the officer. "This man has left a suicide note, and he wants whoever reads it to know its authentically from him. It's a rather old custom practiced by the more radical elements of the..."

The officer suddenly rose from the body and turned to Marcus. "Sir, if this man was willing to do something as drastic as cut off a finger just to authenticate a suicide note, and if the dagger you showed me came from him, then I would suspect this man to be a member of some really fanatical organization, probably the Sicarii. As I was about to say, commander, oftentimes members of such fanatical organizations attempt to prove some point or another by taking their own lives after cutting off some part of their body to authenticate that the note came from them."

The investigations officer turned and looked again at the body lying on the cell floor. "Wasn't this man a member of Jesus' inner circle, the so-called twelve?"

"Yes," Marcus replied. "And now, I have a question that I would like your opinion on. Wouldn't you think that a man — a cunning man — who died with his knife and this silver still on him was trying to make it very clear who and what he was?"

"Absolutely, commander. You can be sure he knew that once we identified him as a colleague of Jesus, we would take his body and examine him thoroughly. He is definitely sending us a message from beyond the grave."

"And what do you think that message is?"

"I believe, sir, that he is telling us who he is and that he had something to do with someone in the temple, something for which he was paid. We know that Jesus was arrested by people associated with the temple, and we know this man was a follower of Jesus. We also know that Jesus and the temple authorities did not see eye to eye on many important theological and philosophical issues, and they were the ones who brought the original charges against him. Yet this man is found dead, with monies from the temple treasury found on him. There was a rumor floating around that Jesus was set up by someone and that it could have been someone from the inner circle. I would be tempted to deduce that if this theory is correct, Judas was the inside traitor working for the high priest. The problem with this theory is that if Judas were a member of the Sicarii, he would never sell himself to the temple."

Marcus considered all that he was told. "Do you think Jesus knew that one of his followers was a member of a violent terrorist group like the Sicarii?"

"I don't know if he knew or not," said the young officer, "but I know there was nothing in Jesus' public message that supported that kind of philosophy. Jesus was absolutely opposed to violence. We often had our people infiltrating the crowds, and he never preached anything to do with violent overthrow."

"That's what I believe also," said Marcus, "which means that maybe our dead friend here was playing both sides against the middle. He probably used the temple people by allowing them to believe that they were using him. What I don't know is why. Maybe he hoped that if he somehow got the temple to get us to execute him, or got the temple to hurt him in some way, then that would force some sort of action to take place. Maybe he believed that Jesus had developed enough fame so that if he were executed, the people would rise up and try to overthrow the occupiers."

"Or maybe," said the investigations officer, "Judas felt betrayed by Jesus because he refused to rally the people around the idea of a violent overthrow of Rome."

"Could be," said Marcus, "but in any event, he appears to have infiltrated Jesus' inner circle with the specific idea of using him for his own plans, whatever they were."

Marcus once again considered everything that was being said. "I suppose if you believed you could somehow steer the most charismatic preacher to hit this area in years around to your way of thinking, or somehow use your in with him as a way of getting the temple to feel it was safe to move against him, thus causing a revolution, you might feel as though you were controlling all of the cards. From a fanatical revolutionary point of view, it's a pretty good plan."

Marcus started toward the door. "I would think that if you were going to deliver a note to someone, you would send it to some member of the press. Don't you agree?

"Yes, sir, I do."

"Who would you send it to?" asked Marcus.

"I would probably send it to David Ben Leven of the *Judean*," said the young officer. "Actually," he continued, "I personally would send it to one of the outside news agencies covering the story about the death of Jesus. That way I would be sure that we Romans could do nothing to interfere with its getting reported. But if I know the Sicarii, they would never send anything like this to a Gentile publication, so they probably sent it to the *Judean*. They know that we give more latitude to the *Judean* than to any other press and that it would be particularly hard for us to suppress news about anything dealing with the death of Jesus with so much foreign press in town."

As the two men started up the stairs, Marcus said to the officer, "Remind me to put you in for a promotion."

"Thank you, sir."

Marcus called the sentry and told him to form his detail and go and remove the body. "Take him first to the infirmary. Then if no one comes for him by nightfall, take him out the back way and unceremoniously dump him in Potter's Field," he said.

Marcus then told the investigations officer: "Don't repeat anything we talked about. If anyone inquires about the body, tell them that members of the family came and took it away and that we have no idea where."

Next Marcus called out to Vergas: "I want twenty men in five minutes."

"Yes, sir," said the captain.

Marcus knew that if indeed there was a note, the recipient would probably already have it. He wasn't exactly sure what he would do if it was the *Judean*. "It depends on just what the note says," he thought to himself. As the men he requested started to assemble he suddenly had another chilling thought: "How did Sejanus know about the note? It was probably only a hypothesis," he thought, "but he sure made it sound like he knew through some kind of supernatural means. That's probably why he is who he is."

Marcus and the squadron of men began to make their way toward the center of town to the building that held the offices of the *Judean*. He still believed that the business about the young soldier who got sick during the actual execution of Jesus was probably nothing serious. He told himself that he would get to that some time later that day. What began to press upon his nerves more and more was his upcoming visit with Demetrius.

As he remembered the address where Demetrius was being held, he was thankful it was right outside of town. He would not have liked the idea of riding all the way to Capernaum, all the while thinking of just how he was going to confront his old friend. He wondered if he would be allowed to question him alone. Sejanus had said that no one would be allowed to question the centurion but himself and Marcus. But what if Sejanus had someone there to check up on Marcus? He began to think he was getting a bit paranoid. He also began to get uncomfortable because he realized that there was something else bothering him, something having nothing to do with Sejanus.

The questions he had begun asking himself after his meeting with Sejanus began forcing their way into his consciousness again and began to gnaw at him: What if Antoni Demetrius, the loyal soldier and practical, honest man, said to him that this Jesus really did heal his son? What if he said that this man did it because he really was some sort of holy prophet? How would he handle that? Marcus did not believe in such things. He believed in only what he could see and what he could touch. He believed in knowing human nature and how best to exploit it. The conflict he was now facing was that Demetrius was the very man who had helped him shape this way of thinking. If

Demetrius had changed, what did that mean for the very ways that Marcus thought about the world?

Demetrius was extraordinarily honest, even about his own deceptions. When he had to sell a piece of his soul to get ahead, he never tried to pretend he didn't know what he was doing. "You must always give up something to get something," he was fond of saying. But truth was never for sale with Demetrius. Some believed the reason he never rose even higher in rank was because he was too honest. He had risen about as high as an honest man could. The type of honesty that Demetrius possessed could quickly become a liability, once a truly high level of office was attained. One could only imagine what a pain it would be to have a truly honest man in a place like the Roman Senate.

"So what happens if this man whom I know so well turns to me," Marcus thought, "and says that he had a supernatural experience resulting in the health of his son, and he sincerely believes it was because of Jesus? What will I do with that information? How can I not accept it when it comes from Demetrius, who never has lied to me?"

As Marcus came closer to town, he suddenly began to perspire as his mind began racing faster and faster. If Demetrius said Jesus was indeed a "messiah," then Marcus would have to accept that that was what Demetrius really believed. And since Marcus knew Rome would never accept that notion, that news, perhaps along with Demetrius himself, would have to be buried. "And my role in all of this," Marcus thought to himself, "would then be to have to help cover it up. Now there's a thought: I would have to help cover up the truth about our killing a god."

Marcus kept going over this new scenario time and time again. His mind kept racing back to the same point: Wouldn't it be something if the Jews who believed in Jesus being a god were right? Wouldn't it be something if there really was one God, and he really did have an only son, and he really was sent to earth, and the Romans killed him? "And," Marcus pondered, "wouldn't it be something if my role in this cataclysmic event is to act as the agent of the cover-up?"

That thought began to both bother him and strangely amuse him at the same time. In a curious way he felt he would have much preferred to have been the one to have executed Jesus, if indeed he were some kind of god, than to be accused by the gods for all of eternity as being the one who helped mastermind a cover-up. What a reason to be damned: not because he stood face-to-face with a god and put him to death for the good of the empire, but because he acted as a co-conspirator in a cover-up.

Just then Marcus felt consumed with shame: he was an officer in the mightiest empire on earth, and yet he was pondering shirking his duty because of personal feelings about his friend or even worse over some god.

The face of Sejanus came into his mind: the image of a man who was tall and straight and fearless. His dedication to the empire was obvious, and there was no force on earth or in heaven that could ever dissuade him from doing his duty to Rome or to the emperor. Did he fear the gods? More than likely, the gods would have reason to fear him if ever they had the gall to suggest that he do something that he did not deem good for his emperor. Even emperors feared Sejanus, for they dared not conflict with what Sejanus understood as his duty toward Rome.

And now in this test of loyalty, Marcus was called upon in the name of duty to investigate everything that happened surrounding the death of Jesus and Rome's involvement in it. And yes, if necessary, he must even investigate the role his closest and dearest friend may have played in whatever happened. He believed his dearest friend would be most ashamed of him for forgetting in a moment of weakness that duty must be put above all else when one is a soldier in the empire. If in the course of performing that duty, life, happiness, and even the possibility of eternal salvation were lost, then that was the price one must be willing to pay, with gladness, for the sake of preserving the good of the empire. To act in any other way would be an act of disloyalty, and indeed unpatriotic. Loyalty was what joined him together with all of the men serving in the empire; it was the glue that kept Rome strong and able to face all enemies, foreign or domestic. They were strong because they had one goal, to serve the empire, no matter what the personal cost.

And if he and all of his comrades ended up in some eternal netherworld because of their service to the empire, then it would be a price well worth paying. For while on earth, they reigned supreme over countless lands. There was no power greater than Rome. These simple people knew nothing of honor and so now found themselves subjects in their own land to this mighty empire. Romans did not call upon gods to bless their work but relied on the power and might within them. If gods exist, then Rome's might must be a sign of the gods' blessings on it. And if other gods exist and stand against the power of Rome, then those gods weren't worth fearing, for if they could not stop Rome's might on earth, then they would have no victory over it in death.

Marcus found strength in the patriotic lecture he was giving himself. He began thinking about the epic poem *Paradise Lost* by Milton and started to recite parts of the speech Lucifer proclaimed while shaking his fist in defiance to the heavens when, after losing the great battle with God, he found himself forever an occupant of hell. Without realizing it, he started reciting the speech out loud:

> Farewell happy fields,
> Where joy forever dwells! Hail, horrors! hail
> Infernal world! and thou, profoundest Hell,
> Receive thy new possessor, one who brings
> A mind not to be changed by place or time.
> The mind is its own place, and in itself
> Can make a Heaven of Hell, a Hell of Heaven.
> What matter where if I be still the same,
> And what I should be, all but less than he
> Whom thunder hath made greater? Here at least
> We shall be free; the Almighty hath not built
> Here for his envy, will not drive us hence.
> Here we may reign secure; and in my choice
> To reign is worth ambition, though in Hell:
> Better to reign in Hell than serve in Heaven.

"What matter where," he thought, "if I be still the same. A Roman, an officer of the imperial army of the emperor. It is better," Marcus thought, "to reign while serving the emperor than grovel and serve a God."

He thought that if this assignment forever changed his life and meant that he could no longer enjoy the comfort of friendships and even loves as he once had known them, then he must be prepared to give up joy for duty and, in so doing, find an even greater joy within.

As they drew near the building that housed the *Judean*, Marcus suddenly realized he had been withdrawn and silent too long and shook his head back and forth.

"Are you all right, commander?" asked a soldier in the squadron.

"Fine, soldier, just fine."

"What's the matter with me?" Marcus thought. "I know Demetrius better than anyone. There is no way he's going to end up telling me he has become a convert of Jesus. If he were here in town, he would have done his job as professionally and as calmly as anyone in the garrison. He would have acted as I must now, as a Roman officer. I don't know how all of this got started, but I'm sure that by next year this time, Demetrius and I will be enjoying wine in the streets of Rome together, the same way we did when we were young and at the academy."

He truly wanted his hopes about his friend to come true, despite the sense of unease he could still feel in his gut. He sensed that for the first time, something bigger than the empire was closing in on both him and his friend, and try as he would, he could not shake the feeling of impending peril.

– CHAPTER FIVE –

"WHEN YOU AND YOUR BUDDY Commander Marcus get together for your little drink, be sure to tell him how much we Jews appreciated his giving us a lesson in Isaiah's suffering servant motif," David said with a smirk.

"Now now," replied Gerry, "you have to admit that was pretty good. He probably waited a long time for an opportunity to spring a quotation from one of your own prophets on you."

Gerry turned to the camera crew and told them she needed to put a tag on the story of the news conference. It was still the middle of the night in the States, so Gerry knew the spot wouldn't be aired until 6 A.M. at least.

"David, don't go away, I need to do a quick tag for this story. Guys, how's the light?"

Gerry waited for word from the crew and began speaking into the camera: "This is Gerry Simmons, WXOT foreign correspondent. As you heard, there are more surprises in this shocking story. Judas, one of the twelve, it appears committed suicide this morning. Further, it seems initial reports of strange phenomena at the time of Jesus' death were simply rumors. As soon as more news becomes available, we'll report it here. . . ."

"Get that off to the station and meet be back here in one-half hour," Gerry said, and the crew sped off toward the studio. "What do you think of this Judas business?" she asked David.

"I think we ought to find out where they have taken the body, and then I think we need to talk to whoever found it."

"Those are my thoughts exactly."

"You mind if I stop at a phone and call my office? Some of us reporters still have to work for a living," he said, and they both laughed. David went over to a nearby phone. When he returned, he looked a little pale.

"David, what's the matter?"

"I think you and I might want to go to my office right away."

"Why?" asked Gerry. "Aren't we going to try to find out who the shepherd..."

David cut her off and said, "Let's go."

There was a sudden seriousness in David's manner that told Gerry she should do as she was told.

"I've already asked my secretary to send someone over here to meet your crew and to tell them where you're going," he said without the slightest humor in his voice. That more than anything made Gerry wonder.

After David and Gerry entered the small building that was the home of the *Judean,* they went immediately to his office and closed the door. His secretary sat by his desk and appeared quite shaken.

"Are you all right?" David asked her.

"Yes, I was just a bit startled."

"Where is it?" David asked.

"I put it in your desk drawer."

David opened his top desk drawer and retrieved a brown paper bag. He carefully pulled out the contents, which consisted of a large, rolled-up piece of paper wrapped in a cloth of some sort. David removed the cloth and very slowly began to unravel the paper.

"Will somebody tell me what the hell is going on?" Gerry said, but just above a whisper.

David kept slowly unrolling the paper until at last it was almost completely flat. It was then that they began to see traces of what appeared to be blood on the paper. And then, there it was — a small portion of a human finger, apparently cut just above the knuckle.

"What the hell is that?" asked Gerry.

David looked long and hard at what was on his desk. He then turned to Gerry, and for the first time in days a gleam was back in his eyes. "It's the note, my American friend, it's the note."

Gerry's eyes widened, and she said in almost a whisper, "You mean the suicide note, from Judas?"

"Yes, and it appears he wanted to make sure we knew it was authentic. I guess he figured he wouldn't be in pain all that long anyway."

Gerry sat down in a nearby chair. "I know it's a little early, but do you think we could have a drink?" The secretary got up and said, "I thought you'd never ask. Remember, I opened this, and not with the careful suspense you two did. I almost lost my breakfast. I still don't know how I managed to roll it up and put it back in the bag."

Gerry looked again at the note on the desk, and even though she was a veteran journalist, she still found herself avoiding looking at the bloody stump that was once part of a finger.

"Who delivered it?" she asked the secretary. "How did it get here?"

"I don't really know who delivered it. When I got to the office this morning, I found it stuck in the mailbox outside the front door. I just assumed it was a parcel of some type. We get stuff left for the paper all the time."

Suddenly, David let out a loud whistle, followed by the word "Damn!"

"What?" said Gerry with great anticipation in her voice.

"After forty years in this business, there are few things left to surprise me, but this one I must admit came straight out of left field. I should have seen it right away. The finger was a dead giveaway. Do you notice anything about the signature, Gerry?"

"It's signed Judas Iscariot," answered Gerry, a little puzzled at what David was getting at.

"You leave us for a few days, and already city life has dulled your reporter's eye, my friend. Look closely at the name."

Gerry got up from her chair and took a closer look at the name. It was only then that she noticed the change. Instead of the word "Iscariot," there was written the word "Sicariot," Judas Sicariot.

"What does this mean?" Gerry asked with great curiosity.

"Well, my friend, let's first of all agree that even a man in great pain both physically and mentally would still know how to sign his name correctly, agreed?"

"Of course."

At this point David turned to his secretary and asked if they could be left alone for a moment. He then turned to Gerry and said, "If my guess is right, Judas must have been a member of the Sicarii party. They are so called from the Greek word meaning assassins. If this is so, Judas was a member of one of the most radical revolutionary groups in Israel. They get their name from the small knives they carry under their robes known as *sicae* and have been known to assassinate Romans whenever they get the chance. No doubt he used his *sicae* to sever his finger. Notice how clean the cut is? This letter could answer many, many questions, my friend, many, many questions."

Gerry found herself wanting to ask a thousand more questions, not the least of which was, Why, after being a journalist here for so many years, was this the first time she had ever heard of such a group? However, she decided instead to get to the more immediate matter at hand, the letter itself.

Gerry and David both stood over the letter and began to read. The writing was not completely legible, and some of it tended to ramble a bit, so it took both of them some time to get through it. The letter read:

My name is Judas, son of Simon and a member of the "twelve disciples of Jesus," as we were called. I have removed the smallest finger of my left hand and have enclosed it in this note, so that you may know I am in fact who I say I am. By the time you get this letter, I will be dead. I will take my life in an area where my body is sure to be found. When you examine my body, you may look at my hand, and see that what I have told you is true.

First let me say that I believe from the bottom of my heart that God did anoint Jesus of Nazareth to become the messiah, the son of God, and the liberator of our people. In the three years I spent with this man, I have seen, with my own eyes, the power of the Almighty work wonders through him. From the moment I first met him, I believed, even before he himself became fully aware of it, that he was the Christ, the one whom the prophet Isaiah foretold would be our deliverance.

But a short time ago, I also became aware, through the power of God, that all we were taught as children of Abraham about the coming of the messiah might not be fulfilled unless we mortals helped to bring it about. I began to see that God could indeed raise a man up from among us, just as he did with Moses, to be the chosen deliverer of Israel, and yet he who was chosen could refuse to follow his anointed mission and indeed shrink from the mighty task set before him. When such an event takes place in history, it often falls upon one less blessed, but perhaps more faithful, to act for the fulfillment of prophecy.

I now know that my whole life was a test leading up to this moment. I believe that God did put me to the test to see if I were worthy to follow the Master and be ready to assist him, lest he falter in any way to ascend to the heights of the heavens, so that he might return with his angels and rid our land of those who would once again try and enslave the chosen people of God. It is for this reason that I was led to become a member of the Sicarii, to prove to the Lord God that I would do anything asked of me to help bring about the day when we would live as God has promised in a land of milk and honey, rather than in a land filled with pagan Roman infidels. Once the God of our fathers saw that I was truly willing to give my life to him and his people, he then led me to Jesus so that I might act as the instrument of his divine conquest, lest he falter from God's command.

Jesus, in his last year, began to totally reject the kingship of this world and even began to reject the mission that he would be ordained to lead in the next life. Although he was blessed, he began to stray from the divine mission to wipe the earth clean of those who did not believe in the Lord God, and he began to speak instead of another mission calling for brotherhood even among those who are Gentiles. He began to reject God's command of an eye for an eye, and he began to preach salvation even to the accursed Samaritans, who we are taught to curse even in the temple. Jesus swayed so far from the path that he even healed the son of a Roman soldier, a son who would one day grow up to kill Jews as his father did.

It was for this reason that God instructed me to set into motion the events that would lead to the death of Jesus, so that he might return and fulfill his true mission upon the earth.

Let me say here that there is no measure for the contempt I hold for all those who believed they could buy from me my loyalty, either from my Master or from God. Know, those of you who gave me money to betray my Lord, that you did not use me; it was I who used you.

Let all who see, observe that when the message of God is not obeyed, death and chaos are always the result. Those who believe that the Romans are our brothers, look at what they did to the anointed one. Those who believe that the high priests who get rich in the temple are our brothers, look at how they conspired to kill the holy one. Those who believe the kings and princes are our brothers, look at how they readily joined in the plot to kill the anointed one. And even those who believe that all of the twelve understood and were brothers, look how they all fled when faced with the martyr's death of true believers, like that of the anointed one.

You might ask why I have taken my own life. I have taken it so that I might join he who was crucified. Now I know that Jesus truly understands what his mission is, and indeed will return to rid the earth of those who do not bow down to God. I go to be with him so that I might return at his right hand and, with the angels of heaven, slay the infidels who rape our land.

I go to join Jesus. Beware, oh children of Sodom, the day of the Lord is at hand.

Judas Sicariot, servant of God

Gerry sat back down in her chair and took a long, deep breath. David kept going over and over the contents of the letter. Finally Gerry said to David, "What do you make of all of this?"

David looked up from his desk, turned toward Gerry, and returned the question: "What do you think of all of this?"

"What do I think? I think the guy was a twenty-four carat fruitcake, a fanatic with delusions of grandeur. I think he was half-past crazy, going on nuts. That's what I think of our late friend Mr. Judas Iscariot, or Sicariot, or whatever the hell his name is supposed to be."

Gerry found herself speaking louder and getting angry, though she didn't quite know why. The last time she felt this sort of inexplicable anger was when Jim Pratt began to tell her the details surrounding the death of Jesus. All she knew was that Judas's letter made her angry. Maybe it was because she had covered so many stories in the past about people like this, people who were capable of blowing up buildings with children in them because they believed that they were driven by some higher sense of purpose than the rest of the world. Maybe it was because she was embarrassed that a whole terrorist organization existed for years right under her nose and she didn't know about it. Or maybe she was just tired of people like Jesus ending up dead while people like Judas ended up self-proclaimed heroes on the six o'clock news.

In any event, she calmed down, took a sip of the wine she had asked for earlier, and waited to hear what David would say both about the letter and undoubtedly about her outburst.

"I tell you," he said, "I too believe that the person who wrote this letter is crazy. The difference between us is that while, like you, I don't excuse the craziness, I do, unlike you, take the cause seriously.

Most men aren't born crazy; most men are driven crazy. And to simply point the finger at the symptom, without recognizing the cause, does no one any good. The problem with you, and indeed with most of the Western world, is that you have no idea what it's like to live in an occupied land."

Gerry began to protest with a clear tone of indignation in her voice: "You're going to tell me that I don't know what oppression is? Me, who always had to be twice as good at just about everything, in order to..."

David cut her off: "I didn't say you didn't know what it was like to be oppressed; I said you didn't know what it was like to live in an occupied land. There's a difference. Suppose when you returned to America, you found out that Russia or some other country had somehow come in the middle of the night and completely taken over your country. Suppose you were suddenly told what you could read and what you could wear and where you could or could not worship whatever God you happen to believe in. Would you still feel that everything should be dealt with rationally, or would you begin to believe that revolution in some form or another might need to take place? In fact didn't you and the British have a slight disagreement that produced just such people as our dead friend here?"

Gerry again began to protest: "Well, first of all, my ancestors didn't come out all that well on either side of the American revolution, so the analogy doesn't quite hold as much water for me personally. But still, I do believe there is a world of difference between people like Patrick Henry and these creeps."

"Why?" asked David. "Is it because you believe we are freer under Rome than America was under the British? Is it because under the present system we are allowed certain freedoms, such as this newspaper? Do you believe that if tomorrow I began publishing a series of articles calling for the death of Pilate and the overthrow of Tiberius I'd be allowed to remain in business very long? The point is that it doesn't matter how many freedoms we are allowed; it is the fact that someone other than ourselves is giving us permission as to what may or may not happen in our own land. And when those who should be in the forefront of ridding our land of such oppression become willing participants, fearing that any other course of action might endanger their own political status in this land, well, it all can become insane enough to drive men crazy."

"Are you trying to tell me that you believe this guy Judas was some sort of patriot?"

David smiled and said, "I'm trying to tell you that he was probably a man who started out with a hunger for freedom and justice and ended up frustrated to the point of madness. What is it that the black American poet whose work you showed me last year wrote? I can't remember his name, but I loved his work."

"Langston Hughes," Gerry answered.

"Right. Well, I will never forget that beautiful image he created when he wrote the words, 'What do you do with a dream deferred?' You remember — it's where that line 'a raisin in the sun' comes from."

Gerry laughed a little. "Yes, I remember. I introduced his poems to you, remember?"

"Well, Gerry, this is a land filled with people who every day see their hopes for freedom dry up like that raisin in the sun. That will produce different effects in different people. Some will learn to wait. Many will join factions and different political parties. Some will learn how to exploit the situation. Some will become Zealots. And some will go mad. But most often the ones who go mad are the ones who start out with the greatest hopes and the greatest courage. I would bet you that the reason Jesus was attracted to Judas in the first place was their hearts were probably alike. They both had a fire in them. They both proved that they were willing to sacrifice all that they had, including their lives, for what they believed in. And do not forget, my friend, that there were many, including the people in the town where Jesus was born, who believed he was as deranged as we now judge Judas to be. And if you call suicide madness, ask anyone who knew how the system works around here what it meant for Jesus to come to Jerusalem and pull that stunt at the temple. That was as suicidal as hanging yourself from a tree."

"Who knows?" Gerry said. "But while I would love to spend the rest of the day discussing philosophy with you, it seems you and I have a more immediate situation to deal with, and that is what do we do with this note. My crew should be here shortly, and I know I want to have the exclusive on this, but should we call the police and let them know we have it or let them read about it in your newspaper or see it on TV?"

David was about to speak when he was interrupted by the interoffice phone. He picked up the phone and heard his secretary say very calmly that there were about twenty Roman soldiers waiting outside, and the head of the contingent requested his presence immediately. David was about to tell her to tell them he would be right there, thinking that he would hide the note back in his desk until they were gone. Before he could finish, however, he heard a short knock on the door. Without waiting for a response, a Roman soldier entered. "Ah, look who I found, my two favorite reporters," said Commander Marcus, as he walked in and closed the door behind him.

Marcus gave a quick smile toward Gerry as he walked over to the desk where the note was resting and looked at it without picking it up. David sat in stony silence as Marcus carefully read through it.

"Well I'll be damned," he said. "The kid was dead right. Judas was a member of the Sicarii."

He turned toward the two reporters and said, "My investigations officer came up with his, shall we say, Judas's rather odd political affiliations a short time ago. It was his opinion that Judas wanted not only the press but everyone to know that he was really a fanatical terrorist working both ends against the middle. He left a trail of clues big enough to drive a reporter's ego through, including the finger bit. He was some piece of work." He paused and then went on: "I must admit that we always thought that if anyone was working some kind of double agent thing, it would have been Simon. It just goes to show you, you can't trust anyone these days."

Gerry smiled and asked, "What happens now?"

"Well, Gerry, I'm afraid we have to confiscate the note, and I must ask you not to print or report any of this on TV until it's cleared with the Roman authorities. Somehow they knew about the possibility of the note, and it did not take much to figure out that if someone like Judas was to deliver it to the press, he'd send it to this noble establishment. Nevertheless, I have here a restraining order signed by the emperor's representative making it a crime against the empire for the contents of this note to be made public before it has been officially cleared by Rome."

Marcus held Gerry by the arm and walked her toward the door. But he still said what he needed to in earshot of David: "Now, Gerry, I want you to do something for me. I want you to promise me that you will not let this information get out until I have a chance to clear this upstairs. I don't believe it's against our interest to have the world know about Judas, and I feel reasonably sure that I can have this released back to you within a matter of hours. Now I'm telling you this because I know you're a reasonable woman and because we know some other reporters in this room sometimes forget that, like it or not, Rome still is the ultimate authority in this part of the world."

From across the room David said, "Oh no, commander, I can assure you that I am constantly reminded of how much freedom we don't have because of Rome's occupation of our land. Please be assured that as long as you are here, we will always have men like Judas blowing up buildings and turning themselves into self-proclaimed martyrs."

Marcus smiled and continued speaking to Gerry as though he had not heard anything: "Therefore, I am asking you, for the sake of this publication, which we all know has far more leeway than most, and for the sake of everyone's well-being, that you please allow me the chance to clear this with the Roman authorities. As you can guess, things are pretty touchy in the high command right now, and the people who sent me to fetch this note I would not cross for anything in this world. Believe me, I know what I'm talking about. So please talk some sense into your colleague and get him to check his own martyr's complex for a few hours. Because if he ends up on a cross, I doubt he'll get as much worldwide attention as Jesus is getting. *Capiech?*"

Marcus opened the door and ordered one of the soldiers to come in and collect the note. He then turned to the two reporters and said, "After all, I would hate to lose the opportunity to read constantly what slime we are from the best supermarket tabloid in the Middle East."

Marcus shook Gerry's hand and reminded her once again that he would enjoy getting together and having that drink once all this blew over. He then left with the other soldiers.

Gerry turned to David and shrugged her shoulders. "Well, that's that. I still believe we'll be able to put out the inside story on this once Marcus has it released back to us. And I believe he is right: the empire won't lose any sleep over the world knowing Judas's true identity."

She turned to look at David, whose face revealed pure detestation. He was quiet for some time, then got up and poured himself a drink. He did not say a word for a full sixty seconds. Gerry knew that when David was like this it was best to let him alone.

When he finally did speak, it was to say one word. He took a drink and without looking up from his glass uttered the word "Bastard!"

– CHAPTER SIX –

Tiberius Julius Caesar lounged on a low couch in the great hall at the palace of the Roman emperor. Although he was a decorated war hero who had been emperor now for eighteen years, he was still insecure in his power. The stepson of the late great emperor Augustus, Tiberius knew he had become emperor by default: Augustus had simply had no one better to leave the empire to. Many in Rome viewed him as unworthy of the position, adding to his insecurity and ruthlessness.

Tiberius pondered what this whole Jesus affair meant to Rome and the empire and then asked an aide: "What have you got for me on this business in Jerusalem?"

"Not much, your highness; the investigations are still going on. His Lordship Sejanus is leading the investigation, as you ordered, and he has put in charge locally a commander named Marcus to find out all there is to know from the Jerusalem side."

"Who is this local commander, Marcus?"

"His file is on your desk, your highness. He is a good officer: ambitious, bright, and loyal to the empire. He will do whatever it takes to find out what went on. His orders are to report directly to Sejanus, and to no one else. We expect to have his report within the week."

"Not good enough. I want it within the next two days. Tell His Lordship Sejanus that I want him to go down there personally and spread around some of that celebrated fear that he is so famous for. I want some answers, and I want them now."

"Your highness, His Lordship is already there, and he has promised to stay in the area until the answers you require are given to your satisfaction."

Dealing with Lucius Sejanus was not one of the emperor's favorite pastimes. Many believed that Sejanus was even more powerful than the emperor himself. He was also a real Roman insider. Tiberius knew that if he were ever overthrown, the coup would be led by a man like Sejanus. He knew Sejanus would never do such a thing for his own power and glory. Rather it would be because he became somehow convinced that the emperor was no longer "good for the empire." The emperor dealt with Sejanus as one must deal with a fierce dog: no matter how afraid of him he was, he refused — by sheer force of will — to show that fear. If he ever did, Sejanus would devour him. There were also times when the emperor felt that Sejanus obeyed his commands only out of respect for the office, not out of any personal respect for him. All this troubled Tiberius deeply and led him to consider ways to destroy Sejanus before Sejanus could destroy him. "What if," the emperor thought, "one day the man no longer lived up to his office? Perhaps there might be some way to use all of this business in Judea to my advantage." The key would be found most likely in Sejanus's protegé, the man Sejanus personally sponsored to become governor of Judea, the man who in some way might be held responsible for all of this mess: Pilate.

The emperor had always believed that the procurator of Judea was not made of the "right stuff" of real leaders. Pilate had never known how to lead. He was appointed to his post only because Sejanus insisted that Pilate be given something of importance. Judea was the least important post the emperor could assign him, believing that once there, he could not get into too much trouble. Now an international incident had arisen that could have been avoided if only Pilate had either used some backbone or used some common sense. "Remember, Sejanus," thought the emperor, "he is your boy. This could all prove to be an interestingly messy situation should one choose to exploit it."

On the other hand, there was a legitimate untidiness that had to be handled here as well. Putting aside his feelings about Sejanus, the emperor knew there was a problem of damage control. He had to find out if this was going to be as much a problem for the empire as some of his aides suggested it might be. He knew the press would be pounding down the palace doors looking for answers to all of this. The press secretary could only do so much — eventually the emperor would have to make a statement.

It made the emperor long for the good-old days, before an emperor had to worry about politics. But then he remembered that those times never really existed, times when sheer might could be used to answer a lot of otherwise unanswerable questions or to extinguish those who might answer the questions. Things tended to be a bit more barbarous back then, but certainly more honest. Now "diplomacy" had to be used in all things at all times. "Oh, we can still kill as many people," he thought, "but we must do it now with diplomacy. We can still enslave, oppress, murder, torture, whatever, as often as it serves the majority's purposes. But we must do it now with diplomacy. And what is diplomacy as far as the average Roman citizen is concerned? It means we must find words and phrases that sound good and that convince both our people and other governments that that which they know is true is not true at all. In earlier, better days we would have simply called out the army and proclaimed with spears at the ready: 'Yes, we killed your Jesus of Nazareth, and we did not do it because we were afraid of him or because we thought he was right and we were wrong but because we are Romans, and we can do what we want. Why? Because we are the biggest, toughest, bravest, and strongest empire on earth. And we know the majority of you will support us as long as you get whatever cut you believe is due you. Was it a mistake to kill him? Was he innocent or guilty? Who cares? The deed is done, and we cannot waste time worrying over spilt blood, for we have money and power and other vital interests we must get on with.' Instead, today we must call out an army of word warriors. We must explain to people whatever they want to hear. Not the truth, mind you, or even the near truth, but we must paint the picture that will absolve ourselves and our allies for what we have done. What hypocrisy."

The emperor wandered over to a nearby chair and sat down: "I remember," he thought, "when I was growing up hearing the stories about how members of the senate plunged their daggers into the body of the greatest Caesar of them all, the great emperor, Julius the First. I remember hearing of all the sanctimonious politicians waving the banner of Rome high as he lay there dying, telling everyone what a sacrifice they had just endured for the goodness and glory of Rome. Never for their own wealth or glory, no never. Caesar lay dead, yet they claimed to be the victims. Marc Antony was right to rally the people against them.

"And now we've got this. Suddenly, you hear words like 'great man' and 'great prophet,' and people ask, 'How could your government let this happen?' The man was a two-bit, dime-a-dozen Jewish preacher who happened to get a little more press than the rest of them. He was a mosquito who could have been quietly swatted with a fly swatter. Or better still, he could have been left alone to preach about love and universal brotherhood until he was ninety. After all, like most of the people who wander the land trying to convince man that he is somehow better than his greedy warlike behavior suggests, he would have soon become more of an entertainment feature than a threat to anyone. Instead, thanks to that idiot in Judea, he was run over by a steamroller and flattened out to be bigger now than he ever was in life."

He walked over to the table and poured himself some wine. He turned to his aide and asked just what time the others would be there.

"They are here your highness; they await your command to enter."

"Have them wait awhile," said the emperor. He drank and then said to the aide: "Do you know they're building a city and naming it after me?"

"Your highness?" said the aide, somewhat puzzled by the question. Everyone in the empire was aware of the city being built in honor of the emperor. It was considered a great diplomatic conquest that the Jews, a people conquered by Rome, would now build a city and name it after the emperor himself.

"The Jews are building a city complete with a castle near the hot springs, and they are naming it after me. It shall be called Tiberias. Herod has so decreed it himself."

The aide said: "I am well aware, as is all of Rome, that His Majesty King Herod is building the city Tiberias. It shall stand for a thousand years as a testimony to your highness and the marvelous achievements your administration has accomplished."

"Yes, I see, you may go. I shall call you when I'm ready." With that the emperor dismissed his aide.

"And why is this conquered people doing me and Rome such an honor?" the emperor pondered. "Is it because those savage people have finally understood that if it had not been for us, they, with all their factions and Zealots, would have torn themselves to shreds by now? Have they finally understood that if it had not been for Rome, they would have been occupied by someone with far more ruthlessness than us or would have become victims of those blood-sucking temple fanatics, who use religion to exact from their people far more than we expect from them? Is it because they're willing to admit that they have not had a just administration since their great king Solomon? Or is it that they believe that Rome can be bought and that I can be bribed by naming a city after me? Is it that they believe that I am so desirous of being liked that I would allow anything to happen, as long as I can still have someone, somewhere, even the Jews, name a city after me?

"These Jews are nothing if not clever. They're survivors. They would have to be in order to endure after so many years of occupation. They know that even though I am emperor, I am not loved as my stepfather was. They know that if either of my mother's two children from her former marriage had lived, I would not be emperor today. Could it be that they believe that I am so lonely and in need of acceptance that I would become everlastingly grateful to His Majesty Herod for this 'honor' and then would allow myself, and indeed Rome, to become instruments of their deceit? Perhaps even now they are hovering in their temple saying: 'Yes, we used your procurator, and in doing so, we realize that we have used you and Rome. And if you dare give us any static over this Jesus business, we'll name that city we are building in your honor after someone else.'

"Oh, be careful, foolish people. For if indeed we find out that this was all a plot to make us look foolish in the eyes of the world, we will crush you and your city and leave your bones to rot in that desert you call home."

The emperor walked over to a cord and pulled it, summoning his personal aide. "Tell the council to enter," he ordered. The aide bowed and left the room.

As he waited, the emperor continued to think of the matters in Judea: "What does Pilate think of me? Does he believe that all I am about is bricks and mortar, cities and monuments, all of which will turn to dust not very long after our bones decorate the parched earth? Did they use my city, Tiberias, as a pawn in tricking him to do what ill-served Rome? Did Pilate not know that as long as he served the best interest of Rome, the empire would always support him? Did he believe that we could be swayed from that support if they who are occupied and under our authority threatened to go over his head and come to us? He is procurator, damn it, and when in Judea, he is Rome. Have we begun to be like the very people we have conquered, ready to sell our kingdoms for personal greed or our honor for personal safety and gratification?"

At that moment a large door — emblazoned with the images of lions and other wild creatures — opened and members of the emperor's governing council began to file into the room. One by one, they bowed before the emperor and gave him a salute, "Hail Caesar!" and then stood behind the chair at the place reserved for them at the table. The emperor walked to the head of the table, sat down, and waited for a second or two before inviting the others to be seated.

The emperor liked to watch all of these generals, senators, and very high-ranking Roman officials, many of whom he felt believed they were better suited to run Rome than himself, all standing waiting for him to allow them to be seated. It was one of the small things that reminded everyone that he — and no one else — was emperor.

"Gentleman, please be seated. You all know why we are here, so let's get right to it. At present, General Sejanus is in Judea finding out firsthand just what happened and what role Rome played in the matters leading up to the execution of Jesus. We know that he was executed under Roman law, but just what he was charged with seems a bit sketchy. At first it seemed to be a purely Jewish matter, things dealing with their gods, their notion of messiahs, and so on. Then somehow the matter was turned over to us, and he was convicted by the governor, I am told at first reluctantly, of sedition and treason. It seems that he was next handed over to the Jewish people as some sort of sacrifice in accordance with their local feast or something. And then, in some way that's not yet clear, he ended up being executed by Roman authorities. Since we have not gotten all of the facts just yet, I do not want to spend this meeting dealing with fault or even facts about what did happen there. What I need from you at this point is suggestions about what to do in terms of the press and the PR problem that this could conceivably have for Rome.

"As you can imagine, our ambassadors are calling in from all over the world asking what they should tell the press. Already General Magnus put his foot in it by suggesting that we would never do anything so dumb as to execute Jesus, only to be told minutes later that in fact we did have a hand in it. The ambassador in New York had agreed to meet the press, fully ready to deny any involvement on the part of Rome in this whole affair. We got to him just in time. But we can't keep the press waiting on this very long or else we not only will look guilty, but we will look like fools. And you know, gentlemen, I will not stand for that. Your comments?"

At that, various members of the council began to speak, but one man outshouted the rest: "Your highness, first and foremost, whatever happens we must never be seen by the world as failing to support our local representative in Judea. We must back the governor there and leave no doubt in anyone's mind that we will always support our local Roman officials."

A second councilor rose and spoke: "Your highness, I for one believe this whole affair is an outrage. What is the whole purpose of capital punishment in that part of the world? It is to act as a deterrent against anyone breaking the law. The law, gentlemen. What makes Rome a civilized empire is that even though we are strong, we do not throw our weight around in the occupied territories with no rhyme or reason. This is not the Rome of thirty years ago when we simply took what we wanted without feeling the need to be a just people. No, today, gentlemen, we must become a nation of law. And those who break the law, and only those, deserve the ultimate act of punishment. However, if the law can simply be manipulated by any group who so desires, then we are no better today than we were in the days before we wrote those laws. If we show the world that capital punishment to us is simply another expedient political tool — to be manipulated either by us or by those whom we place in power — it makes the people in these territories feel that their lives are not worth preserving and that they can be put to death at any moment for anything. It, therefore, becomes no deterrent; it simply becomes another form of political maneuvering. If you can die for having views different from the temple, why not risk death for something more important in their eyes, such as overthrowing the government, or killing soldiers as often as possible? I say that if anyone should be brought to trial, and indeed executed, it should be those responsible for letting this whole thing happen."

A smattering of applause broke out from some of the members of the council. The emperor turned and looked sternly at the councilor. "And would you have me execute Pontius Pilate as well? He, after all, is the ultimate one responsible in Judea."

Another councilor began to speak: "Your Highness, with all due respect to my lord councilor, I disagree. I believe that those responsible for Jesus' death ought to be given Rome's highest honor. Unlike some of you in this room, I had the opportunity to hear this preacher speak, and I tell you he was a dangerous man, a man who threatened our vital interest in that part of the world. The Jewish priesthood did exactly what needed to be done."

One of the other councilors rose to his feet in protest: "Surely, my lord councilor, you do not believe all of those Jewish myths surrounding this man, that he was their long-lost messiah come down from heaven to establish the new world order with their God as king? Were you worried that the ancient prophesies might have come true if Rome did not put this man to death in the nick of time? Gentleman,

I believe Jesus may have found his first Roman convert, right here in the council of the emperor."

At that a few of the councilors began to chuckle, but the councilor who spoke previously remained calm. When it was quiet, he began once again to speak. "First of all, my lord councilor, if I were to become a convert to whatever religion Jesus was espousing, it might surprise you to know I would be far from the first Roman to join him. Even here in Rome there are many who believe in this man, and now that he is dead, he will become even more famous. But when I speak of dangers to the empire, I speak of the way Jesus began to show the priesthood up for what it indeed is. Why, my lord councilors, do we allow the Jewish monarchy and priesthood to exist? Why have we never insisted that their structures be broken down or their religion be outlawed? It is but for one reason: we keep them intact because they provide a valuable service to the empire. Through their religion they keep a sense of order throughout the land, and that sense of order helps Rome maintain control in the area. We keep them in power, and, in turn, they keep us in power, without the needless bloodshed and force that we would otherwise have to inflict in order to sustain our presence. The only control the priesthood has over the people is their ability to hold their theology over their heads like a sword. Any mortal enemy, no matter how strong, can, under the right circumstances, be defeated. But gods, gentlemen, gods are harder to defeat. And from my understanding of the God of their forefathers, he is one not to be trifled with."

The councilor had gotten everyone's attention and went on: "If Jesus is perceived as being a spokesman for their God, and he begins to tell them that what the priests and the scribes are telling them to do is somehow different from what their God wants, then the effectiveness of the temple comes into question. And the temple authorities know that their usefulness to us would then come into question. They know that if their effectiveness comes into question, then it might force us to make, shall we say, some modifications in the way we do things concerning them. They decided to look out for their best interest, and in so doing, they looked our for ours as well.

"Your highness, we must never forget that the priesthood is motivated by the most basic of all human instincts, self-preservation. However, if they were not so afraid of losing what they have come to believe is precious, they might just come to understand that we need them as much as they need us. What would have happened if

Jesus had somehow convinced the majority of the people that he was indeed the messiah and that the time for standing up for truth and freedom was at hand? What would have happened if he had gotten the majority of the people to believe that their God was ready to protect them and that somehow their God was once again ready to take on another modern empire, just as, according to their traditions, he did with Moses and the Egyptians? If the movement had gotten bigger, sooner or later the priesthood, motivated by that same self-preservation, might have moved farther away from us and closer to the people. Then what could we have done? Send in the army, massacre thousands of people? What would we have done in the aftermath of such an invasion? I tell you we would have had a bigger PR problem on our hands than we do at the moment. Thus, I say to all here present that we all know the time for using brute force is fast coming to an end. We must now use as much diplomacy as we do steel. It was far better for Jesus to die, and precisely at this time, when he could still be seen as a martyr, but before he became too uncontrollably dangerous. I tell you most solemnly, my lords, the temple did the right thing."

As the councilor took his seat, the emperor kept hearing the word "diplomacy" ringing again in his ears.

The emperor began to speak: "Gentlemen, whether or not you agree that this Jesus had to die, and whether or not you believe that the priesthood acted in their best interest, or in ours, we still have a delicate situation on our hands, and we have to make a statement to the press. So if you will kindly limit your remarks to the issue at hand, I would be most grateful. I assure you that this problem will be with us for quite some time, and we will have ample opportunity to discuss the merits of Jesus' death then."

The emperor knew that despite all of the polite words he used, everyone in the room understood that it was a direct order to be obeyed immediately.

"Your highness, I believe the key to all of this as far as the public is concerned can be found in our governmental referendum labeled the Cultural Noninterference Act, which was ratified by the general council and signed into law first by your father just before his death, and later re-signed into law by your highness. It clearly states the following: 'All countries under the protection of the Roman government shall in no way be forced to give up any of their particular laws, whether religious or secular, as long as they do not interfere with the rule of law set down by Rome. In such cases where there is no conflict to the vital interest of the Roman government, Rome shall assist in any way possible the fostering of local customs and beliefs, but will do so only at the request of the legitimate local representatives of the nation or nations under Roman subjugation.' Now, it is quite clear, your highness, that this was a local matter, and we were clearly asked to assist in carrying it out. We are obligated by law to help the people in any way they ask us as long as it does not interfere with our vital interest. And even if some in this body now believe that perhaps executing Jesus was not the wisest thing to do, we can still clearly make a case that we acted within the laws of the treaty signed by your father and the Jews. We can even go so far as to say that we decry the violence. The governor of Judea tried in vain to put a halt to the proceedings, but it would have clearly been a violation to the occupying treaty if we had refused to assist the Jews in carrying out a part of their religious ritual and customs."

A general sound of agreement arose in the room. Another member of the council spoke: "I believe that might indeed be the ticket, your highness. It was after all Rome that took away the local government's right to perform executions on its own. If Jesus had broken a religious law and was found guilty as a Jew of the offense, Rome could have been accused of completely ignoring the rights and freedom of the temple authorities if it had not given in to their request. And the temple represents the very heart and soul of the Jewish people."

"I must protest, your highness," said another councilor. "Jesus was not tried and convicted of some religious matter, at least not according to what I have heard from the media. He was convicted of treason against the state. How can we say...?"

The council member was interrupted by still another member: "It was still a Jewish matter," he protested. "Rome only acted in accordance with the treaty. That is all that matters."

A brief argument broke out between the two council members, but the emperor stood and lifted his hand for silence.

"Gentlemen," he said, "even though we are still waiting for a full statement from the governor, I did receive a short while ago a preliminary report on just what took place at the trial, at least at the public trial involving Pilate. I think you ought to hear this, for it may have a bearing on the very topic we are discussing." The emperor picked a report off the table. "This came to us from one of our agents who had infiltrated the crowd that yelled for the death of

Jesus. Pilate, as you all know, was always a bit dramatic, but in this instance his sense of drama may have paid off. According to the report, when Pilate pronounced sentence he did a very interesting thing. I quote, 'The governor had a bowl brought to him in full view of the people, whereupon he proceeded to wash his hands before the crowd. He proclaimed in a loud voice, "I am innocent of this man's blood," and then ordered that Jesus and the water be taken away at the same time.'"

Many of the councilors in the room looked up in surprise. "He actually did that, in full view of everyone?" said one of them.

"Yes," said the emperor, "so the obvious question is: Do we have enough here to give this to our friends over in room 17B, I mean, enough to let them handle the mess in their usual manner?"

At once a collective sigh of relief arose. Even though no one at the table said anything, everyone knew precisely who the folks in office 17B were and what they did best. For a new type of official had emerged in the empire: people whose sole job was to put "spin" on the most unpopular events and turn them around so that they meant something different. Yes, between the treaty and Pilate's dramatic gesture, there was enough to be given over to the spin doctors.

Something about these spin doctors bothered most of the council members, including the emperor. Spin doctors in some ways marked the beginning of the end of an era dominated by the old-time power brokers in the empire. The rise of the spin doctors meant that the old-timers could no longer simply lead by power and treachery or even cunning. Instead, from now on the empire would rely on a type of slickness, a sort of flimflam that left everyone feeling a bit less certain about the truth.

To many of the old-timers, there was a marked difference between the old-time propaganda chiefs and this new breed of huckster called the spin doctor. Propaganda had long been considered a noble part of warfare. When Rome conquered a people, the system conquered their body while, through propaganda, the propagandists worked on conquering their spirit. The latter were also a part of the machinery that helped keep the Roman people cheering the army on, closing their eyes to whatever atrocity the army might commit, as long as it was for the honor and glory of Rome. And it had been considered an art to filter good propaganda out into the masses.

In fact some of the resentment felt by the old-timers resulted because the spin doctors had helped to reveal an awful axiom to them: people are eager to be absolved from responsibility, and any good lie will do for many, as long as it keeps them from having to take responsibility for what is going on in their world.

Perhaps the most disillusioning aspect of the new era was that it was no secret to anyone just what the spin doctors were employed to do: their job was to lie openly. Having a spin put on a story was simply an expected and accepted part of life in the modern empire.

But still, there was, at the conference table, this collective sigh of relief, because no matter what anyone thought of the spin doctors personally, they all knew that this action on the part of Pontius Pilate was the sort of move the spin doctors could manipulate with ease.

"Your highness," said one of the members, "as head of the department that oversees 17B, I know that this is the sort of thing our people can turn to our advantage. I am sure there are people in my department who can come up with a statement for the press that will be both satisfactory to your highness as well as good for public relations later on. I can give it to my people and have something on your desk within the next three to four hours."

Once again there was a murmur suggesting collective agreement and relief. Finally, the council member who originally protested the whole affair stood and asked to be heard: "Your Highness, I agree that we may be able to handle the press if we put the spin doctors, or word warriors, or whatever you wish to call them, on the case. But it still does not address the larger questions this whole affair raises. For while we may be able to fool the press, we can not ourselves be fooled. The fact is that Jesus was a reasonably good man who spoke a lot of simple truths and was killed for it. And the people who wanted him out of the way didn't care about the good of the empire but cared simply for their own greed and nothing more. No one at this table has to care, as some supposedly do, whether he was some sort of god or savior. We here are much too intelligent for that kind of musing. The fact is, he did nothing to warrant death by Rome. He was no real threat to us. Remember, the treaty also talks about conflicts with our vital interest. I have yet to be convinced that Jesus was a threat to the vital interest of anyone in this room. And even if he had been a threat to us, as some here have suggested, that should have been determined by us and no other authority. All of this talk about what kind of threat he was to the Jewish priesthood and how he could have become a threat to Rome is talk that I have heard for the first time at this table. Unless I missed a meeting or two, we never, at least to my knowledge, determined he was a threat to the empire before."

At this point one of the other council members interrupted by asking what the point of this speech was.

The reply came quickly: "The point I am making, my lord council members, is this. I believe, as I said, that Jesus was basically a good man, even though I did not agree with him on some things. He spoke a great deal about universal brotherhood, caring for the poor, feeding those who were hungry. He tried to get those poor, miserable, occupied people to believe in something other than the squalor that is their lives. Has it gotten to the point that to say and do those things in the Roman Empire warrants death? Did any of you here ever hear any reports of Jesus raising an army to march against Rome? Has anyone here ever heard of reports about his planning to overthrow the temple authorities? Any information of that nature would have indeed earned our swift and most severe reprisals. In fact, even when challenged on the point of paying taxes, an issue that could have had a direct connection to his relationship with us, he refused to tell the people to withhold them.

"No, gentlemen, until all of this took place, to most of us sitting at this table Jesus was merely an interesting character, a preacher with some notoriety perhaps but nothing more. And despite what I have heard at this table this morning, I know that privately many of you thought he was indeed quite interesting as well.

"The fact is, it was not we who wanted him dead, so how come we are the ones who put him to death and now have to get the spin doctors to help get us out of this mess? How is it that one of our procurators, no matter how dramatically he tried to make it seem differently, was the one who sentenced him to death? It was still our soldiers who marched him up that hill, was it not? It was our soldiers who, according to my information, put a lance in his side. It was our men, but somebody else's idea. Whose? I can tell you this. Whoever masterminded this whole affair did not do this because they cared about the honor and glory of Rome. And that, gentlemen, is why I am indeed concerned about this affair. We will handle the press, but for the good of the empire, we must know truly what has happened here over this weekend."

The council member took his seat and felt for the first time since he entered the room that he had truly made his point. All eyes turned to the emperor, who spoke in a low and calm voice: "I agree with my lord council member, and I assure you that this matter will be fully investigated. As I said at the beginning of this meeting, General Sejanus is already in Judea conducting a full-scale investigation of the events. And knowing the general as you do, I am sure you will agree with me that we will be up to our necks in either answers or corpses in a short time. However, I do believe we are in agreement that for now our first priority is to make a statement to the press. Is it agreed that Pilate's action is enough, with the right spin put on all of this, to tie his and thus our actions to the Cultural Noninterference Act?" There was a general nod of agreement around the room. "Good. Please see that this is given to the right people, and spread our decision around to all of our ambassadors that all comments regarding this matter are to be tied in to the Cultural Noninterference Act. I want this to go out immediately. I don't want people like General Magnus shooting off their mouths about Rome's policies on TV, making matters look even worse than they are already. And by the gods, get this to Pilate. Make sure he knows our decision before someone from the press gets to him. He is to make no, I repeat no, statement to the press without first checking with us. Has he said anything to the press as of yet?" Someone in the room answered that he had not. "Good," said the emperor. "That is the smartest thing he has done so far."

The emperor then dismissed the council members, and in a few moments he sat alone in his chamber. "You know, of course," he thought, "the council member is right. Someone has clearly and cleverly used Rome." He wanted to believe it was the Jews; they seemed to be the most logical choice. But something kept telling him it wasn't the Jews. And then, for some inexplicable reason, he was suddenly swept with apprehension. Suddenly, the emperor of one of the most powerful empires since Alexander the Great, or the Great Khan, felt that he, and all of Rome, was no more than a tiny, insignificant part of some great scheme that was going on around him and that as of yet he could not explain. He felt Rome was merely a pawn in a great game that was being played, and all that Rome was, its history, its conquest, its grandeur, was nothing more than the material of this one tiny pawn on some galactic board. Rage coupled with fear began to swell up in the emperor. "Who would dare treat us this way?" he said out loud. "Who would dare?"

Finally, he reached for a chalice filled with wine, and, taking a sip, he thought, "Well, at least we are off to a good beginning on this. I have done what I needed to do; now let's see what comes out of Judea."

He rang for his aide. "What's next on the calendar?" he asked and went on to other imperial business.

– CHAPTER SEVEN –

Marcus, Vergas, and the other soldiers attended to various details relating to the investigation and the press until evening, when they headed back toward the barracks. Near the buildings, Marcus said to Vergas: "I want you to take the men and return to the barracks." He spoke with an extra note of authority. "I will be back sometime either later tonight or tomorrow morning."

"May I ask the commander where he can be reached in case of emergency?" asked Captain Vergas.

"How curious," thought Marcus. "Since when does the beast Vergas care where I go? Usually, I could go to hell for all he cared. Now all of a sudden he wants to know where I can be reached. Either this is the greatest testimony ever of the power of Sejanus to inflict discipline through fear or I am really getting jumpy."

"I'll be away on business. Please try and hold the empire together until I return, captain." With that, he turned his horse swiftly around and rode off toward the countryside.

Marcus felt it was useless to try and speculate any further on this whole Demetrius business. He began to feel a sense of urgency about getting to this meeting. Where he had earlier felt great apprehension about seeing his old friend, he now felt a sudden rush of enthusiasm. It was either that, he thought, or simply the sense of wanting to get it over with. Finally, he approached a little-known road several miles outside of the city, turned right and went down a small, narrow street where, after about fifty feet, he turned right again. He could see a small house in a clearing just a short distance away. Even though it was by this time quite late, and hardly anyone save a shepherd or two should be around, he nonetheless slowed his horse considerably as though he felt the need to brace himself for something. Marcus checked the piece of parchment containing the address of the house where Demetrius was being held. This was the right house all right. "Where are the guards?" he thought.

As Marcus got off his horse and approached the house, he suddenly saw what appeared to be a rather old man walking with a stick near the entrance. The old man came toward Marcus and said rather loudly, "Can I help you, sir?"

Marcus told the man he was looking for a friend of his and thought he might be in the area.

"Friends are a good thing to have," the man said, again in a rather loud voice, suggesting that his hearing was a bit faulty. "What's your friend's name, sir? Perhaps I know him."

At this point, Marcus was a bit confused and getting a little annoyed. He once again took the parchment out of his breastplate and looked at the address. He turned to the old man and said, "Listen, my name is Commander Marcus, and I am looking for..."

At that moment, the old man took hold of his arm and said in a quiet firm voice, "I know who you are, commander. Please accompany me to the entrance of the house. When we get there I shall turn and walk away. You enter the house. Centurion Demetrius is inside."

As Marcus turned and looked at the old man now holding his arm rather tightly, he noticed for the first time the faint outline of an imperial-class military sword hidden beneath his garments. Marcus was disturbed by this. What disturbed him most was being caught off guard by a Roman soldier disguised as an old man. One of the prerequisites of becoming an officer (and staying alive in this part of the world) was developing an ability to look beyond the obvious and to do so quickly. Many a Roman soldier had been found in the early days of occupation dead with a knife in his ribs because he could not distinguish the beggar from the assassin. Marcus believed that a week ago he would have spotted the old man for a Roman officer from half a mile away. He prided himself on his ability to size up a situation and then usually take advantage of it. Yet if this man had not been a soldier, he would have found himself lying in a pool of blood, watching his life pour out onto the ground of this land he hated so.

This little episode told him much and worried him even more. It told him that before he went inside, he had better remember that he was there to do a job, and a part of that job was to size up the situation concerning Demetrius and the Jewish prophet. "No matter what I think of my friend," he thought, "I would do neither one of us any good if I go in there and leave my professional ability to think and analyze outside."

As they reached the door, the old man turned away and Marcus went inside. The room was dimly lit and sparsely furnished. The curtains were drawn, and the flame in the lamp was barely flickering. On the table sat a half-eaten dish of fruit, bread, and cheese. A small bottle of wine was completely empty. The room was empty. Marcus walked into the bedroom, and there lying face down on the bed was his friend Antoni Demetrius. When Marcus saw him, his heart sank a little. This was not the man he last saw in Capernaum.

"Demetrius, wake up. It's me, Marcus."

Demetrius stirred a little, then slowly turned over and peered through half-drawn eyes to see his old friend. At first Demetrius didn't say anything. He just looked at Marcus with a blank stare. But then he shook his head a bit and began to focus, and only then did he begin to smile a little.

"Marcus," he said. "I knew they would send you. I was hoping they wouldn't, but I knew it would be you. Give me a moment to wash my face and I'll be right with you. Forgive my appearance, but I didn't have a chance to grab a change of uniform before I suddenly became a guest of the Praetorian Guard. I know you have a lot to ask me, and I also know you have work to do. Marcus, don't worry about all of this, just do your job. No matter what comes out of your visit here, remember you have a duty to the empire. Just give me a minute and I'll be right with you, commander."

"What's this 'commander' crap?" said Marcus. "And I don't need anyone telling me about duty. I already learned that stuff from the best there ever was or ever will be. I learned all about duty from you, remember?"

Saying that felt good to Marcus. He wasn't sure if he was becoming so intimidated by all of this that he might begin to sell out something that had been as precious as anything ever was to him, his friendship with Demetrius. As Demetrius rose a bit unsteadily to his feet, Marcus reached out to steady him. All at once they suddenly embraced each other, and for a minute it was like the hundreds of times before in all of the places where they had come upon each other. For a brief moment there was no Jesus, no Sejanus, no miracles to explain. There were just these two close friends and comrades, fellow officers in the army of the glorious Roman Empire.

After a short while Demetrius emerged from the washroom looking a bit better, but still appearing worn.

"So," said Demetrius, "who called you in to do this 'find out if Demetrius has gone nuts and become a danger to the empire' job? I know Sejanus has a hand in this. Did he send one of his top-brass henchmen to fetch you in the middle of the night?"

"I'm afraid not, Demetrius. This seems a bit more serious than you know. Sejanus came to see me himself. He has personally given me orders to find out directly from you just what happened between you and Jesus. Apparently word got out from someone that Jesus helped Tarius get over an illness. Rome is quite uptight with this whole Jesus affair. They are not sure whether the Jews got that idiot Pilate to play into their hands by having us execute Jesus, thus making us look bad in the eyes of the world. Not that we ever cared much what anyone thought of us before, but still, this thing has gotten a lot of attention. This business with you is just a small part of it. Look at this." Marcus pulled out the ring Sejanus had given him and showed it to Demetrius. "He wants me to question everyone and determine just what happened. I suppose I should thank the gods that I was away when it all happened, but for some reason I have been picked to try and come up with the answers to things that, between you and me, I don't even know half of the questions to."

Demetrius looked long and hard at his old friend and then began to shake his head. "Marcus, I am surprised at you. You know how the empire works. They picked you for this job because you are absolutely the right person for it. You hold a command high enough so that you can speak and question with authority, and thus be grandly rewarded if you come up with the right answers, or be royally sacrificed if you come up with something unsatisfactory. You know Rome isn't going to take any of the responsibility directly for this, considering that this took place in one of the provinces. And for sure, they are not going to blame the governor for what happened. They'll back Pilate in public to the hilt. If an investigation takes place, headed by you, and all is found to be in order, at least in enough order that the press and the politicians feel satisfied, then you should make out like a bandit. But be careful. If they need to find a scapegoat, you could find yourself living in one of these luxury cottages like your old friend here. Marcus, you know I love you as a brother. That is why I tell you, be careful, and no matter what you feel about me, or anyone else, do your duty to the utmost. Play it absolutely straight, no matter what. It may be the only thing that can save you if all hell breaks loose over this."

"Demetrius, I need to find out about this business between you and Jesus. What happened? What was wrong with Tarius, and what did Jesus have to do with all of this? And I need to know most of all why Sejanus would feel that whatever took place between you and Jesus would somehow make you unfit to serve in the empire. I mean, with your record, how could anyone doubt your loyalty to Rome? It's not like you've suddenly become a convert of this evangelist."

"That's where you're wrong, my friend. I have not publicly embraced this man's teaching, but I believe Jesus was more than a faith healer or a good preacher. I believe he was who many said he was: I believe he was the son of God."

Marcus once again felt like he had been caught off guard. Demetrius's words fell on Marcus like a series of blows: he took two steps back, turned, walked toward the door, opened it, called to the old man, and asked him to look after his horse for the night and to secure for him some food and several bottles of wine. He closed the door, turned to his friend, and said, "We're going to have a long night together."

He sat down and said: "OK, Demetrius, tell me what happened, from the top."

Demetrius rubbed his forehead, searching for the right words, and then began: "About two years ago, we received at the garrison word that a young preacher was making his way to Capernaum. He had apparently been working down in Nazareth, without a great deal of success, partially because he grew up there, and you know that old line about a prophet not being honored in his own land. However, we had received intelligence reports that he could become dangerous because he seemed to be the brightest, most capable evangelist to come from around these parts in years. There were of course all the usual reports about miracles and signs that circulate when one of these Jewish soothsayers gets some notoriety, but Jesus, right from the start, had an air about him that seemed potentially..."

Marcus cut him off in midsentence: "I know the background on Jesus. I read all the so-called intelligence reports. What happened between you and Jesus?"

"When Jesus came to Capernaum, my unit was assigned to monitor his activities. We watched him all the time. It seemed as though once he got out of the small town of Nazareth and into the big city, things just opened up for him. He began to attract huge crowds. I never saw anyone who could work a crowd like Jesus. I saw grown men with families, who had full-time jobs, drop what they were doing and join his crusade right on the spot. While I believed he was just a man, I was entranced watching him in action. I'm not sure just how much formal education he had, but I never saw anyone ask him a question about Jewish law that he did not answer.

"There were times when stooges from the temple would dress up as common people and try and get him on some point of law. We of course knew right away who these guys were, and I always believed Jesus could spot them a mile away. But he would listen to their questions and sometimes put his hand to his head as though he was suggesting that this was going to be a hard one. Then either he would sit back and tell one of these devastating parables that would have the crowd roaring with laughter and approval or he would just flat out level the guy with some straight, honest truth that, no matter where you were from, you could not disagree with."

Marcus noticed that for the first time since he had been there, Demetrius looked bright and alert. He seemed to be gathering strength from retelling these stories. Marcus also noticed something else, something disturbing: for the first time there was a part of his friend that he did not recognize.

Demetrius went to the window and looked out. For a moment the light in his eyes left him. It was as though he suddenly picked up on his friend's feeling and felt sad for the distance he knew this might be creating between them. He also knew that this kind of talk probably did not help his chances of getting out of whatever mess he was in with the empire. Then suddenly he laughed and called Marcus over to the window. He pointed to a hillside and said to him, "See those mountains over there. I saw Jesus pull off one of the greatest stunts I have ever seen in my life, right up on those hills. I have to tell you this story; you'll appreciate it.

"I'm sure in your intelligence reports you have heard of the now-famous miracle of the loaves and fishes, or the feeding of the five thousand, or whatever name it goes by in Judea. Well, first of all, it was more like fifteen hundred than five thousand, but there was a miracle performed right up there on those hills. But you know what? It had nothing to do with magic whatsoever. It had to do with guts, knowing how to work a crowd, and skill. We had heard that Jesus was going to make this major policy speech, and so with the usual Roman heavy-handedness we put several of our people, including myself, into the crowd to witness what took place. People came from all around to sit up on that mountain and listen to Jesus.

"Now you know how folks travel in these parts, stashing a small piece of bread or dried fish for the journey. Well, after about four hours, people began to complain of feeling a bit hungry. Yet when Jesus asked if anyone had any food, everyone in the crowd looked around at everyone else as if to suggest that no one had a bit of food on them. Then this kid came up to Jesus, and he took out some small loaves of bread and a few pieces of fish and handed them to him. Jesus said to this kid, 'Why are you giving me this?' The kid said he wanted to help feed all the people who had come from so far to hear Jesus speak. Jesus said that if he gave all he had, he would have nothing for the journey home. The kid said that he believed what Jesus had to say was so important, he would sacrifice his dinner and go hungry later so that others could stay longer and hear more of God's messenger. Jesus thanked the child and put the food into one of several large baskets that were sitting nearby. While continuing to emphasize the fact that the kid gave everything he had, Jesus turned to the person next to him and, looking him right in the eyes, asked if he might be able to spare anything. Well, the man, after seeing that the kid gave everything, reluctantly reached into his sack and put into the basket a small piece of bread and some dried meat. I'm sure it wasn't all the guy had, but Jesus thanked him and then turned to the next guy. All the time he kept talking about this kid, and how he gave everything, and what faith the child had.

"One by one, people who had no intention of being caught without food for the journey home gave a small portion of what they had, not wanting to appear entirely selfish after seeing what the kid did. And the whole time, Jesus never stopped talking about how much this little child was willing to give in order that others might be fed by the truth of the kingdom of God. Well, by the time they got around to the last man, they had collected so much food, they couldn't have eaten it all. And what was really a nice move on Jesus' part: he took all of the remaining food and gave it to the kid who gave the original loaves and fishes. It was beautiful. Jesus knew that if those people just stopped being so greedy for one minute and shared just a little of what they had with someone else, there would be enough for everyone. That's when I began to really admire the man. That's when I saw something in him that I had never seen before."

Marcus stared at his friend. He admired the talent that Jesus had for working a crowd and in fact had witnessed other events similar to this one himself. And yet it still did not explain what had led Demetrius down the road that brought him to this point. Demetrius saw the look on his friend's face. He knew it was time for total truth. "How was your vacation?" he said to Marcus.

"What?" Marcus responded.

"You went to Jericho, right? How was your vacation?"

"It was fine, but what...?"

"Did you notice anything missing in Jericho this time?"

"Missing, what was missing? Demetrius, I have to get at the truth of all of this in order..."

Demetrius cut him off with a wave of his hand and pulled up a chair very close to Marcus. "What I'm going to tell you is classified, and it might cost me my life. I think, however, that you have a right to know this information. It will explain my behavior, and it might shed some light on why Sejanus himself is giving this matter more attention than you might think it deserves. Sure, Jesus' death at our hands is an embarrassment to the empire, but so what? No matter how much flak we catch about this, it should all be over in a matter of months. Everything will return to normal, and the politicians will all do what they must do. It's a great news story, but who will remember any of this in five or six years, right?"

Before Marcus could answer, Demetrius began to shake his head no. "What happened here will be remembered ten thousand years. And a handful of people in the empire know it; one of them is Sejanus. Sejanus is a true patriot. He not only cares deeply for what Rome is today but cares how it will be remembered throughout history. He believes Rome has given much to civilization and wants it to be remembered for all of its works of art and culture, as well as for its military strength and genius. What he fears is that from now on Rome will be remembered simply as the empire that executed Jesus and will be forgotten for everything else. What angers Sejanus even more is that Rome might have been duped into all of this by the Jews."

Marcus began to laugh a little: "I understand the strain you are under, my friend, and I know that a lesser man than yourself would probably have cracked in half by now. But I really think you're getting a little nutty over all of this. I assure you, Demetrius, that ten thousand years from now, no one will have ever heard of Jesus, Sejanus, you, me, or anyone else connected with this whole mess."

Demetrius smiled and stood up. "Let's go for a walk, Marcus. I believe they will let us at least walk around the grounds here. I'm sure that our horses are being, shall we say, well looked after, and, therefore, they know we, or at least I, can't go very far."

"Fine," said Marcus, "the fresh air will do us good."

As they got up to leave, Demetrius turned to Marcus. "You still don't know what was missing in Jericho do you? Your old teachers at the academy would be quite upset at your powers of observation, or should I say your lack of them."

As they began to stroll around the house, Marcus noticed a sense of relief coming over his friend's face as he began to tell his story: "Several months ago an incident took place in Jericho that few people observed, even though it took place in a crowd of people. It was written up as simply one of the reported miracles of Jesus, but this one was no trick, no instance of mind over matter. This was real, and only a handful of people know about it or its significance. I happen to know about it by accident, because even though I had been assigned to cover Jesus when he was in Capernaum, I just happened to be in Jericho on leave when Jesus came into town. Being the good officer that I am, I decided to watch his activities. Besides, Helen was out shopping, and I had had enough of that for one day. Now whenever you and I vacationed together in Jericho, what was the first thing we noticed at the gate of the city, every single year for fifteen years?"

The answer suddenly struck Marcus: "The beggar! Of course, the blind beggar sitting at the gates of the city, asking for money."

This had become so noticeable because he stood in such stark contrast to that beautiful resort city by the sea.

"But this time, you didn't see the beggar, did you?"

"I guess I really didn't notice. I mean if I did notice he wasn't there, I suppose I just figured he died. He was after all kind of old, and beggars don't often live long lives in this part of the world. Anyway, what's he got to do with all of this?"

"The fact is, he didn't die, and the reason he was no longer begging at the gate is because he is no longer blind. Jesus cured him."

Marcus gave Demetrius a look of suspicion. "You know I don't believe in any of that stuff, but I suppose it's possible to help someone who's suffering...."

"Hold it, Marcus. I know what you're thinking. You're thinking that perhaps if someone like Jesus, who is believed to be a great messenger of God, lays his hands on someone, and that person wants to believe and is desperate enough, then he might be able to over-come his illness purely by believing and allowing his mind to overcome physical obstacles, etc., etc. I know all that stuff and believed most of his miracles were of that nature. It's what the imperial psychologists use to explain all these types of so-called miracles. I read all of the material they put out too you know. But that's not what happened there."

"OK," Marcus said, "how do you know? For all you know this guy and Jesus could have been in this together. Although I suppose to pose as a blind man for fifteen years is a little too much to suspect of anyone, maybe the man that day was an actor dressed up to look like the beggar. Who knows? But I still don't understand what this has to do with you."

"No, this was no stunt. And only Sejanus and a handful of people outside of the emperor himself know the story behind it. And I am not even sure the emperor knows the whole story. This, after all, involves the Roman Secret Service, and you know how secretive they are."

Marcus felt a pain in the pit of his stomach. "Now," he thought, "the Roman Secret Service is involved somehow. What next, the American CIA?" Marcus turned toward his friend and with a heavy sigh asked, "What does the RSS have to do with all of this?"

"When Sejanus was a young captain working his way up the ranks, he worked as an intelligence officer for the RSS. He was extremely cruel and efficient at his job. Well, about twenty years ago, the empire got wind of a plot to kill several high-ranking officers serving in Jeri-cho. Through sheer brutality, they began to learn the identity of some of the ringleaders of the plot. One of the leaders was a brilliant scribe by the name of Bartimeus. It seems he acted as a spy for the network and funneled information back to the other ringleaders. Well, he was caught and imprisoned. The officer in charge of the interrogation was Captain L. A. Sejanus. He tortured Bartimeus, relentlessly, until he told the whereabouts of the rest of the leaders. He then had each one executed right in front of Bartimeus so that he could see and re-member what took place. After he had killed the last man, he turned to Bartimeus and said that those deaths would be the last things he would ever see, so that they would remain with him forever. He then picked up a dagger and blinded him with it. He was later released and thrown out into the streets of the city. Seen as a traitor by some in the city, and having had his lands confiscated by the state, he soon became a beggar out on the streets. Bartimeus was the beggar always seen by the gates of the city."

Marcus did not quite know what to make of all of this. But something inside of him was making him feel a little sick. At first he wanted to argue about the reality of the so-called miracle. But Demetrius was adamant.

"Marcus, the man had no eyes. He wasn't suffering from a case of glaucoma or some other form of eye disease — he had no eyes."

Demetrius halted for a second, faced Marcus, and went on: "Well, that day when Jesus came into Jericho, on his way into the city, he walked right past the old beggar. When Bartimeus heard Jesus was near, he began to shout and scream like a madman. The people around him tried to shut him up — you know how snooty these Jericho people can be — but the man kept shouting at Jesus until Jesus stopped and told someone in the crowd to help the beggar up and bring him over to him. I'm telling you, Marcus, I saw this with my own eyes."

They walked to a low bench and sat down, a statue of Mars on one side of them, a statue of Venus on the other side. Demetrius seemed amused by this, grinned, and went on: "Jesus asked the beggar what he wanted, and the man said he wanted to see again. People laughed; they thought he wanted Jesus to get him on public assistance or something. My first thought was that I was going to issue a pretty good report on the incident, disproving once and for all any legitimate healing power Jesus may have claimed to have. Even though I knew we all knew the stories concerning his miraculous cures were untrue, I thought this would be a chance to authenticate his powerlessness. You see, I knew the man was blind in a way that could not be healed.

"At first I expected that Jesus would in some clever way convince everyone present that the beggar could not be healed for some mysteriously prophetic reason. I knew whatever the reason would be, Jesus would cleverly come up with something convincing. But I said to myself, 'Prophet, you aren't going to get around this one. You make this guy see, and you really are doing something.' I was prepared for anything to happen, that is, anything but what took place. You see, Marcus, when the blind man asked to see, Jesus asked him if he really believed he could cure him. The man said, 'Yes, I believe in you.' And Jesus cured him."

Marcus looked terribly sad for a moment, but then seemed to pull himself together, and Demetrius continued: "But it was not just the healing of the blind man that got me to believe; it is the way he did it that affected me so profoundly. And strangely enough, being a Roman soldier had much to do with it. You see, it was precisely all of my training, my years of commanding other men, even to their deaths during combat, that made me believe that this man was who some said he was."

"And what did he do?" Marcus asked with some forced skepticism. "How did he make this 'miracle' happen?"

Demetrius stared into Marcus's eyes: "He ordered it," he responded. "He gave an order that the man should see, and some thing or some one obeyed that order."

At this Demetrius got up from the bench and looked to the east, where the very first hints of dawn were showing. They began slowly walking toward the front of the house.

"Marcus, despite all of this, you know me better than anyone on earth. You know I am not one to give in to irrational behavior. You know I am not one to believe in anything that cannot be proven. And you know I am military through and through. So if I tell you this, you know I believe it to be true. More than anything, you know I would never lie to you. I am telling you that if you had been there, you would have noticed exactly what I did. Jesus was able to give an order, and it never occurred to him for an instant that it would not be obeyed — just like it never occurs to us that our men won't obey us. It didn't matter that what Jesus ordered was impossible. What he asked for had to be obeyed because he ordered it done."

Marcus once again felt himself getting impatient. "How do you know about the blindness and Sejanus's role in all of this? I mean, even if people found out that this man was punished, for espionage, how could anyone find out about Sejanus's role in it. There are few people who even know the RSS exists."

"I know because I was there when it happened."

"There?" Marcus shouted. "How could you have been there? I've known you for twenty years. I never heard you talk about this."

"True, but remember — I was two years ahead of you at the academy. This happened just before you arrived. As a cadet, I was assigned a field duty one summer to help patrol the area in Jericho where the incident took place. I was to act as an observer, of course, and not in any way to engage in combat. It so happened that the centurion I was assigned to was the man who led the raid on the area where Bartimeus was arrested. Since he was the arresting officer, he was a witness to much of the interrogation. Since I was assigned to him, I was also allowed to be present. As you know, only the top 3 percent at the academy were allowed to participate in such operations back then. And you know in those days, I was the most gung ho, pro-empire student the academy had. Yet none of us was prepared for the cruel, cold, efficient work of the RSS.

"When things started to get rough, I was offered the chance to leave, with no dishonor, but I wanted to see how the enemies of the empire would be dealt with. Those who stayed were sworn to absolute secrecy under order 3476 of the National Empire Security Code. To violate any part of NESC would have meant instant execution for treason in those days.

"Well, I willingly signed an oath and was permitted into the interrogation. I will never forget the sight of that man being blinded. The only thing that kept me from throwing up was that I believed the good of the state was more important than anything else. As I said, we were all sworn to secrecy, and shortly after that, they disbanded the program that allowed cadets to get such up-close and personal insights into what really goes on in occupied lands, but I never forgot what I saw that day. Nor have I ever forgotten the face of Sejanus. Even though at such a young age I was horrified at what I witnessed, I also admired the way Sejanus worked. He did not do what he did because he was sadistic, as some believe he is today. There was no joy or pleasure in his face, nor was there sorrow or guilt. It was duty, plain and simple. That is one reason why he is so feared. He has proven all of his life that he will do whatever is necessary, to anyone, if the good of the empire is at stake."

By this time they had returned to the front of the house. Marcus did not want to walk anymore. He was once again feeling slightly hurt and a bit surprised. Demetrius had never told him this story. They had both traveled to Jericho many times and had always seen the blind beggar together. How could his best friend have kept the origin of this man's blindness from him? He too understood duty, but still there was something disheartening about his friend putting duty above their friendship. It reminded him of the things his friend had said to him when he had first arrived. All that stuff about duty over friendship. Until this moment, it all sounded like harmless military rhetoric. Now it left a hollow feeling in him.

He suddenly felt the need to become very military himself. He was not ready to try to reconcile all of the information he had heard about the man with no eyes being able to see. He could not face that just yet.

Right now he told himself that he was concerned about his friend, the empire, and putting an end to all of this as soon as possible. Somehow he knew that things were never going to be the same between them again, and that left him angry, sad, and afraid.

"Demetrius, tell me about the incident between you and Jesus."

Demetrius understood the tone of his friend's voice, and he too knew what was happening. He felt sorrow over Marcus's resentment and anger. Yet he felt even greater sorrow that Marcus could not understand what he was telling him. He wanted to shake his old friend and say to him, "Don't you understand what I am telling you? Jesus made a man see who had no eyes. We tore them out of his head twenty years ago, and Jesus ordered them to return, and they did." He wanted Marcus to see that the only reason he broke his sworn vow after all of these years and told him the story was that he loved Marcus and wanted him to begin to comprehend what was happening right then in their lives.

Demetrius began to slowly and deliberately speak, this time as though he was reporting an incident to a superior officer: "After I returned from leave, I went back on duty in Capernaum. What I saw in Jericho gave me nightmares for some time, but I tried desperately to rationalize what I had seen. Then one day I came home and was told the horrible news: my son had fallen ill and was dying. You know we had lost our daughter shortly after she was born, and now my son, my only son, was dying. You know how much we love our son. During this time I continued to have dreams about the incident in Jericho, but for some reason they began to turn from nightmares into dreams of hope. I kept seeing Jesus order things in my dreams, and they would come true. One night I dreamed he ordered an end to war, and suddenly, all of the wars going on between the empire and the border towns, or the fighting between the neighboring states, just stopped. One night I dreamed he ordered an end to sickness, and, suddenly, there was no more sickness. I thought I was going insane.

"Well, our son's condition began to become desperate; he was failing fast. I had always believed that I understood death and was prepared for it in any shape. But somehow this situation was totally baffling. You see, on the one hand, I couldn't stand the fact that my son was suffering and dying, and it seemed there was nothing I could do. And yet, on the other hand, I wasn't worried. I knew Jesus was going to be in the area, and — maybe it was because of those dreams — I knew I would ask him to help my son, and that he would. I know this seems strange and nonsensical. I am a Roman soldier, and I also know that if Jesus had said that he would help my son only if I gave up my allegiance to the empire, I would not have done it. Yet I knew if I asked him, he would do it, and without strings. Don't ask me how I knew, but I just did.

"When he was through preaching, I walked up to him and introduced myself and asked him if he would cure my son. In one part of my mind I expected him to look upon me with great suspicion. I expected him to say, 'Go take a hike you Roman murderer.' I guess I half expected that reaction because it is what you or I would have done had we been Jewish messiahs in a land filled with Roman occupiers. I mean, after all, we took over their land, as was our right; we took away their freedom, killed who knows how many of their citizens. Why the hell would any Jew want to help one of us?

"And yet there was something else in me that knew if I asked him, he would do it. And so I asked him, and without hesitation he said he would, and asked me where I lived. I told him he need not come to my house because I believed that he had the power to order my son back to health. I told him I knew how power worked, because I am a man of power, with people under my command. I told him that when a Roman soldier gives an order, it is obeyed without question. I told him I had seen him before, and that I knew that if he only gave the word, my son would be healed. He reached out his hand to mine as if to shake it, but instead held it tightly in his. While holding my hand, he put his head down for a few seconds, almost as though he suddenly went deep into thought, like he was trying to find out something about me by holding my hand and reading my mind. Then in a few seconds, he looked up at me and smiled. He said to me that I had great faith, but it was not a faith that I had gotten all on my own. He said that I should not abandon that faith, no matter what happened to him, or what might happen to me. He told me my faith was there for a reason. He looked very seriously at me for a moment, and then he broke into a big smile. 'Go home,' he said, 'the order is given. Tarius will be fine, and one day he will make his father proud.' At that he turned and walked away with his followers. I never saw or talked with him again. He left Capernaum for Jerusalem. Shortly after that, he was executed.

"When I returned home, our son was well. I knew he would be, and he was. I knew it because Jesus had possessed the same air of authority that I saw in him when he healed the beggar. Yet I was not entirely happy. There was something about the way Jesus said that my son would one day make his father proud that left me uncomfortable because I had the feeling Jesus was not talking about me. I also wondered if what I had done could somehow be seen as threatening to the empire. The answer to that came shortly after the news of Jesus' death reached Capernaum. That's when I suddenly found myself here."

Marcus felt disoriented, but for the first time he saw a glimmer of hope. He drank off a glass of wine and said: "Demetrius, we'll discuss miracles some other time; I need to know this now: you say that you did not tell Jesus that you would be a follower if he helped Tarius get well?"

"That is correct."

"Then are you still loyal to the empire?"

"Yes. Of course I am."

"And what if one day we are given orders to put down any revolt that these followers of Jesus might try and instigate because of our role in all of this? Will you still faithfully execute your orders without hesitation, despite what you think you believe Jesus may have been?"

"Marcus, I can promise you this: if the day ever comes when I feel I can not faithfully execute my duties as an officer in the emperor's services, I will resign my post. I will never speak out against Rome or the emperor. On this you have my word. Even Sejanus knows that if I give my word, I will keep it or die."

"I'm afraid that if you break your word to him, that is exactly what will happen, my friend." Marcus looked out of the window and saw dawn spreading.

"I will go back and tell Sejanus that I believe you are fit to serve and command. I will not mention anything about the beggar, and whatever happened between you and Sejanus twenty years ago is between the two of you. I am glad that your son got well, and, frankly, I don't care how he got better. All I need to know is that I can go to Sejanus and tell him that, according to my best judgment, you are no threat to the empire and, indeed, are fit to serve."

With that Marcus stood up and headed for the door. "When this is all over," he said, "we'll sit down over some wine and talk more about it. I think everything will be all right. By the way, have you told anyone else about your belief in Jesus?"

"No," said Demetrius.

"Good, keep it that way. At least until this all blows over. Better yet, in the name of the emperor, I order you not to discuss any of this with anyone until further notice. Is that understood?"

"Yes, sir," answered Demetrius.

"Good. I'll get you out of here as soon as I can. Give my love to Helen and your son. I really am happy that he's all right."

As Marcus went to leave, Demetrius held his arm. "Marcus, the beggar had no eyes."

"Yeah, I know Demetrius, just remember you're under orders from now on. I must go. Be well, and may the gods be with you."

"And may God be with you," was Demetrius's reply.

Upon hearing that response, Marcus suddenly feared that despite everything he would try to do for his friend, he would never see Antoni Demetrius again. He tried desperately to remember the words from *Paradise Lost* and all the stuff about giving up friendships for the sake of the greater glory of Rome. But for some reason, all he could see was the face of his friend. In that moment, he hated what he believed Jesus had done to them both.

– CHAPTER EIGHT –

GERRY HAD JUST RETURNED to her hotel room. She was over-joyed by the fact that a few hours after Marcus had left with the suicide note from Judas, he did indeed have it returned (minus the finger) to the office of the *Judean* with written permission to print it and broadcast it over TV. Gerry had gotten hold of the camera crew and had gone on the air live with the exclusive story. David had put the story on the front page of the evening edition. They had both scored a big scoop on the rest of the media.

"Well, what do you think of the commander now?" Gerry had asked her old friend. "He told us he would release the note back to us if we waited, and he kept his word."

"He's still a bastard," had been David's reply.

That, of course, did not surprise Gerry in the least. She had left for her hotel feeling delighted with the day's events. She had just sat down on the bed when the phone rang. The voice was unfamiliar.

"Ms. Simmons? I have some information about this Jesus affair that I think you might be interested in."

"What is it, and who are you?"

"Come on, Ms. Simmons, be real. What I have is some information about the trial. An eyewitness. Someone who was there and can tell you firsthand just what happened. Someone who can tell you of the, shall we say, peculiar things that took place during the trial."

"Why are you telling me about this, why not David Ben Leven, or someone local?"

"I'm telling you because, first, I know that when you worked here, you were always straight with your sources and reporting; and, second, I believe this story is worth some money, and Ben Leven wouldn't give you the steam off his own piss. However, if you're not interested..."

"I'm interested," she said and paused while the voice gave her an address. The person on the other end of the line then abruptly hung up.

Gerry stood by the door of her hotel room staring at the piece of paper with the address on it. It was in an area of Judea that was known for being sometimes dangerous. And at this hour of the night...

A tide of questions rose within her. Why on earth would she consider going out in the middle of the night to meet with some strange character in a seedy part of town? Was she simply being a good investigative reporter, or was she once again just trying to prove something, either to herself or to the world? Hadn't she proven enough already, at least to herself? The most disturbing question centered around whether or not her fears were based on her being a female correspondent. One voice inside her said, "If you were a man, would you be afraid to go?" Another voice inside said, "If you were a man, would you be afraid not to?"

She began to think of all the novels she had read as a young woman in which reporters would often meet people in dark alleys or sleazy, waterfront bars to get the "real scoop" on Pulitzer Prize stories. She was reminded of people like Woodward and Bernstein meeting characters like "Deep Throat" in darkened car garages. It always looked so good in the cinema and read so well in books. But the simple truth of the matter was that even in the Middle East, she had never been called upon to meet someone in a dark alley in the middle of the night. Sure, she had had her confidential sources when she worked here. But more often than not, she met them in coffeehouses in the middle of the day, or in restaurants for dinner, not in back alleys.

She also began to think about the equally romantic notion of good reporters being able to trust their instincts in these situations. She thought that if she wanted to get this story, she had better bury her instincts, because right now, her instincts were telling her to forget this stupid idea and get into bed.

Instead of following her instincts, she caught a cab and went to the address she'd been given: the address of a small, rundown motel in a seedy part of town. She had put in a call to New York and was authorized to pay a "reasonable" amount of money, depending on the story. She was also told what seemed like ten thousand times in a fifteen-minute phone conversation to "be careful." She hated to admit it, but she now felt less secure about this venture than she did before she called New York. "Well, you loved this place because of all of the intrigue," she mused. "Well, you've got it, intrigue à la mode." She got out of the cab, looked around, and within seconds a man emerged from a darkened section of the alley.

"I'm Alan," he said, blankly. He was a young street hustler. After looking him over, Gerry did not believe his story was going to be worth more than twenty dollars and some lost sleep; but she decided to play the scene out.

"Look, pal, it's late, and I have a lot of serious work to do tomorrow, so what's your information? What can you tell me about the trial?" Gerry was getting impatient; she was tired and scared. She wasn't really sure what the character connected to that ominous voice on the phone was supposed to look like. She only knew that this kid wasn't it.

Alan looked at Gerry and knew immediately, with the kind of wisdom a street broker of information learns right away (if he wants to live more than a few days and do business in the Middle East), that she believed she was wasting her time. "I don't know anything about the trial," Alan said.

Gerry turned to walk away in disgust when Alan called out to her: "But there is someone in one of these rooms here who could tell you everything you would want to know about it."

Gerry turned and looked at Alan. "Yeah, and who, located in the Jerusalem Hilton here, could tell me anything about the trial?"

"That's what you're paying me to find out."

"Look, pal, I'll give you twenty bucks; you give me the room; I'll talk to him, go home, and we can all get some sleep."

Alan took a step closer to Gerry and said, in a very composed voice, "No, you won't. You will give me five hundred dollars. And you know why? Because I'm going to let you talk to him first. If you think the information is worth the money, you pay it. If you don't, forget about it. But if you agree the story is genuine, the price is five hundred American dollars. Agreed?"

Gerry thought this was really strange. A street hustler like this guy was never willing to give anything away for free, unless he knew the players very, very well. He must have also known somehow that if she said she would pay the money for good information, she surely would. He must also believe — no he must know, without a doubt — that whatever or whomever he had stashed in one of these seedy rooms was going to be worth every penny.

"Let me get this straight, pal. I get to talk to this source first, and if I think the information is worth it, then I pay you five hundred dol-

lars. And if I don't think it's worth it, then I don't pay you a thing—
I pay you nothing?"

"You got it, 'pal,'" said Alan, imitating Gerry's sarcasm.

Gerry was about to agree when a haunting feeling swept over her.
Along with everything else bothering her about being here in the middle of the night, she was also still a bit unnerved with this whole thing
about Judas and the secret organization. She began to think, "What
if this guy is a member of the Sicarii and has decided to make me
an example of just how extreme they really are? What if, instead of
only killing Roman soldiers, they've now decided to kill Western reporters?" She tried to calm her nerves. "Come on," she thought, "this
Jesus execution is one of the biggest stories of the year, if not the
decade. And now you may have a lead that others would kill for...."
She suddenly wished she hadn't used that word.

"Look," she said to herself, "you're a reporter. People don't kill
reporters. That would be a little extreme, don't you think?" "Yeah,"
she heard a voice answer from within. "You mean like in the word
'extremist.'"

Her thoughts were suddenly interrupted by Alan's voice: "Look
over there, down the alley." Gerry turned around and looked down
an alley. At first she didn't see anything, but soon she made out the
outline of a shadowy figure. Before she could really comprehend what
she was seeing, Alan spoke again.

"Look at the other end of the alley." When Gerry looked the other
way, she saw another figure. She was sure she had not seen the shape
before. When Gerry turned back, Alan simply said, with no emotion
in his voice, "Look, lady, if I had brought you here to kill you, you
would be dead already. Room 114."

In a strange sort of way, Gerry felt better. She began to think,
"What a strange world this is. What a strange time to be alive. Here
you stand in the face of a potential threat to your life, but somehow
knowing that the threat is real and not just in your head makes you
feel safer than not knowing."

"Well," she said to Alan with a smile, "it's nice to know that you're
not a dumb guy, because killing a reporter would be real dumb. If your
information is good, you'll get your five hundred dollars."

Alan never cracked a smile. He just repeated the words "Room
114," walked over and sat on an old trash can, withdrew from his
shirt what looked to be an old newspaper, and began to read.

Gerry turned, walked to room 114, and knocked on the door.

"Come in, Ms. Simmons," came a voice from the other side. The formality of the voice stunned her. She had expected a hoodlum, not someone addressing her as "Ms. Simmons."

"Oh great," she thought, "he knows me by name. Hey, I have an idea. Maybe the Sicarii are not out to kill Western reporters. Maybe they are out to get *this* Western reporter."

Gerry turned the handle of the door, walked in, and was immediately surprised by what she saw. There in a corner of the room stood a very distinguished looking, well-dressed man who looked to be in his early sixties. He wore very fine clothes and a yarmulke on his head. His beard was well groomed and not particularly long. One could tell, even by the way he stood, that he was well mannered and cultured. Gerry knew that whoever he was, whatever he had to say would be worth the time and effort.

"Won't you please sit down, Ms. Simmons. Please forgive the rather melodramatic cloak and dagger approach for getting you here. I assure you, this is not my usual method of operating, but this place is owned by a relative, and I did want to assure that our meeting would be held in utmost privacy. I hope you were not unduly frightened by your having to travel to this neck of the woods at such a late hour."

Gerry thanked him for his concern (after squelching a small urge to ask him what he meant by that remark and whether he would have said the same thing to a man; the impulse to ask him that made her smile). She asked his name.

"I cannot tell you that just yet. For now I will only tell you that I am a member of the council, and I am from the town of Arimathea. It probably would not take much for you to use the information I have just given you to track down my name and find out my background. I must ask you, however, not to do that, at least not yet, and that you give me your word you will not."

Gerry agreed, at least for the time being.

"My sources tell me that you are a journalist one can trust, and that you do not break your word once it is given. If that is so, I must ask you to promise me that you will print only the information I will give you and never reveal your source. Your disclosing your source would mean my death, and the death of my wife and children as well. But even more important than that, it would give certain people a chance to try and discredit the information I am giving you. Because of certain actions I have taken on behalf of Jesus, I have already cast a certain amount of suspicion on my loyalties."

"Sir," Gerry said, "first, I must tell you that I am primarily a TV journalist, although my station is owned and operated by a company that has a newspaper connected to it. If I were to do a story on your information, there would have to be a taped record of what you say. Now, if you don't want to have the story on TV, I'm sure that if your story is worthwhile, I can get it in print. But I must inform you as well that it is very difficult to print stories and have them believed when at the end of each paragraph you must constantly use the term 'anonymous sources.' If you do not tell me your name, you, sir, are an anonymous source. If your story proves valuable, I must also pay the gentleman you hired to fetch me a considerable amount of money. In order to do that, I must wire my editor in New York. He is going to want to know the reliability..."

"Do not worry about Alan. He is my nephew and a good boy at heart, but my sister has let him grow too fast and has not kept him well enough insulated from the elements of the street. I will take care to give him the two hundred dollars we agreed upon if your editor decides either that what I have to tell you is not worth the money or that the conditions are not agreeable to him."

Gerry thought to herself, "Two hundred dollars? Why that little..."

"Please understand, Ms. Simmons. I don't care how much immediate attention what I am going to tell you gets on your TV station or in the newspapers. What I am more interested in is that somewhere there is an official record of just what took place at the trial of Jesus of Nazareth. If it makes the front page of your newspaper, fine. If it ends up on page one hundred, that is fine also. Frankly, that is where I would prefer it end up for now. I of course could never give an interview on camera. But wherever it ends up, there must be a record of it somewhere. I know someday that record will become part of an important document, and that document will serve generations of humankind in some way."

For Gerry, the last sentence seemed to ring of unfulfilled hope and darkness. The man's words should have had a joyous ring, but they seemed surrounded by pain and sadness. Gerry believed that in this part of the world people seemed often prone to speak in broad, cataclysmic sentences that seldom made a lot of sense. It suddenly reminded her of the thing she admired most about the now dead Jesus of Nazareth. To be sure, Jesus spoke that way also, but he often added something else to it, some small, human element that somehow made his words all make sense today, here and now, even to the most common people. Jesus possessed something, for lack of a better word, call it "light." "That's what it was," Gerry thought, "light that brought brightness to this world of constant impending."

Suddenly, for some inexplicable reason, Gerry began to remember her few encounters with the rabbi from Nazareth. She had not covered many of the Jesus events, but she had seen him on at least a few occasions and had heard him speak on several others. Unlike the man before her, there was always something certain and immediate in Jesus' voice. It was never, "One day, everything will be all right if . . ." His message always seemed to be in the present tense. He always made people feel that hope had arrived, that the breakthrough was happening in that instant. And for some strange reason, the word "light" kept coming back to her. When this council member, along with so much of Palestine, spoke of hope, it was as if their only hope was hope. When Jesus spoke of hope, it was as if he was the giver of hope, but never in what might someday come to pass. It was as though he was himself proof that hope was a dividend that indeed could pay off if never given up on, and for an awful lot of people, Jesus was the proof that hope was not wasted.

At that moment another picture entered her thoughts, an image that seemed to undercut all this message of hope. It was the picture of Jesus' body hanging from a cross on Golgotha, commonly translated to mean "the place of the skull." "He's dead," Gerry pondered. "Died 3 P.M. Friday. That's why we're all here. That's what this big news story is all about. That's why I am in this stinking motel room talking to this strange, well-mannered council member who will not even give me his name."

She suddenly remembered the feeling she had had while waiting for the elevator in New York, that feeling of anger that she could not quite apprehend. She started to feel that perhaps Jesus was not such a good fellow after all. "What happens now," she thought, "to all of those people who held on to that hope and now realize that hope is only a wish still ungranted? For most people, that hope will become more of a sore in their lives than a salve. And what would have been wrong with letting these poor, miserable slobs have a few more years of promise before snuffing out the best glimmer of hope they have had in a hundred years? Maybe the reason men like David Ben Levin never believed in Jesus was because they have seen far too often what hope shattered can result in."

Gerry remembered seeing Jesus enter a rather heated argument with a group of men who thought like David. They believed that Jesus was basically a good man, but they had accused him of bringing false hope to the very people who needed hope most, the poor. They accused him of taking advantage of those who have the least, the most susceptible to any kind of message of hope. It was the only time she thought she caught a glimpse of anger in Jesus' face. Jesus said to them that they were right on one level. The poor have very little choice; they have nothing; and, therefore, they are much more open to the possibilities that God would be there for them.

But he also commented that people like themselves could receive even greater blessings than those living in poverty if, with all of their university degrees and their fine homes and season theater tickets, they too realized that without God, they had nothing. "But," he told them, "you hide your emptiness behind bigger and better possessions. You mask your own need for God's love behind esoteric, self-serving dialogues about the poor. You need God in your hearts, but absent of that, you think you carry him in your wallets."

"It's interesting," Gerry thought, "how a few comments passed in a conversation could spark a whole group of connections in the mind." For instance, she had never made the connection before, but it was right after that incident that Jesus used the phrase for the first time in public, "Blessed are the poor in spirit." She also remembered that that day was the only time she ever personally felt a little uncomfortable with one of Jesus' analogies.

"Do we have a deal?" The man was staring at Gerry, a bit bewildered by her long silence.

"I'm sorry, what did you say?"

"I said, 'Do we have a deal, Ms. Simmons?'"

"Yes, fine, fine. I cannot promise you this will make it on the air, or that they will print what I send them, you understand, not having heard just what it is you are going to tell me about the trial, but they usually do if the story is worthwhile. And I will put it through without mentioning your name."

"First, let me say this about myself. I am a scribe, a lawyer to some of your listeners. I have always had great reverence for the law. We are a people of laws, from the book of the Exodus, to Leviticus, to Deuteronomy. The law, Ms. Simmons, to us is everything. It covers the way we dress, the way we eat, even the manner in which we greet one another. Every manner of prayer and sacrifice is covered in our laws. Take away the law from us, and you take away what it means to be the people we are. The law is given to us by God and can only be changed by God. It is meant to last one hundred million years, even longer if it is what God desires. It is not meant to be altered to suit anyone's purpose, no matter how pressing the need might seem at the time. Ms. Simmons, I am here to tell you that the trial of Jesus broke the laws given to us regarding how one is to be tried in our courts. And I saw people who I believed felt like I do, like every Jew who believes in the God of Israel must feel, break the law of God."

Gerry interrupted: "I had heard that it was illegal to hold a trial for a capital offense at night."

"It is more than that. According to the Mishnah, it is illegal to hold any trial on the eve of the Sabbath. To do so is an affront to the Sabbath itself. But there is even more. According to the law, no sentence of death can be pronounced on the same day as the trial. Jesus was tried and sentenced to death on the same day. Even the place where the trial was held was illegal according to our laws."

"Where was the trial held?" Gerry asked with some puzzlement. "Wasn't it held in the official chambers where trials are always held?"

"No, it was not. The trial was held in the home of the high priest himself. That too is against our laws."

"Can you tell me what happened that night and at the trial itself?"

"I, along with all of the other council members, was called to the house of the high priest. We were told there was a matter of urgent business that we had to attend to. I did not fully know what was going on, although when I arrived, I had the feeling that many other council members did know. We were told that Jesus had been arrested and was going to be tried right there in the house of the high priest. When some of us protested, we were told to keep silent, and to our shame, we did. Jesus was then brought in, bound like a common prisoner. He was accused of blasphemy, and various witnesses were brought forth to testify against him. One by one they began to speak. However, it became very clear that the witnesses could not agree just what Jesus had done wrong. They began to argue among themselves. You see, Ms. Simmons, that should have been the end of it. Once witnesses disagree, the charges, according to our laws, must be dropped. One could clearly see that there had been no true prior examination of the witnesses. That too must be done according to the law. There must also be an independent agreement of testimony. It was obvious that was not the case."

"So, sir, you're telling me that all of these things you mentioned are part of your legal system, and none of this was carried out in the case of Jesus?"

"That is exactly what I am telling you, Ms. Simmons. And there is more, something that as a scribe I found unbelievable. When it seemed like the case was falling apart, Caiaphas, the high priest himself, began to take over the role as chief prosecutor of Jesus."

Gerry looked up from her notes in surprise. "There was a bit of a rumor on the streets about that, but you're saying Caiaphas did in fact take on the role as the inquisitor?"

"Yes, he did. I know you see the gravity in that statement. It would be like going to a courtroom in your country and having the judge take over the prosecution of a case while still sitting on the bench in judgment."

"Can you tell me what Jesus' behavior was like during all of this?"

"For the most part he kept silent. Jesus knew that we had no real case against him, and so he remained quiet and let the prosecution defeat itself. And he was under no obligation to make any statement that could in any way be used against him. One by one the witnesses perjured themselves without any help from Jesus. Even while he stood there, in the middle of the floor tied and bruised, he still in his silence was smarter than the whole Sanhedrin put together. At least so it seemed, until Caiaphas pulled one very dirty trick, and Jesus did the first dumb thing I ever heard or saw him do."

"What happened?" asked Gerry.

"The trial was going badly, as I said. Two witnesses came forward and said that Jesus had boasted that he would destroy the temple and somehow himself rebuild it in three days. The council members began to laugh at the absurdity of trying a man for blasphemy because he threatened to tear down the temple on Monday and have it standing again by Wednesday. The whole thing seemed farcical. While no one could be sure just what Jesus had meant by that remark, or even if he had indeed said it, one could be sure he had spoken metaphorically in some manner. While it is true that we are strict in our laws, we are not barbarians. The only way that blasphemy charge could have had any significance would have been if Jesus was speaking literally— which would have meant he was claiming he could perform that feat because he was God."

Gerry interrupted, "But some people I spoke with claimed that toward the end he *was* claiming to be the son of God."

"He was always rather careful about making that claim in public. We had heard that he said it, but he never said it to any of us. Besides, he never in any way encouraged anyone to worship him personally or be anything other than a good Jew. He never preached any other religion but Judaism. Oh, perhaps some of his interpretations were a bit, shall we say, liberal; nonetheless, he still preached Judaism. He went to the temple and observed the Sabbath. He did sometimes break certain of our laws and way of life, but never anything that we could point to that was truly grave. If we put to death every Jew who broke some portion of the law from time to time, this country would be empty of its people in a matter of months."

"Yes," Gerry interrupted, "but did Jesus say he was the son of God, or the messiah, or give some indication that he was more than an itinerant preacher on the night of his trial?"

"Well, I am getting to that, Ms. Simmons. As I said, once the charge about the temple was made — and it looked at that point that desperation was about to set in over this circus we were calling a trial — the high priest did something that was most despicable, and Jesus did something that was very dumb. Caiaphas stood up and walked over to Jesus. At first he screamed at him: 'Didn't you hear what they said? Are you going to answer these charges or not?' But Jesus remained silent. Then Caiaphas walked slowly behind Jesus and said to him: 'I charge you under oath by the living God: Tell us if you are the Christ, the living God?'"

"What did Jesus do then?"

"He gave a very ambiguous answer, and then he said something that put the nails into his own hands. He said to Caiaphas: 'It is you who have said it,' and then added, 'but I say to all of you: in the future you will see the Son of Man sitting at the right hand of the Mighty One and coming in clouds of heaven.' That was it; it sealed his fate."

Gerry again looked up from her pad. "I don't get it. If that's all he said, why was that so damaging? It seems to me that he still never confessed to being your messiah."

"There was a very important reason why what he said was so damaging, Ms. Simmons. It has to do with Jesus' beginnings as a preacher. He was initially brought to our attention because of a near riot he was supposed to have initiated in his hometown of Nazareth. It was said that it was there he first began making claims about actually being the messiah. He reportedly stood up to read the scriptures, and when he read from the prophet Isaiah, who speaks about the coming of the

Holy One, he ended the reading by declaring that in some way the scripture was actually referring to him. It was never made clear what he really said, and we were never able to fully substantiate it, but that was the beginning of our scrutiny of him. Well, when he answered the high priest that dark evening of his trial, he quoted the scriptures in the same way he had supposedly done back in Nazareth. He used the phrase 'Son of Man sitting at the right hand of the Mighty One.' That comes right from the scriptures and speaks again about the coming of the Holy One."

"Sir, forgive me, but I'm still not sure I see the point. It seems that even if he had quoted scripture, he still did not say that he himself was this Son of Man, only that the day was coming on which all of you would see whoever 'the Son of Man' refers to coming on some clouds. And, in fact, I believe you said that it was the high priest, not Jesus himself, who implied by his question that Jesus was the messiah."

"Ms. Simmons, how well do you know the scriptures?"

Gerry suddenly felt she was back in Sunday school and, as always, had not read the lessons she was supposed to. She was hoping the scribe was not going to ask her any questions about the scriptures, because this was one test she was sure to fail.

"Well, I have read some..."

The scribe understood this as an admission of lack of knowledge of scripture and explained himself: "You see, Ms. Simmons, the particular passage Jesus quoted comes from the book of Daniel. And it is a passage that speaks of the Son of Man being given particular authority over everyone and every nation. The scripture talks about Daniel's great vision of the beast that symbolized the ancient powers that ravaged our land. Then it speaks about the Lord, our God, destroying the beast, while at the same time appointing one 'like the Son of Man' to be king over us all. Daniel writes:

As I looked, thrones were set in place, and the Ancient of Days took his seat. His clothing was as white as snow, the hair of his head was white like wool. His throne was flaming with fire, and its wheels were all ablaze. A river of fire was flowing, coming out from before it. Thousands upon thousands attended him; ten thousand times ten thousand stood before him. The court was seated, and the books were opened. Then I continued to watch because of the boastful words the horn was speaking. I kept looking until the beast was slain and its body destroyed and thrown into the blazing fire. The other beasts had been stripped of their authority, but were allowed to live for a period of time. In my vision at night I looked, and there before me was one like a Son of Man, coming with the clouds of heaven. He approached the Ancient of Days and was led into his presence. He was given authority, glory, and sovereign power; all people, nations, men of every language worshiped him. His dominion is an everlasting dominion, that will not pass away, and his kingdom is one that will never be destroyed.

Even before Gerry could sort out fully the meaning of all she had just heard, she could not help but admire the way this man was able to quote scripture from memory. He just began to quote it as though it was as natural to remember that passage as it would have been for him to remember his name. There was passion in his voice as he quoted the book of Daniel. He did not speak any louder than he had before, but still there was something different in his voice when he spoke.

"So what you are telling me," Gerry said, "is that when Jesus quoted this passage from Daniel, it was perceived as his way of saying that he was indeed the one all the prophets spoke about, and if I understood the inferences from the reading, he was also proclaiming to be the king of all peoples and all nations, not just the Jews."

"Partly correct, Ms. Simmons. What Jesus did was to strike at a collective nerve that runs through all of us who are priests, scribes, and Pharisees. You see, Jesus was a good man in many ways. I myself admired much of what he said. But he had one terrible fault. He was extremely intolerant of the position all of us find ourselves in here in this occupied land. I suppose it had something to do with his youth. He wanted everything to change overnight and saw anyone who did not agree with his method of doing things as traitors or cowards. He never had an appreciation for the way things must work in the real world.

"Despite what he would often say in public, we are not all bad people. Much charitable work goes on in the cities and towns, and much of that work is done by dedicated rabbis and Pharisees throughout the land. But we are under the occupation of Rome. That does not give us the freedom to do all we would like to do. And every member of the Sanhedrin feels the conflict between preaching the scriptures but having to do it in such a way that we do not offend Rome, which quite literally could destroy us all by closing down all of our temples and forcing us to become wanderers in the desert. It is within Rome's power to declare Judaism an outlawed religion. There are some who would argue that in this day and age, something like that could no longer happen. I dare say to you that those are the same people who would have argued that what happened to Jesus could no longer have happened either.

"Still, even the most conservative member of the council struggles constantly over how much compromise, if any, should be taking place between our duty to God and our duty to assure the survival of the temple and all that that represents. For many of us, those two positions are one and the same. Very few of us take that responsibility lightly. It gnaws at us constantly, and we pray daily for guidance from God.

"What Jesus did when quoting Daniel was to quite openly suggest that all of the council, all of the Sanhedrin, and all of the temple leadership had turned into the beast of Daniel's dream. I don't know if he meant to literally suggest this, but he implied that he believed that we had reduced ourselves to the level of the barbarians that ruled and ravished our country during the time of the prophet Daniel. Worse, his statement suggested that God was going to appoint him the king and ruler of us all. It suggested the coming of a new age in which all that we represent would somehow be ushered away, and the Son of Man, appointed by the Ancient of Days, would rule over us all. It was simply too much for the council members to ignore.

"You must remember that this was all said at a time when Jesus, by simply keeping his mouth shut, could have quite possibly gotten out of this alive. Even when Caiaphas charged him under oath to answer, he still could have gotten out of it if he had been smart enough to know that no one can be forced to give testimony against himself. But instead of keeping quiet, he uttered those words, knowing that they could spell his doom. His words made the council members feel as though he was arrogant, as if he was saying that he could not be harmed by the collective weight of the whole council. He made many of us feel as though we, who have lived and died for Judaism, were nothing but a bunch of dogs, to be disposed of by God through the appointment of himself as the Son of Man. This coupled with that 'Good Shepherd' nonsense..."

Gerry interrupted, "Good Shepherd? What about the Good Shepherd? I had heard that Jesus had referred to himself as a shepherd looking over the people of Israel. Surely no one could have found that particularly offensive. In fact, that was one of the first terms of endearment used to describe him around the world, was it not?"

The scribe glared at Gerry, wide-eyed, frozen, enraged. He got up and walked toward a window, trying desperately to regain his composure. Gerry raced back through the last few minutes of conversation. What did she say that had gotten this man so upset? Finally, he began to speak: "It is amazing to me how you in the West love heroes. You crave heroes, no matter what the cost. But seldom do you take the time to consider what the price of being a hero is, either to the man who would become one or to the people who are affected by the individual."

Gerry watched intently as he waved his hand, seemingly in disgust. She had no idea just what was happening here and why this talk of the good shepherd had suddenly seemed to turn this cool professional into a smoldering pit of anger. She wanted to ask him some questions but decided to wait and let this strange little scene play itself out. "Please forgive me, Ms. Simmons. All of us are a bit tired these days, and, I am afraid, a bit stressed out. Read the book of Ezra, Ms. Simmons. Read chapter 34. You will see that Jesus' use of the term 'Good Shepherd' was not an innocent pastoral allusion. When he used it, it was meant as a biting, satirical criticism of all of us who are wandering through this desert of occupation while trying to lead our sheep away from the wolves of Rome. It was meant to suggest to the crowd listening that we have all become hired hands who, because we are paid, will not risk our necks for our people. And once again the parallel solution is for God, as he does in the book of Ezra, to replace all of the present shepherds with a 'Good Shepherd.' One who will 'do the right thing,' as that young filmmaker in America called his movie. Don't worry, Jesus' inference was not lost on those of us who live and work in this part of the world. It hurt many of us deeply, that kind of talk. Still, we have been attacked before, even by many of our own, and — as hard as this may be to admit — many of us felt that Jesus' attacks on us weren't without foundation. You see, Ms. Simmons, most of us believed that Jesus used his knowledge of scripture to throw back in our faces our own laws and teachings as a way of getting us to live up to our responsibilities as leaders and shepherds of our people. And while you would never get anyone of us to admit it today, some of us actually welcomed the challenge. Jesus had begun to get many of us to think about what we had become. Many secretly admired his cleverness at using scripture. Believe it or not, for some of us, he was indeed beginning to make some sense. At times he was a breath of fresh air, even though fresh air can sometimes be cold and biting. It is why I believed he could have gotten enough members of the council to vote against his being put to death if he had only kept quiet.

"Oh, to be sure, there were some on the council who genuinely had it in for Jesus, and no matter what had transpired, would have voted for his death. There were some who believed that it was truly right, just, and helpful toward our salvation to have him eliminated for the good of the temple. Others wanted him out of the way because he exposed some of the corruption that ran through the temple, but I believe that was a relatively small minority. But when he stood before us and quoted Daniel, he tore all of the grounds from beneath the council members who would have helped him."

"Why?" asked Gerry. "I want to be sure I really understand why that quote upset all of you so much."

"Because, Ms. Simmons, at that moment, Jesus went from a man who could be seen as working tirelessly for the welfare of all of God's people, even if you disagreed with him or believed he was just a bit misguided, to someone who really seemed to believe he was God. He went from a sort of civil-rights-activist rabbi, who was motivated by passion and love for his people, to someone who was doing all of this because he believed he was the Son of Man. He turned into someone who perhaps began to believe his own press clippings and was now suffering from delusions of grandeur. It was simply too much for the council to bear."

"Sir, if you believe all of this, and I have no reason to doubt your word, why are you here? I don't see why you bothered to tell me all of this about the trial and your laws. It sounds to me as if you believe Jesus had gone crazy."

"I tell you these things for three reasons. One, as I said, we are a people of laws, and no matter what Jesus did, that can never excuse us from doing what we did. I cannot say with certainty whether we used the law to serve God or to serve ourselves. I know there are some who would disagree with that assessment, but that is how I feel. Even if we believed Jesus guilty of the most obscene blasphemy, he should have been brought to trial in the usual manner. Jesus was one of us; he was a Jew and deserved to be treated with all of the rights afforded him by our laws.

"Second, I am not sure that we ever heard the whole story from Jesus himself. We never had a chance to question him specifically on just what *he* meant when he said what he did. Right after Jesus quoted Daniel, the high priest, sensing what had happened, seized upon the opportunity and tore his cloak, a sign of great torment for us, and whipped the crowd present into a frenzy. He ended the trial right there on the spot, claiming there was no more need for witnesses. At that point, we ceased being a tribunal and became a lynch mob. In the cool light of morning one can think that perhaps Jesus' quoting of Daniel was part of some greater defense he was about to put forth. Maybe he was genuinely hurt and tired and didn't know just what he was saying. I don't know. But I do know that what happened at that trial, and the way we convicted him, was wrong. It was wrong, wrong, wrong."

Gerry sat and pondered the look on the man's face. He had a far-away look in his eyes. There was something else going on in the rabbi's soul. Everything he had said made sense, but still there was something more, something the man had not said. The story up to this point had left some disturbing questions unanswered.

For one thing, it did not explain why this man felt that a record of all that he had said could someday benefit the world. "All of human-kind" he had said when Gerry started the interview. To be sure, what she had been told would make a good news story: "Council Breaks Own Laws in Order to Convict Jesus." "Jesus Quotes Scripture Suggesting He Was the Son of God." But there was still something missing. For instance, why the secrecy? If he were to go public with this, surely the other council members would band together and publicly deny the charges, and that would be that. The story would get a little press and then in six months be forgotten. And what had he done that would make him feel his life might be in danger if his name was a part of this story? He talked about having already cast a certain amount of suspicion on himself because of "certain actions" he had taken on behalf of Jesus. What actions?

"Sir," Gerry finally said, "you must excuse me, but I have been a reporter for a long time. And if you will pardon my saying so, something doesn't add up here. I know on the surface this seems like a perfectly good news story, and I can assure you I will do all I can to have it aired as well as printed, just in the manner we agreed on. But I feel there is another shoe here somewhere."

"Another shoe?" said the council member. "What do you mean, another shoe?"

"It's an old American saying. When something is not complete, and we know there is more to come, we say that we are waiting for the other shoe to drop. It has to do with living in apartments back home and hearing the person above you at night take one shoe off and let it drop to the floor, and then a few seconds later hearing the other one. If you only hear one, you find yourself waiting for the other to hit the floor before you can fall asleep."

"I see," said the council member. "That's a good saying. It sounds like something we would say. You know we are a people rich in wonderful sayings. Are you sure the people above you were not Jewish?"

For the first time there was some laughter in the room, albeit a somewhat uneasy laughter. It did help break the tension for a few seconds. Then there was silence.

At last the man spoke: "Ms. Simmons, there is perhaps another shoe, but I can only let it drop off the record." The rabbi paused and smiled a little, proud of the way he had just appropriately used this new saying so creatively. "I am sure that what you are hearing in my voice is a certain amount of passion, and perhaps you feel that what I have told you thus far doesn't seem to warrant so much of it. Well, in some ways, Ms. Simmons, you are wrong. I am very passionate about the law. To those of us who believe, the law means everything, as it did to Isaiah, Jeremiah, and all of the prophets before us. But there is more, . . . and this I will only say if you give me your word that it is off the record."

Gerry knew that she had little choice here. A no to that request would surely mean the end of the interview.

Once assured by Gerry that what came next would be held off the record, the council member continued: "This morning, I went to the office of the governor and asked that the body of Jesus be allowed to be buried in our family crypt. Because of Jesus' lifestyle, Jesus really had very little money, despite all of his fame. I gave that as the excuse for burying him in our family tomb. The real reason, however, was that I wanted one of us on the council to do something that would make up for the role we had played in his death. I realize that may sound awfully hypocritical, being responsible in some ways for his death and then offering him a free tomb to be buried in. But my motives really were pure. I can only let history be the ultimate judge as to my motives in this matter. I dare say that we scribes stand to go down in history as a most villainous lot, but that simply is not who and what we are. It is all in the hands of God now anyway. You will help record that history, Ms. Simmons. Remember as you write that it was one of the council members who told you the truth about all of this, a member of that very same council that condemned Jesus."

"You mentioned there were three reasons that you wanted a record of this, so far you have mentioned two."

"The other reason will surprise you even more," he said. "Particularly in light of everything you have heard me say here this evening. The truth is..." He paused, thought for a few moments, as though he was about to let something pass his lips that once said could have a terrifying effect on him. It was as though he was about to admit something for the first time to himself that would unleash a force that he felt might consume him forever. He never said the words, but several times he had a look that suggested he wanted to say, "Forget it." Finally, he took a deep breath and said the words that so troubled him: "I am not truly certain that Jesus was not exactly who some said he was. I am not certain in my own heart that Jesus was not in fact the Son of Man, the messiah whom the prophets foresaw."

The other shoe not only had dropped, but had landed with the force of an earthquake. While it was true that many of the poor, and a few of the liberal well-to-do, had become ardent followers of Jesus, and while it was also true that some even supposedly believed he was the messiah, Gerry had never heard any member of the council, or anyone in authority, dare say they thought he was some kind of god. To hear this kind of talk come from a scribe and a member of the council was absolutely astonishing. It was also strangely unsettling.

They had been talking for the better part of an hour now, and by this time Gerry had begun to feel rather comfortable with this elderly gentleman. She had forgotten somewhat the call in the middle of the night, the meeting with the street punk called Alan, and the way he had told her he could have killed her if he had wanted to. She had begun to forget all that because this scribe seemed normal and rational. He seemed to have a legitimate concern about the law, from a lawyer's point of view, as well as a concern about how history would treat his peers. But now, with this new revelation, everything seemed to become strange again, and even a bit terrifying. She once again began to fear for her safety and suspect she might be a part of an extremist plot that might leave her scarred or even dead. To dispel this feeling she talked: "Sir, why do you feel that there may have been a chance that Jesus was anything more than a good preacher and public activist? I must confess, this takes me by surprise, even more than what has happened here over the last day or two."

"I know this must sound strange coming from me," said the scribe, "and please understand me, I am not saying I believe he was the messiah. I am merely saying I am not so sure he was not. You must remember that we are a people who believe that God will send us a messiah. That is something none of us can deny. A messiah has been promised us. So why not Jesus? He certainly ended up much like many of the prophets foretold. I know you think this is strange because I am a man of reason, an educated man. I am not one of the poor, the people who are supposed to be most prone to believing in 'deliverers.' When I say I am not sure he was not the messiah, I say so because to dismiss Jesus out of hand, without even considering the possibility, is to dismiss the whole idea of messiahs. It is to say that the whole idea is absurd.

"Tell me, Ms. Simmons, is there anyone who could be presented to you as the messiah, who you would not think was a phony or a fraud? Is there anyone who could come to you and present himself as being healed of blindness, or cured of demonic possession, whom you would not dismiss either as a charlatan or as someone unknowingly yet actually cured by means of science or psychology? Would you give any credence to the idea that someone born on this earth could actually be the messiah that God promised us?"

He let the questions take hold and then continued: "I believe that the same skepticism that you possess, we on the council and in the temple also have fallen victim to. We all say we believe in the coming of the messiah, but I am not sure that anyone whom God would send to us could ever live up to what all of us, with our different ideas and prejudices, expect a messiah to be. Looking back on our relationship with Jesus, every rumor of miracles and wonders we as a council heard about, we automatically dismissed as being untrue. We had a logical explanation for everything we heard out of the ordinary. We, the men of faith, had become men of logic. And I ask you, Ms. Simmons, how logical is it to believe in this day and age that God would send us a messenger from heaven, a savior, a messiah? To believe it as a matter of faith, that is fine. To believe it as a matter of logic in a real world, that would not be so fine. We all must say we believe in a messiah, but to say we have ever seen one would cause great scandal."

The scribe turned and once again looked toward the window. His profile spoke of sadness. Even though Gerry's mind was still racing to make sense out of all of this, she also had to fight an urge to try to comfort the scribe. She sensed, however, that the man would view any words of comfort as insulting or condescending. Still, her heart went out to him because he seemed so troubled.

"Perhaps Isaiah was right," he finally said. " 'I have come so that the deaf may hear, the blind may see, and the poor may have the good news preached to them.' Only the poor people, Ms. Simmons, only the people living in the tenements, the people living in poverty who feel the heat of oppression most, only they seem to see something in Jesus the rest of us could not. Did you know that even some members of his own family thought he was nuts? I don't know, maybe he was. Maybe I am. Perhaps..."

The scribe suddenly turned to see the look on Gerry's face, and at once cleared his throat and stood up. "Ms. Simmons, I fear I have been rambling, and worse: I have gotten off the point of this meeting. I believe whatever Jesus turns out to be, he will surely become a figure in history. I also believe his life and death will be an important historical point in future times. How his trial was conducted, for good or for bad, should be a part of that record. Except for those who were at the trial, you are now the only person who knows what truly went on. I do not believe we have the right to take this to our graves. A record of this should be made for posterity. However history judges Jesus, and for that matter, all of us who played some role in this, this record will in some way play a part in that judgment. Write your story, Ms. Simmons. As we agreed, I ask you please not to cloud the issue with all of my later ramblings about messiahs and the like. The record of the trial will speak for itself. I want to thank you for coming at this late hour, and I hope that this information will prove useful."

Gerry knew the interview was over. She stood up, facing the scribe. "Sir," she said, "I promise not to use your name as you requested when I report this story, but I sure would like to know for my own records what your name is."

"It's Joseph, Ms. Simmons. Put that on the news, and I'll be dead shortly thereafter."

Even though the words were ominous, Gerry noticed the man said them with a wry smile. By this time the scribe had skillfully ushered her to the door and opened it. "What should I do about the money?" Gerry said hastily, as she was going through the door.

"Don't worry, Ms. Simmons, someone will contact you." With

that there was a quick goodbye, and all at once Gerry found herself standing again in front of room 114.

She stood there for a minute and then with a start looked around to see if she was alone. She was. "Where were Alan and his comrades?" she thought. She looked up one side of the alley and down the other, but they were nowhere to be seen. Gerry made her way toward the main street where she caught a cab. She had two strong feelings about what had happened: the first was that she sensed she had a great story to report; the second was that the whole affair gave her a bit of the creeps.

She reached her hotel and went to her room. She turned on the all-night news station to see if any more news about Jesus had come up since she was away on this story, but nothing new had developed. She checked her messages and saw that the king had scheduled a news conference for the next day, as well as the governor. She noted that she must make sure to make both of them and then file a report for the evening news show. She was not sure just what to do with the story that was just handed her, but she decided to wait till the morning to figure it out. Shortly thereafter, she fell asleep with the TV on.

About four hours later, around 5:45 A.M., she was suddenly awakened by a tone on the TV announcing a breaking story. The story seemed to reach into her sleep and pull her into consciousness. She sat straight up in bed, and apprehension swept over her just as she was able to make out the words of the reporter: "In other news, police are investigating the death of one of the leading temple officials in Judea. Joseph, a scribe and council member from the town of Arimathea, was found early this morning dead in a Lower East Side alley far from his home. He had been stabbed. It appears robbery was the motive."

– CHAPTER NINE –

As Marcus rode back into town, he focused on who was next on his list. First he would see the high priest Caiaphas, then Herod, and then the governor. He had contemplated marching in to see the high priest with a large contingent of troops, to show him he was not fooling around and wanted some straight answers. But then he thought better of it and decided to go and see him on his own. As he rode up to the temple gate, he was greeted by members of the temple security staff. They all bowed their heads and politely greeted him as though he was a dignitary. He could almost feel the mocking words said under their breath as he rode past each one. He knew there was no love lost among the temple people for a Roman officer, only fear followed by hate.

The temple (which was actually known as the "second" temple, the first having been destroyed by Nebuchadnezzar in 446 B.C.) was a massive structure made even more so by the recent order of Herod to have the temple go through a vast restoration that amounted to practically a rebuilding from the ground up. It had, however, been in a constant state of renovation for over forty-six years. Therefore, carpenters, builders, and workmen of all sorts were constantly running about the exterior of the building.

As he approached the main entrance to the temple and proceeded to dismount, he was met by the personal servant of the high priest.

"Can I help you, sir?" said the servant.

"Tell your master that I am here to see him and wish to do so now."

"Sir," said the man, "I do not know if the high priest is available. I believe he may be in prayer."

At that Marcus grabbed the servant by the collar and glared into his eyes: "You tell your master I wish to see him now. Tell him I am here at the direct order of his emperor and will see him either here now or later in one of my jail cells."

A look of genuine fear swept over the face of the servant as he wrestled to get free of Marcus's grip. Roman officers never treated temple officials so roughly, and the servant had been caught off guard.

"Sir, I will do what I can. Please let me go!"

Marcus released the man, who scurried away into the temple. Marcus had grabbed the servant because he wanted to impress upon all concerned that the upcoming investigation was very serious and that all protocols were off. But he suddenly became concerned about his behavior. He was acting a bit more brutish than was his nature, even if the strong-arming was just an act, a way of setting a tone with the high priest in order to cut through all the fancy footwork that the high priest would engage in as a way of avoiding the truth. The high priest was known for that sort of thing. Still, something kept telling Marcus he had played the part a little too well just then, and, indeed, he had enjoyed the bullying. That was not like him, and it troubled him. Above all else, Marcus prided himself on being a professional. He believed that he — unlike some of the mercenaries Rome was forced to hire from time to time in order to fill out the ranks of the army — was 100 percent military, a professional soldier, just like his best friend, Demetrius. "Demetrius," he thought, "I strong-armed that servant because of Demetrius, my best friend, sitting in a room dazed and waiting to see how my report to Sejanus will play upon his future."

Marcus vowed then and there that he would indeed get to the bottom of all of this Jesus mess. He now had a personal stake in getting at the truth. Though he believed that after a while all of this would blow over, and the rest of the world would soon forget what had happened, he knew this incident would affect the rest of his life. He knew because his friend, his brother, was caught up in all of this, as a result, life would never be the same again, for either of them. That was the real cause for the apparent anger welling up inside him, the fact that something over which he had no control, a crucifixion that took place on someone else's watch, was affecting his life profoundly.

Marcus felt he had been robbed of something that none of these people, Jesus, Sejanus, or even the emperor, could possibly know about: true friendship. Marcus believed that most people never really have friends; they have acquaintances but not friends. He believed that most people would often come close to friendships, but some of the most intimate ones were still somehow fraught with conditions. He remembered "friends" he had made growing up as a child, other children who often promised to be best pals for life. He remembered that with all of these children, there always turned out to be something that one soon learned must never be said, or some gesture that must never be made. If that line were crossed, the friendship would cease, and joy would be replaced by emptiness.

But Marcus also believed that if the gods were to so favor you, you might someday meet someone who bonds with you in a way that no other person in the universe can. You meet that individual who becomes your friend, and from that moment nothing can ever come between you. He understood how profoundly a man could love a woman and his children, but he still felt that no one ever gets to see your heart and soul like that one comrade, that friend whom you would call your brother but who in fact becomes closer than any sibling can be. Marcus believed he had a friend like that in Antoni Demetrius. Even though they now served in different parts of the region and did not see each other as often as they did when they were younger, still they could at a moment's notice pick up their friendship from whatever point they left it, because they were that close.

And now, something had happened that might change all of that. And that something may have been caused at least in part by the man he was about to see next, the high priest Caiaphas. He was supposed to be there to question Caiaphas in a most diplomatic way and find out all he could about what happened on Thursday evening. Yet in his heart, he knew he didn't want to do that. What he really wanted to do was to grab him, much like he had the high priest's servant. Only he wanted to yell in his face, "What have you done to my friendship, to my brother whom I love, my life?" and then cut his throat.

He was mercifully brought back to earth by the remembrance of the icy voice of the man who had given him his orders. He remembered the voice of Sejanus, who had somehow found out about his feelings for Herod and had reminded him that he must never again let his personal feelings interfere with his duty to the empire. For the first time in his life, he welcomed the distracting feeling of fear that General Sejanus alone could instill in men. He welcomed it as horses would welcome the pain when cattlemen of old used to bite their ears as a way of diverting their attention from the pain of being branded with hot irons. However, even Sejanus's malevolence was not enough to fully take away the feeling of personal anger and hurt that was quickly developing inside of Marcus.

Just then the high priest's servant returned and told Marcus he could enter the building and await the high priest's presence. Marcus knew that even if Caiaphas was ready to see him, he would still keep him waiting. There was a saying he remembered from the academy that the Romans always reminded each other of. It had to do with a play on words. They would say, "Always remember that the Middle East is a sick part of the world." They would pronounce the word "sick," but they were referring to the letters S.I.C. The letters stood for Strategy, Intrigue, and the game of Chess. They would teach all the cadets that if you wanted to survive here, you needed to know something about all three.

First, nothing of consequence happens in the Middle East by accident. Everything is part of an elaborate, well-planned strategy to achieve something often quite obscure. So if you hoped to survive there, you always had to find out who was behind whatever it was that had happened. Once you learned that, you learned to look beyond an apparently simple event such as the murder of a soldier, or even the death of Jesus, because often it was only a part of some greater and still unknown strategy designed to accomplish something in the future.

Second, never forget that intrigue is like the air in the Middle East; it surrounds you constantly. Therefore, no local was ever to be trusted with sensitive information. Anyone could be an agent for someone else, and you never knew just who.

Third, Chess. A good chess player always thought five and ten moves ahead of his opponent. Sometimes it was better to give up a bishop in order to capture a queen. Chess was actually taught at the academy. It was a course required by all upperclassmen. It was part of your final exam. If you could never win a game of chess, you were not considered militarily smart enough to command.

Just then the high priest entered the room. He was grinning widely as he approached Marcus. "Commander," he said with a warm yet transparently insincere smile. "What a pleasant surprise. Welcome to God's holy temple. Won't you sit down? If you like, I will ring for some refreshments."

Marcus thanked the high priest for his hospitality but graciously declined. He wanted to get right down to business. He wondered if the high priest would comment on his harsh treatment of his servant, but Caiaphas never uttered a word about it.

Marcus began: "I have been ordered by the emperor to conduct an investigation into the events surrounding the trial and subsequent death of Jesus. I must warn you that Rome is not pleased with the

way events took place. As you can see, Judea is now crawling with reporters, and the whole world is asking how a man like Jesus could end
up executed at the hands of the Roman government, when apparently
he was charged with some crime that had nothing to do with Roman
law. This situation has the potential to blow up in all of our faces, and
you can truly bet your life the emperor will not rest until he knows all
that has happened here."

"Commander," said the high priest, "you are blowing this thing all
out of proportion. Jesus broke our law, and his offense was one pun-
ishable by death. Rome has taken away our right to administer the
death penalty ourselves, so we had to go to your governor and ask
him to do it. The governor was kind enough to grant our request;
Jesus was put to death; and that was that. All of this hype in the news
media is exactly just that, hype, which in a short while will blow away
into the desert sands. I for one believe you have come to the wrong
place for answers. I suggest if you or Rome has any questions regarding the legality of what was done here, go to your governor. He was
the one who issued the ultimate order."

"I assure you," Marcus answered, "I will see Governor Pilate in due
time, but right now I am here with you and would appreciate your
giving me all of the help in this matter you can. It is my understanding that when you first brought this matter to the governor, he turned
down your request to have Jesus executed. Later, at your insistence, he
complied with your request. I would be interested to hear in your own
words what transpired to change his excellency's mind."

"I can only hypothesize, commander, but I suppose we were able to
make a strong enough case against Jesus, and the governor was able
to see our point of view."

"And just what was the case you made against Jesus? What had he
done in your eyes to make him so dangerous as to warrant his being
killed?"

"Jesus was a psychopath. He was willing, due to his delusions of
messiahship, to jeopardize all of our lives and even our very souls as
a people in order to gain fame and fortune for himself. He would
have surely become a revolutionary had he not been stopped when he
was. What your governor did was to take steps to nip in the bud a
potentially dangerous situation, thus avoiding bloodshed and tumult
in the streets of our city. He was smart enough to realize that we
as a people know about these false messiahs and the mischief they
can cause. Once it was explained to him how dangerous the man had

become, he took our advice and put an end to his life. That is all there is to the story. Soon the press will find out just what kind of person Jesus really was; they will become disillusioned with him and the story, and it will be over. Any more questions I suggest you ask your governor. Now if you will excuse me, I really am quite busy. This is after all a very holy time of year for us."

Caiaphas stood up as if to end the meeting, but Marcus asked him to return to his seat. Both Marcus and Caiaphas knew that it was really a command thinly disguised as a request. For the first time the high priest lost his composure just a little, for he hated being told what to do. It was bad enough he had to suffer the insult done to his servant, and thus to himself, but being ordered about by this Roman infidel in the house of God was more than he could stand.

"Why do you feel the man was so dangerous?" asked Marcus. "Had he done anything different lately, something he hadn't done over the past three years? According to my sources he preached no violent over-throw of the government. Could all this have been something personal between you and Jesus? Did he have something on you or the temple? Why did you so badly want him dead? Surely you must have known the scandal putting Jesus to death would have caused worldwide."

"Jesus was executed in accordance with your laws because he had become dangerous. I told you that."

"I know, you keep saying that, but as of yet I do not know why you felt he was so dangerous. And dangerous for whom? Did you have some secret information suggesting that he was about to raise an army against Rome? If so, why was it not reported to me or one of my deputies? Our surveillance reports on Jesus were quite up-to-date. None of us had heard anything new about his activities. And if he had for some strange reason become a violent revolutionary, do you think we would not have been able to defend ourselves against whatever Jesus would have thrown at us? Somehow, in my tour of duty here, I have never felt that Rome was in danger from the likes of Jesus and his little band of followers. I know he was quite popular among a lot of your own people. I dare say, from an outsider's view, that he may have been more popular than you seem to be. Might that have been the danger, that he was getting even more popular among the high priest's people than even the high priest himself?"

Marcus thought that would have sent the high priest into a rage, but instead the high priest only began to smile slightly, as though he knew he was about to capture an important piece on the chessboard.

"Commander, it is not by popularity that we minister to our people; it is by the will of God. And as far as Jesus' so-called popularity is concerned, he was not as popular among our people as the commander would like to believe. In fact, I suggest Rome investigate some of its own people before you go tossing that ridiculous nonsense around the temple. From what I hear, even some of the commander's own close personal friends have been seen in the company of Jesus before he died. We of course know it is not our place to question why officers of such high rank in the imperial army would be heralding the name of this potential threat to Rome and the emperor."

Marcus felt as though he had been stabbed. Could the high priest be talking about Demetrius? Could he have found out about his relationship with Jesus? Was he the one who somehow got this news to Sejanus, thus putting his friend under suspicion and house arrest? Ten thousand high priests in Marcus's eyes could never measure up to the likes of one Antoni Demetrius. "You snake," he thought, "you viper's brood. If you were half the man Antoni is, you would be twice the man you are." Marcus knew he had to think quickly because he would soon be engulfed in emotion. He was wounded, he realized that, but he also knew he must recover quickly. He of course knew what he wanted to do, but killing the high priest was not an option at the moment. "What a news story that would make," he thought, "especially with all the press in town. Besides, it would only help embarrass the empire."

Marcus knew he had to fight back. He also knew it was time he started acting like a Roman officer again. He knew the next shot was his, and he took dead aim. "Is there anything else you would like to add to your statement?" he asked the high priest.

The high priest looked a bit surprised. He had expected Marcus would fight back somehow, so thrown off balance that the fight would be easy from here on in. He knew how close Marcus and his comrade in Capernaum were, or so he had been led to believe by the spies who reported the incident, and was surprised Marcus did not go into a rage.

"As I told you, you can report to the governor and find out any other information you wish," said Caiaphas.

Marcus thanked him and headed for the door. He turned and took out the ring bearing the insignia of the emperor. "By the way," he said, almost casually, "I don't believe I will go to see the governor just yet. I am to report my findings to the emperor and to General Sejanus.

The emperor ordered that all new information be reported at once. I'd better give Sejanus my report right away, and then go on to see the governor. Besides, I'm sure you know how the general likes to be made informed of things right away, and no one keeps Sejanus waiting."

Marcus could see the concern come over the face of the high priest, for he too knew of the infamous Sejanus. He also could not help but be concerned about any report reaching the emperor without first being filtered through Pilate, whom he fully expected to back him.

"And what might I ask will the commander say to General Sejanus?"

"I will tell him that it is my belief that you and the temple are behind all that has happened and that in an attempt to embarrass Rome, you instigated this plot. I'll tell him that, furthermore, it is your considered opinion that large-scale numbers of Roman officers have become traitors here in the region and have converted to become followers of Jesus. I'll say that while I believe you're motivated by pure hatred of Rome, and therefore your actions need to be fully investigated, maybe you felt it had become your responsibility to help clean up the Roman army, just like you felt it was your duty to remind the governor, in public, of his duty to Rome. Finally, I will tell him that it is my professional opinion that you and other members of the council felt that this episode would so embarrass Rome that it might afford you a political advantage."

Caiaphas's eyes widened. "But that is not true," he screamed. "Besides," he continued, "all of this was approved by Pilate himself. Are you going to tell the emperor that Pilate acted wrongly in this matter as well? Will you tell them that you think he is part of this plot to embarrass Rome?"

"I have been ordered by the emperor to get at the truth, and that order came directly through General Sejanus. Do you think the emperor would have me lie about anything I find here? I am to report my findings truthfully; those are my orders. After that the chips will fall where they may."

"But you are lying," screamed Caiaphas. "I never said anything about massive defections to Jesus. I had nothing to do with any plot to embarrass Rome. You cannot report such a lie. Besides, if you do you will be condemning your own governor. He will go down with the rest of us; I warn you, commander."

Marcus knew he now had Caiaphas cornered and frightened, and he wasn't about to set him free.

"It really does my heart good to see how much concern you, as part of an occupied people, seem to hold for the welfare of our officials. I will also add that to my report. But between you and me, let me let you in on a little secret. Did you know that the reason our illustrious governor came to power was because he was the protegé of General Sejanus himself? For some reason, he has always held a soft spot in his heart for Governor Pilate. Perhaps the governor did not act with the clearest of judgments in this matter, and some disciplinary action might even befall His Grace. I can't really speculate on such high matters. After all, I'm only a soldier carrying out the orders of his superiors. But on the way here I heard something very interesting. It seems there is a small, little-known treaty that was signed several years ago by your people and the empire. It is called the Cultural Noninterference Act. I am told that Pilate is about to announce that he backed your plan to kill Jesus because he did not wish to interfere in your barbaric culture and felt somewhat duty bound to act on your request. I don't know if that was indeed the real reason; I was hoping to find that out for myself. But based on that treaty, Rome is already willing to back the governor in the press. So you see, even if Pilate didn't do this thing for that reason, he'll now say he did, and that will provide him his cover."

"And Sejanus? He will forgive Pilate, at least for now, for he truly likes the man?"

"Ah, but the last conversation I had with the general concerning the temple seemed to suggest that he did not hold you in quite the same regard. In fact, well, let's just say he had had his suspicions about your role in this whole affair right from the start. I'm sure you'll be hearing from the emperor once I hand in my report. I'm also sure you'll be hearing from General Sejanus as well. He may even pay you a personal visit. In fact, I'm sure that once he reads my report, a visit from him will almost be a sure bet."

For a moment there was silence in the room. Caiaphas knew he had been beaten. He was, after all, a Jew, and these were Romans. He knew that in the end it mattered not what kind of agreement he and Pilate entered into. When it came right down to it, Romans would all stick together and leave him and his people out to dry. He suddenly remembered the words of the prophet Habakkuk, who cried to the heavens: "How long, oh Yahweh, must I cry to heaven and you will not answer, must I call to you and you will not help?" He felt, like so many of the prophets, that God was putting him through a test. "Why so many tests?" he thought. "Why so many tests?"

Although Caiaphas sensed he had been beaten, he also knew his next steps would be important. He needed a moment to think his next move through, and so he stood up and said: "Excuse me for just a moment. There is indeed a matter of urgency I have to attend to. I'll be back in only a few moments." Marcus stood and watched Caiaphas go to the door, open it, and move into the hall. In the hall Caiaphas leaned against a wall and drew in a deep breath, thinking. His mind wandered as he began to contemplate the road that had led him to the temple and to this point in his life. Ever since he had been a child, he had promised God he would serve him. Always, since his first visit to the temple, he knew this was where he was called upon to live out his life. He had loved God with all of his heart, right from the beginning, and swore an oath that if ever God would allow him to become a priest, he would follow God wherever he was asked to go. When he became high priest, he never had any thought of lining his pockets with silver. He truly only wanted to serve God. Unlike his greedy father-in-law, Annas, who had been high priest, Caiaphas took on the job with nothing but reverence and commitment to God's word.

He had become a staunch defender of the faith. He believed that the only way God's loving mercy would ever reach into an imperfect world was through the strict adherence to temple law; therefore, the temple must survive. Nothing or no one was more important than God. He believed that even though man was sacred, no one man was as important as the temple through which God's love and grace enter the world. He believed that in his spiritual heart of hearts, but he also believed something more. He also knew that he alone stood at this moment in history between the Roman world that most of the poor who loved Jesus didn't know and the ruthless Roman world he understood, one that was absolutely capable of exterminating his people purely for the sake of expediency.

Marcus's threats to his existence and way of life had driven home how much the priesthood had diminished since the glory days of the Zadokites and the Maccabees. High priests used to garner such high respect that many of them were civil leaders as well. No one would dare question a high priest as Marcus just had. Acting as civil head as well as spiritual head made sense back then. After all, who could better lead the chosen people of God than someone who was appointed by God himself? And back then there was never the slightest doubt

who picked the high priest. It was God, no other — you were chosen by the Lord God Almighty. Now the high priests were chosen
and served at the pleasure of the king or the Roman authorities who
happened to be in power. Of course Caiaphas could only complain
so much about the present arrangement, for that is after all how he
became high priest. And deep down inside he still believed that he,
too, just like the high priests of old, was chosen by God. He just had
trouble figuring out why God would let scum like Herod, or the infidels like the Romans, have a hand in his reign. He thought the Lord
did indeed work in mysterious ways.

Suddenly Caiaphas's mind began to fill with all sorts of strange
thoughts and memories. He began to recall his slow but steady rise
to the high priesthood. Annas had been the high priest for some
time and, even by temple standards, had grown to become particularly greedy and spiteful. When he retired, everyone thought that it
was because he had simply gotten tired of the rigors of duty. Only a
few knew that he was forced out of office by one of the Roman governors who preceded Pilate. When forced to leave, Annas, always the
schemer, hustled a deal to put his son Simon into office. But Simon
never really wanted to be high priest, and after a short while he left
the office, clearing the way for Caiaphas to take over. Caiaphas had
been high priest for eleven years before this Jesus mess broke out, and
he believed he had been a good one. Under his administration there
had been less corruption (though it clearly had not ceased altogether),
and, in general, most enjoyed a period of relative peace. And most
important of all, temple attendance was up, ensuring that people were
coming more and more to God. That was more than anyone could say
about the way Annas had done things for so long.

Annas, by this time, had become a sort of high priest emeritus, still
holding a certain amount of influence around the temple. But Caiaphas had firmly taken control of the temple and had developed a
good rapport with the Roman occupiers as well. As a result, he believed that as long as he knew the rules and played the game correctly,
he would remain high priest for as long as he wished, thus assuring
the safety of his people. Caiaphas had long felt that Annas, though
his father-in-law, had never forgiven him for ending up in the position that Annas had felt rightfully belonged to him for life. It helped
explain why when Jesus was arrested he was first brought to the old
man rather than to Caiaphas, to whom he should have been brought.
Caiaphas knew that a subplot had been hatched here, but he would

never admit this to Marcus. He believed that was the difference between him and his father-in-law. Caiaphas knew that Jesus had to be eliminated, and he could articulate the reasons why. Annas, on the other hand, saw this only as an opportunity of perhaps getting his old job back. Caiaphas knew that Annas was truly hoping that Caiaphas would somehow louse all of this up by causing an international incident and perhaps lose his job (and maybe even his head), thus clearing the way for Annas to return.

At first Annas had thought that he could somehow get a speedy confession out of Jesus, using his usual heavy-handed methods to deliver the whole package over to Rome, bypassing Caiaphas altogether. Delivering Jesus to the Romans complete with a confession of crimes, perhaps against the state, would have solved everyone's problems. It would have shown Rome just how dangerous Jesus really was while at the same time getting him out of the way without causing Rome any embarrassment. It would also have shown Rome just how capable Annas still was. But Annas was no match for the likes of Jesus. Caiaphas knew that the reason Annas could do nothing with Jesus was because Annas was doing this for all the wrong reasons. He knew the only way one could defeat a man like Jesus was to have the power of God on one's side. Because Jesus was no ordinary man... "That's strange," he thought, "what made me think of Jesus as extraordinary?"

Caiaphas knew that these reminiscences were getting him nowhere and that he simply had to go back in the room to tell Marcus the truth. He stepped away from the wall he'd been leaning against and opened the door. When he reentered the room, Marcus was staring at him, looking for telltale signs of weakness. It was as though Marcus was reading a map that would help him plot a strategy to defeat Caiaphas altogether. Caiaphas decided it was time to get down to the business of trying to save his people.

Marcus indeed knew that he had Caiaphas cornered. He knew that he had stunned him with his last outburst, but he also knew enough about the Jews to know that one blow was not enough to kill Caiaphas's spirit. The Jews had after all lived through many years of occupation and still survived. Marcus knew all about his tenacity, and so understood his next moves were critical.

"Sit down, commander," said the high priest. "I will tell you everything I can about whatever you ask. What do you wish to know?"

"I want to know who orchestrated this whole affair, and why. I want to know how we were dragged into this, and what was said to Pilate to get him to agree."

"My first answer may surprise you, commander, but let me say here and now that I, and I alone, was the so-called 'orchestrator' of all of this. If, at the end of this, you feel someone has done wrong, then that someone is me. If I have misunderstood what was in the best interest of Rome as well as our state, then I am the one who should be arrested. It was no one else here at the temple. I am the high priest, and I alone bear the responsibility for whatever role the Jewish people played in this affair.

"I will not bore you with a long history lesson on the suffering of our people. I doubt you would understand much of it anyway, considering that at present we are suffering under you and your empire. But unlike the way you Romans treat us, I will not dismiss the collective intelligence of your people. I believe you are capable of understanding, at least in theory, how we must feel living under occupation. Every Jew in Israel longs to be free — you know that. Every Jew wakes every day wishing that all of you would go and simply leave us alone and let us be free to love God and our land. And yet every day we awaken to find that we still must live under your tyranny with no end in sight to this nightmare. Unlike the poor, the uneducated, and the ignorant, I believe that this, like all of life, is God's will for us. Why? I do not know. Perhaps we are still suffering for the sins of our forefathers. But when God decides we will be free at last, then we will be free."

Marcus interrupted him. He knew an inquisitor should be patient, but his patience was wearing thin again, and he blurted out: "Get to the point." As soon as the words left his lips, Marcus regretted the outburst.

Caiaphas seethed with anger at the impudence of this Roman official. He wanted to scream at Marcus, "You delivery boy. You flunky of the emperor. I am the high priest. I don't care what you think of me, Caiaphas, but don't you dare speak to the high priest of the chosen people of the Almighty that way!" But he knew he had to remain clam, knew that Marcus's outburst might be part of some game the Roman was playing.

"The point, commander, is this. When people are suffering like this, they are always looking deep down inside for someone to deliver them. They are always looking for a messiah. Let us speak frankly with each other. I know that the only reason we religious authorities are left standing is because you know that we can help control the people. You who worship gods who look like animals know nothing about holiness and divinity. You leave us alone not because you respect our religious traditions but because we serve a purpose. This is no secret among those of us who have to do this dance of survival, and we at the temple have learned the steps well.

"You Romans have never given us much credit as a race of people. You believe we are little more than a sideshow on your way toward world domination. That is why I tell you here and now that neither you, nor Pilate, nor Sejanus, nor your emperor really was ever capable of understanding the true nature of the threat Jesus posed. You never understood the threat because in your arrogance you never believed that anyone could really threaten the mighty Roman Empire. That is what you believed about the armies of Parthia, which is why those armies drove you arrogant Romans all the way back to Rome. You couldn't see the threat Jesus posed because you no longer know what it means to have to struggle for your freedom. It is what will be your downfall someday.

"What did it mean for this so-called prophet to go about our streets telling the people that God had appointed him to bring sight to the blind, to bring hearing to the deaf, and to preach the good news to the poor? To a Roman, that all sounds like harmless theology, and to the Western world it made him sound like a wonderful humanitarian folk hero. But do you know what it meant to my people? It meant that for people who are oppressed, at last God was fulfilling his promise and sending us a deliverer. Do you know who he was going to deliver us from? It was from you and all who would oppress our land. And when Jesus went through the streets telling the people that those of us in authority, the rightful religious leaders, were only hired hands who would run from the wolf rather than stand and fight, and that he was going to be the new shepherd who would protect them from the wolf, do you know who the wolf was he was referring to? You — you are the wolf. You and all of the Roman occupiers. Let me tell you what it would mean for people who must suffer the indignation of occupation to suddenly find themselves under the protection of the Son of God himself: they begin to feel that with God on their side they can do anything. People who have longed to be free all of their lives, but who felt powerless to fight for that freedom, might feel as though the time was right for revolution. They might start to feel that since we temple authorities hadn't delivered them, perhaps Jesus would."

Marcus stood and took a step toward the high priest. "Are you telling me that you as a Jew and a high priest would not have welcomed a revolution to gain the freedom of your own people?"

Caiaphas knew he needed to answer this question with care. He had spoken very boldly to Marcus and knew that he had started down a path from which there was no escape. He had said too much to back away from the defiant stance he had decided to take.

"I am telling you that if Jesus had been the messiah, I would have been in the front line of any revolution to rid our land of your presence. That would have been my or any other person's responsibility as high priest. But Jesus was not the messiah, and until one comes, my first responsibility is to the Lord and the protection of his people. And as long as the Lord God allows you to stay here in this place, he must have his reasons, and I must coexist with you and keep our people from doing anything that would result in their ultimate destruction. To that end, for their protection, I will remain loyal to the agreements between our people and the Roman Empire. I will always council our people to obey the laws, pay their taxes, and remain good citizens under Roman authority."

Marcus went back over to his chair and took his seat. He was not sure he was being told the whole truth, but what he had heard so far made a certain amount of sense to him, at least from the point of view of one who had to walk a tightrope between Israel and Rome, as he knew Caiaphas had to.

"Was there any reason why you believed Jesus had to be put to death at this moment in time?" asked Marcus.

"Jesus needed to die now because, as you know, this is the time of our Sabbath. Jesus' name was beginning to spread throughout the entire Middle East, and pilgrims from all over the region were coming here to celebrate. This time of year our people are most susceptible to believing in miracles, and we were afraid that Jesus might have used this opportunity to stir up the masses toward revolt. I am sure you were aware of Jesus' arrival in Jerusalem. The people were hailing him as a king. The man rode in on a donkey, and still they were throwing palm branches in his path and hailing him as a king. Your people probably thought it was quaint, but to people longing to be free, Jesus was beginning to seem like a conqueror, a hero to the masses. Imagine that scene being played out by crowds ten times that number when our streets became filled with pilgrims from all over the country."

Once again Marcus interrupted him: "But Jesus had never, as far as I know, espoused any revolutionary ideologies. Why did you expect he might do so now?"

"That is where you are wrong, commander. Much of what this man preached was indeed very revolutionary, as far as conservative Judaism is concerned. But even more important, if he had stirred up the crowds enough, the situation may have quickly gotten out of control, and before you know it, riots could have broken out in the streets. He was simply too dangerous and had to be stopped before the Sabbath got fully under way.

"You must understand something. Look around you, what do you see? Do you see Rome? Yes, you do, because you are Rome. Everything you do is Roman in some way. But what is it that the average Jew sees on the street? I don't mean the educated. I don't mean people in the media. I mean the average Jew living here in the city or out in the countryside. They know you are here; that is for sure. But for the most part, they see only a few patrols of soldiers. They see some forts and a few police stations. They do not see, nor do they know, Rome like most of us in the Sanhedrin do. Why not revolt? they might ask themselves. Particularly if they are under the protection of the man who claims to be the Son of God. After all, they might reason, what is there for us to defeat? A few hundred soldiers, maybe even a thousand. They may look around and say, 'There are more of us than there are of them. We are all here in this place; it is the Sabbath; and the messiah is with us. And we are burning with the desire to be free, as all men should be. Why not revolt and do it now?' Having said that, I ask you this, commander. If our people were to revolt and attack the garrisons you have set up, what would have been the response of your emperor?"

Marcus knew that within a matter of minutes, whole divisions would have been dispatched to Judea, and the revolt would have been crushed into the dirt. He knew contingency plans existed to deal with just such an event, and the plan could be put into effect in a matter of moments.

"Yes, commander, I know about your plans. I know about R4–57 and the other so-called riot contingency operations that have been worked out by your governor and your police and military forces. I know that within a matter of hours, whole divisions of soldiers would have swept down on our people and annihilated them in our very own streets. And I know that if you felt so provoked, you would destroy our temple, which to us would be like destroying our very souls. We would cease to exist as a people, and I would go down in history as the high priest who, by doing nothing to prevent this, brought about the destruction of Israel."

For the first time Marcus allowed himself a slight smile. How did the high priest know about the contingency plan to deal with revolts in the provinces? How did he know its name? He knew it was pointless to ask because in some ways everybody already knew the answer.

"If you want everyone in this city to know anything, just classify it a state secret," he said to the high priest.

"Some things never change, commander, especially around here."

"So if I understand you correctly, you are saying that Jesus, intentionally or otherwise, could have sparked riots in the streets by pretending to be your messiah, and the people, feeling they were under the protection of your God, could have felt the time was right for revolution. And, furthermore, you believe that our response would have been such that it would have brought only destruction to your people."

"That is correct, commander."

"Why didn't you come to us with all of this earlier? Why didn't you share your concerns about Jesus with the empire, instead of going about this in a way that was potentially dangerous to us all?"

"Because you had already made up your minds about Jesus and decided that he was no real danger to anyone. We had warned everyone again and again about the possible dangers, although I admit never formally. But you had decided he was nothing more than a harmless preacher, a local folk hero. In fact you even enjoyed how he seemed to get the better of us on occasion. What could we have said to convince you of the danger he posed? Look how hard we had to work to convince the governor of his guilt, and even after all we had said, he still almost pardoned him."

"What about the miracles that he supposedly had performed? What did you make of all of that? After all, there were some pretty impressive reports. . . ."

Marcus suddenly realized the reason he had asked the high priest this question about miracles, and it disturbed him greatly. It was not that he wanted information to add to the report; rather, he was hoping that the high priest of the religion that Jesus was a part of could explain what had happened to his friend Demetrius. He kept hearing Demetrius say over and over again, "Marcus, the man had no eyes." He wanted the high priest to say something like, "Oh, these phony messiahs always do sleight-of-hand tricks that fool the unsuspecting";

or, "These people are masters of illusion; don't let it bother you. Once they are dead, everything returns to normal." He got part of the answer he wanted. Caiaphas stated: "Commander, we have lived through dozens of false messiahs, and I assure you that each and every one of them has appeared on the scene with all sorts of wondrous stories surrounding him. If you believe the stories you heard about Jesus are fantastic now, wait until the stories are told to your grandchildren. By then they will have had him raising people from the dead."

Marcus was suddenly getting very anxious and wanted to wrap us the interrogation immediately. He heard himself repeat the words in his mind, "Wait until the stories are told to your grandchildren." He didn't want any of this to reach his grandchildren. He wanted it to be wrapped up right away, and he also wanted to believe, as some suggested, that this would all be forgotten in a matter of months. He wanted to believe as he did when all of this broke that it would be news for a little while, but then the foreign press would leave, the story would be over, and life would return to normal. Why would any of his grandchildren ever hear about this? But he couldn't help imagining his grandchildren asking him about his role in all of this: "What did you do during the crucifixion, grandfather?" Would they understand what doing one's duty for one's country entailed? Would they understand that patriotism sometimes meant putting aside one's personal considerations for the good of the state? If the tales about Jesus were to survive more than a generation, who would look better over time, the patriot or the preacher?

Marcus suddenly rose from his chair and moved toward the door. He turned to speak to Caiaphas: "I will alter my report to include all that you have told me. I am a thorough man and will leave nothing out."

Caiaphas wanted to press him on just what he would say to his superiors, but knew that it would be pointless.

Marcus turned once again toward the high priest. "So you believe with all of your convictions that Jesus was only a charlatan, who could have potentially been a danger because of his influence among the people? You are convinced that he could have either intentionally or unintentionally caused the people to revolt against Rome, thus causing us to retaliate and destroy your temple? As a member of this man's religion, you can absolutely assure us of that? And we have your word that you acted out of a sense of loyalty to Rome as well as your own people? And you fully realize what loyalty means to us as Romans? ... "

The reaction of Caiaphas to this line of questioning caught Marcus by surprise. Caiaphas exploded with anger: "Let me tell you something about loyalty and about duty, commander. I give you this advice as a spiritual leader, free of charge. You are here because of your so-called duty to the empire and to help Rome find answers that will absolve everyone from everything concerning this affair. You come here to throw your weight around because you believe Rome must always show those whom it occupies what great qualities of strength and duty you possess. And you look down on us Jews because you don't believe we possess such royal qualities. Well, let me tell you something about real duty and about what I really think.

"First, yes, I really believe in my heart of hearts that Jesus was not the messiah. And so I did all of this not to embarrass Rome in any way or to gain any political advantage. I did this to save my people from the potential destruction that I believe would have come from letting this man live and preach his kind of theology to the masses of Jews longing to be free. But to bring about this outcome, I did things that were against many of our own laws. I broke no Roman law, but there are certain laws handed down to us by God concerning how, for instance, a trial should be conducted that I disregarded because I believed this man to be such a danger. Now, I am sure that you, being a Roman, believe that your presence here and what that represents would be my biggest concern. And I must admit to you that, being human, I am concerned about staying alive as well as seeing that we as a people continue to exist. But let's examine the consequences we all might have to endure if the answers you find are not quite satisfactory. For Rome it might mean a certain amount of political embarrassment. For you it might mean an end to a brilliant military career. For my people it might even mean more death and destruction. But none of what anyone faces compares to what would be in store for me.

"Now let me tell you what I risk if I am wrong. I risk being judged by Almighty God. I risk being condemned to the fires of Sheol for all of eternity, as well as having the name of Caiaphas go down in history as one of the greatest villains to have ever lived. I risk having all the good we have done as Pharisees and scribes and council members be tainted for all time because of the course of action I took these last few days. And you must understand, commander, I believe all of this, not as mere religion but as fact.

"But I risk something even greater. If I am wrong about all of this, I risk being judged not by God alone but also by Jesus, and that judgment would be the worst I could imagine. I risk being forgiven. Do you have any idea what it would mean to me to stand before Jesus and have to suffer the indignity of being forgiven by him? You might believe that if I have nightmares, they are about you and Sejanus and your emperor. No, commander, they are about having Abraham and Moses and Isaiah rightfully shout condemnations against me for playing a role in our messiah's death and about having Jesus stand in my defense and forgive me for what I did to him. Imagine, he would pardon and forgive me just like he forgave the whores in the street, the crippled, and the weak in the slums of Galilee. Me, the high priest of the people of Israel, forgiven like a common sinner. He would know that his greatest punishment for me would be not to allow me to burn in Sheol for being wrong about him.

"So you can be sure, commander, that I truly did what I believed was right. He was not the messiah, and I staked more than the wrath of Rome on it. I believe God was on the council's and my side, and he helped all of this to come to pass for the good of the chosen people of Israel. Jesus was a false prophet, and we are all better off without him."

"What about Judas?" Marcus asked. "What role did he play in all of this? Our people believe he might have been the one who betrayed Jesus to your people, but we also figured out that he was a member of the Sicarii. That doesn't add up to us because the Sicarii don't exactly love you establishment religious leaders. I can understand your wanting him dead, but why would they, and how did the two of you come together?"

"I did not know anything about Judas being a member of the Sicarii, and I doubt very much that he was. They would not have very much use for us, and we certainly have no use for them. How did you come to this conclusion about Judas?"

"I can assure you that the information we have concerning his background is unquestionable." (Marcus thought, "Don't worry, it's classified, which means you will know everything that we have in our files in a week or two anyway.")

"Well," Caiaphas continued, "I knew nothing about his political affiliations. He came to us and said that he was disenchanted with the whole affair. He said he understood the danger Jesus was presenting for all of us, and he wanted to help put an end to what he believed was a charade. He also wanted immunity from prosecution if he co-operated with us in getting Jesus arrested. He said that he wanted us to arrest Jesus and perhaps discredit him in some way but that he did not want any harm to come to him. I told him that I was not sure I could guarantee Jesus' safety once the process began. I am sure that he knew exactly what would happen to Jesus once he was arrested. He then demanded money from us, which made us somewhat suspicious of his motives. We offered him thirty pieces of silver, which he took without any argument. And that was that; the rest is history. We were not all that concerned about him because we were closing in on Jesus anyway. It was only a matter of time. However, as I mentioned, the timing was important because the Sabbath was about to begin. We wanted to avoid a lot of needless bloodshed, and so Judas was helpful in getting us to Jesus without a lot of people around him."

Marcus believed Caiaphas's story about Judas because it fit into his theory that Judas was playing both ends against the middle. He decided that he had enough information for now and wanted to end the interview.

"Thank you for your time," said Marcus. "Please do not leave town until you hear from us." Marcus stood up abruptly.

"Where am I going to go?" asked the high priest. "My place is here in the temple. If you want me, you know where to find me."

Marcus headed for the door and left the temple. Once outside, he felt joyful to be away from that place. He was glad to be out among the land and the trees and hoped he would never have to return to the temple again. He then turned west and headed toward his next stop, the palace of the governor of Judea, the home of Pontius Pilate.

Caiaphas returned to his chapel and began to thank God for once again bringing him safely through the sea of dangers known as the empire. He began to quote the psalmist aloud:

> Yahweh, I know you are near.
> You are always at my side.
> You guard me from the foe.
> And you lead me in ways, everlasting.

He suddenly stopped and said to himself, "The Sicarii? Judas a member of the Sicarii?" He thought that it could be possible. He believed that they were a bunch of fanatics who in their heart of hearts could conceive a plot to pit one group of Jews against another. "He probably thought he was using us all for the good of the kingdom," he chuckled to himself. "I'm sure if that was the case, he must be one disappointed dead man to see that he is not in the forefront of some great cavalry charge of angels sweeping through Israel killing Romans on one side of the road and Pharisees on the other. What life can there ever be for those who work against the people of God by working against the temple? How does it feel, oh wise one, to open your eyes not in the heavens with Isaiah but in the dung heap of Sheol with all the false prophets?"

He laughed at the thought and then returned to his prayers, stopping one last time to consider that the Romans probably got their information all wrong about Judas anyway. "Most likely," he thought, "they got it from some spy working for the Roman Intelligence Service who sold them bad information and then took them for all they're worth. 'Roman Intelligence,'" he said with contempt in his voice, "now there's a contradiction in terms."

He believed that this night when he went to bed there would indeed be no more nightmares. Jeremiah and Micah and Moses would all come to him and sing his praises for defending the truth and dispatching the traitors of Judaism. And, for a moment at least, he felt at peace.

– CHAPTER TEN –

"LADIES AND GENTLEMEN, we have a report from our correspondent, Blaine Jennings, on the Parthian border. He is speaking with Simon, who traveled with Jesus, and fled over the border once Jesus was arrested and convicted."

"Good evening, ladies and gentlemen. This is Blaine Jennings. About an hour ago, my camera man and I met with Simon, a member of the inner circle of twelve who worked and traveled with Jesus. He agreed to give us an interview on the condition that we would not do the interview live, nor disclose our exact location. We were also given instructions that the tape could not be aired for at least an hour after the interview had taken place. Once we agreed to those conditions, we were taken to a spot just inside the Parthian border where we met with Simon the Zealot, who was surrounded by a small group of Parthian sympathizers.

"People often wondered just why such a member of the Zealot party would join the likes of Jesus; after all, their ideologies, it would seem, differed as much as night and day. The Zealot party, for those of you not familiar with Middle Eastern politics, has always been seen as one of the most fanatical of the nationalistic religious and political parties in the whole area. They often consider themselves agents of God whose role is to rid the region of 'foreign oppressors' by any and all means necessary. When speaking to any member of the Zealot party, you will find that he will often quote their party slogan: 'No rule but the law — no king but God.'

"Even during his stay with Jesus, Simon continued to be a rather outspoken member of the inner circle, so much so that he was often referred to by both his name and his party affiliation, almost as though it were a first and last name. Thus he was always called Simon the Zealot. When Jesus was taken into custody, it seemed most of the men associated with him disappeared, except for Judas, who was seen in town and who later was found hanging from a tree, victim of an apparent suicide, and Simon, who was seen heading toward the Parthian border. When a representative of Simon contacted us to do this interview, he made it clear to us that it would be the only interview he would give and that after today he planned to disappear deep into the Parthian hills and become a freedom fighter of some kind. Here now is the interview in its entirety:

[BJ]: 'Simon, can you tell us just what took place in Jerusalem?'

[SIMON]: 'Jesus was murdered. What else is there to know? The oppressive Roman government in league with the puppet government of Herod and the so-called temple executed a man of God, the likes of which the world will never know again. Jesus was murdered by them because of his refusal to live according to their rules, the rules of the oppressor.'

[BJ]: 'What do you mean by his refusal to live by the rules of the oppressor?'

[SIMON]: 'He refused to believe that only the powerful and rich are important and that the weak are only here to serve them. Instead he lived believing in the individual worth of each human person. He also believed that if you treat the oppressor with love, that love would eventually win him over and change him toward your way of thinking. In that sense I guess you could call him an unfortunate idealist.'

[BJ]: 'An idealist?'

[SIMON]: 'Yes, Jesus was an idealist. Now I don't say that in the same way you might call a person ignorant or naive. But the Master believed that people could all get along together if only you showed them that love was stronger than hate. He believed that people, if given the chance, would rather live together in peace than kill one another. I will be the first to admit that for a while I believed that he was on to a "new age" way of thinking. That perhaps people could live together and eliminate things like oppression with the kind of philosophy Jesus was preaching. But Jesus was wrong. The kind of philosophy he was preaching always leads to one end, the death of the person preaching it. I loved him; he was a man of wonderful character; but in some ways, I'm glad this happened.'

[BJ]: 'Are you saying that you are glad Jesus is dead?'

[SIMON]: 'Oh God, no. Jesus meant more to me than anyone could ever know. My heart breaks and is filled with sorrow over his death. I am sorry for Jesus and his family; I am sorry for the men and women who gave up their lives and their livelihoods for a dream, only to now find it shattered. But what Rome and those handkerchief heads at the Sanhedrin may have done is to provide once and for all true revolutionaries with the lesson of the century. And that lesson is that Jesus' way of doing things will never work in this world. Because if the Son of God could not pull this off, who the hell ever will? And maybe that's what God had intended us to see all along.'

[BJ]: 'You called Jesus the Son of God. Do you really believe that he was your messiah?'

[SIMON]: 'Without a doubt. I was with him the whole time, and I saw him do things that no mere mortal could ever have accomplished. I have no doubt in my mind whatsoever that he was the Son of God, the messiah that Isaiah foretold. But I also believe that if he came here to try and prove that human beings are somehow capable of turning the other cheek when slapped, then he was either wrong or in conflict with the goals of his Father, the Lord God Jehovah, or his real intent was something other than what seemed obvious.'

[BJ]: 'Why do you say he may have been in conflict with God?'

[SIMON]: 'Because the God of Israel that we grew up knowing was nothing like what his Son tried to preach. And perhaps that's why God could not help him in the end. I mean, look at the difference between the Son and the Father, at least the Father we know through the Torah, when it comes to dealing with humankind. There was never anything in our religion that carried forgiveness to the degree that Jesus tried to teach us. When David came up against the Philistine giant Goliath, he certainly never turned the other cheek. Instead, he picked up a stone and bashed the [bleep] out of the bastard. When God told Moses to tell our former slave masters to let us go from Egypt, he didn't use any nonviolent philosophical rhetoric. First he killed their crops. When that didn't work, he killed their sons. When all else failed, he killed them. And when the Lord God sent our people into the promised land as he had said he would, it didn't matter that it was occupied by the Canaanites. He told them to get out. When they didn't move, Joshua moved in and tore them to shreds, all with the blessings and indeed the very guidance of God. The God we grew up with taught us that what goes around comes around, an eye for an eye, a tooth for a tooth. And when commissioned to do his will, you do whatever you have to, including spill your enemies' blood, to see that God's will is obeyed.'

[BJ]: 'So are you saying that Jesus' ministry was a failure, or that perhaps he never knew what being a messiah was all about?'

[SIMON]: 'I believe Jesus was successful in demonstrating once and for all that there is no peace without freedom, and there is no freedom without revolution. And nonviolent revolutions for the most part do not work. Considering that I believe Jesus was the greatest prophet who will ever walk this earth and the greatest preacher of nonviolent revolution who will ever live, and considering he walked with the power of God at his hand, if he could not make revolution happen without bloodshed, I then believe it is safe to say that it cannot be done. Now what that says about his success or failure as a messiah I leave up to others to decide. But I for one believe in the words of the old song that goes, "God can do anything but fail." Therefore, in my opinion, he must have been trying to teach us something about revolutions.'

[BJ]: 'You keep referring to him as a revolutionary, and yet I never heard that title used by him or anyone else associated with him. Why do you say he was a revolutionary?'

[SIMON]: 'Because he believed that human beings should repent. The word "repent" means to turn around. So does the word "revolution." But the difference between Jesus and other revolutionaries was that he wanted people to turn around because they came to see the goodness in seeking a new direction in their lives. Jesus after all was a great student of the prophet Isaiah, who often tried to teach a repentance based on individuals seeing what was in it for them. And the amazing part is Jesus never wavered from his point of view regarding repentance or even violence, no matter what may have happened to discourage him. When the police came to arrest him, we wanted to take it to them right on the spot. One man actually got into a sword fight with one of the guards and slashed him across the face. Jesus jumped in and admonished our man for resorting to violence. He told him that if we lived by the sword, we would die by the sword. Well, Jesus lived by the dove, and he still died by the sword. The rest of us barely got away with our lives, but they weren't interested in us. They only wanted Jesus.'

[BJ]: 'Can you shed some light on what happened in the hours leading up to his arrest?'

[SIMON]: 'I'll tell you very little about what took place in private between Jesus and the twelve of us. I would never want anything I say here on tape to be used against any of the other men who worked with Jesus. I will tell you this, however: we were betrayed by someone right in our own group.'

[BJ]: 'Who was it, Judas?'

[SIMON]: 'I won't say that either, but it will come out. By the time this was all going down, most of us already knew that the grand and noble experiment had failed. When I found out who the traitor was, I was ready to take him outside and dust him. But once again Jesus stepped in and made us live by the principles of nonviolence. "Turn the other cheek" was more than just an expression for him. I knew he would be dead within a matter of hours after that incident.'

[BJ]: 'Simon, I'm sure some of our viewers are having trouble reconciling the fact that you refer to Jesus as the Son of God and yet at the same time seem to suggest that Jesus didn't really appear to know what his Father stood for or wanted. If he was as close to God as you say, why do you suppose he preached a message that you say was contradictory to the Torah?'

[SIMON]: 'I don't know. I'm not a philosopher, nor do I claim to have the closeness that Jesus himself had with God. All I know is that the message that Jesus espoused as a messiah got him killed and will probably get the rest of us killed as well, and meanwhile the empire, and those who conspired with it against their own people, will live on. The emperor and the traitors of the people show no signs of going away through some process of brotherhood. Until our people learn once again to pick up arms and expel the oppressors from the land God has given us, we will pray and die forever as slaves.'

[BJ]: 'So then are you saying that Jesus was indeed wrong. If that is the case, doesn't that discredit him somewhat from being the messiah that you and your people have waited for so long?'

[SIMON]: 'No, Jesus was indeed the messiah. Of this I am positive. And you seem to keep ignoring the fact that I have also stated that he could have been trying to show us what not to do in order to win our freedom. Sometimes human beings learn more from seeing disaster than from seeing success. I believe that Jesus was trying to show us something about how things change and why some things don't. Like I said, I really don't know all of the motives as to why Jesus did what he did, or why he chose to teach us in the manner in which he did. I do know that I have truly come to believe that the Lord works in mysterious ways. But no one should get from anything that I said that I didn't believe he was the messiah.'

[BJ]: 'Simon, let's get back to the notion that Jesus was a nonviolent revolutionary. Give us, if you will, an example of Jesus' revolutionary nonviolent philosophy.'

[SIMON]: 'I'll give you an example of one of his most revolutionary manifestos, the one that was written up by all of you Western journalists who rushed to print what you called the "Our Father." It was filled with revolution, but most of you all never even knew it. Neither did Rome grasp its significance until much later. But you can bet your life that the Sanhedrin knew what he was saying.'

[BJ]: 'I know the prayer you are referring to. How was that revolutionary?'

[SIMON]: 'First, he stood on a hill surrounded by a mix of different people: Greeks, Romans, and all kinds of factions of our own people, many of whom couldn't stand each other's guts, and then he said that we must *all* begin our prayers by saying "Our Father." Now I for one didn't know or care if he really was talking about all those other people, but for Jews, many of whom have been ruled by factions for years, causing us to be divided and then conquered, that was his way of saying: you had better remember that you are all Jews together; and unless you get your act together and remember that we all have the same God, you will end up at each other's throats while the empire continues to make you all slaves.

'He told them to pray "Hallowed be Thy Name" because he knew that God's name doesn't mean anything to members of the Sanhedrin and to the scribes anymore. They use the name of God to line their own pockets and to build up their own positions. There was a time when to Jews the name of God was so sacred that they believed that if you even touched the tabernacle where the Torah was held, you would be struck down dead. But today, you have all kinds of people claiming to be ministers of God while all they really do is use the name of God to get fat and grow rich.

'But the most revolutionary concept introduced in this so-called prayer was the notion of the kingdom. He told the people to pray that God's kingdom come and his will be done, on earth as it is in heaven. How do you think the people controlling the kingdom of Herod took to that idea? How do you think those bloodsuckers who couldn't get a job shoveling dirt in God's kingdom but who wield great power in Herod's or Caesar's kingdoms felt about Jesus telling the people to pray for the dawning of a new kingdom to come?

'What we believe was that Jesus was telling the people to pray for an overthrow of these petty, ruthless dictatorships and to pray for the coming of a kingdom ruled by God. He was telling the people to go back to the idea that to a Jew, God should be the ultimate king. Not Herod, not Caesar, but God. That is a concept that every member of the Zealot party can understand. No rule but the law — no king but God. That's why the bastards kept trying to make it seem that he was saying that he was a king. He never said that. He was saying to remember that God is the true king. Members of the high priest council have said to Pilate that they have no king but Caesar. People like that are the real blasphemers, but they have power, and you can't pray people like that out of office. You have to remove them by force because they no longer have either the will or the soul to ever change. They are totally corrupted. When you have people like that running the temple, there must be a change, and now.'

[BJ]: 'But if what you are saying is true, then doesn't that mean that Rome had a legitimate case against Jesus? Didn't they have the right to arrest him and convict him of trying to overthrow the government?'

[SIMON]: 'No, because the Romans were not the ones who instigated this whole affair. As I said, they had no idea what Jesus was saying in that prayer. Besides, Jesus tried to get the enemies of the people to repent by peaceful means. If he had called the people to arms, I believe we would have achieved the goals laid down by his manifesto. Instead, he is now dead, and God's people are still suffering under the yoke of imperialist oppression.

'One more thing I must add to what I said and that is this: everyone who worked for Jesus did not see his message as I am now interpreting it to you. I must make that clear. Only one or two of us believed he was as much a revolutionary as I say he is now. The opinion I am expressing is mine and mine alone. I will not have this tape used as a way of prosecuting my friends.'

[BJ]: 'Simon, what do you think the mood is of most of the other men who worked closely with Jesus? Do you believe they are frightened, disappointed, angry?'

[SIMON]: 'I think they are a little bit of all of the above, but mostly, I think they are relieved.'

[BJ]: 'Relieved? that's seems like a strange thing to say. Why do you think they would feel relieved?'

[SIMON]: 'Because I think most of the men feel like they gave it their best shot, and now it's over. I think once things cool down, most of the men will try to go back to doing what they were doing before all of this got started. I mean, hell, for a while it looked as though we were going to change the world. We were a part of the most incredible wave of energy to hit these parts since Elijah walked the earth. We traveled the country and spoke to thousands of people. There were times the crowds were so large you couldn't see where they began or where they ended.

For a while, you could not help but feel that you were a part of history in the making.

'But there were also times when it was extremely nerve-racking as well. Jesus was terrible about security measures. He would never let any of us stop people from coming right up to him. We saw people who looked like lunatics rushing through a crowd toward him. We didn't know if these people were rushing up to assassinate him or what. But he would never let any of us stop any person who came toward him for help. There was one time when we heard of a clear and definite plot on the part of Herod to have Jesus killed. It took us all night to convince Jesus to leave the area and head elsewhere. We got out of there just in time.'

[BJ]: 'You know for a fact that King Herod tried to have Jesus killed?'

[SIMON]: 'Oh yeah, everyone knew that Herod tried to have Jesus assassinated and was pretty close to getting him too. If Herod's brother hadn't gotten word to us in time, Jesus would have been dead months ago. Anyway, now it's over. Jesus is dead; the bad guys won; and it's over. At least we tried to do something. At least we were a part of something, even though it failed. That's better than most of these people sitting on their asses complaining about the empire and the priesthood ever bothered to do. But that's why I say I bet a lot of the twelve feel tremendous sorrow, but also a sense of relief.'

[BJ]: 'Yet still you are saying that you basically view Jesus' ministry as a failure, at least in the way he saw his mission.'

[SIMON]: 'Perhaps on the surface. Again I am quick to say that maybe this was the plan worked out between Jesus and the Father all along. I am not claiming — nor have I ever claimed — to be an insider into the divine as was Jesus. I was but a mere foot soldier in the movement, and proud to have been there. But it certainly is clear to me that nonviolent revolutions are impractical, impossible, and doomed to failure. I still say if Jesus could not make that happen, then no one ever will. This I know. What the rest of it all means I leave to wiser minds than mine.'

[BJ]: 'I once heard Jesus say to a critic of his nonviolent philosophy that if everyone continued to live by the rule 'an eye for an eye and a tooth for a tooth,' all we would end up with is a world full of toothless old blind people. I take it you disagreed with him.'

[SIMON]: 'Well, I remember the incident quite well. What was not reported was that the man answered back, "At least they would be toothless, blind, and free." We never criticized Jesus in public, but several of us had real questions about this idea of turning the other cheek. Still, we believed in Jesus, and he has proven to be right about an awful lot of stuff.

'I remember one particular time when we entered Jericho and came across one of those blood-sucking traders to our people hiding in a tree so he could get a glimpse of Jesus walking by. Not only was he a tax collector for the oppressor, he was the chief tax collector in the area. He had stolen more of the people's money than anyone in Jericho. Do you know when the master saw him hiding up there, he called him out of that tree and invited him to break bread with him in the tax collector's own house? You know for us here in the Middle East, breaking bread with an enemy means you must be willing to forgive all that has gone on between you, and you emerge as friends. When you consider what those bastards do to our people, bleeding them dry for the good of the empire, to even look with kindness on one is to my way of thinking a huge act of charity in and of itself. To eat with one is really turning the other cheek. Even Matthew didn't think that was such a smart idea, and he was in that business once himself.

'When the people of Jericho saw that, many of them were incensed Jesus would do such a thing. We lost a lot of supporters that day. But I tell you this, when that man came out of that house after sharing bread with Jesus, he sure was changed. I never saw anything like it, and I've witnessed some incredible things while traveling with the master. Jesus didn't threaten him or yell at him or anything like that. He simply came into the house of a man who no self-respecting Jew would have ever been caught dead with let alone eat with, and with nothing but love in his heart, shared a meal with him. That simple act of love and forgiveness did to that man what none of the insults or threats of the townspeople could ever accomplish. I later heard that he gave away most of his money to the poor.

'I do, however, believe that because of the way events have unfolded, either he was wrong, which I find hard to believe, or he wanted to teach us one final lesson by what happened to him.'

[BJ]: 'Will you ever believe in nonviolence as a way of achieving change again?'

[SIMON]: 'No, I don't think so. That's not the kind of thinking I came into this movement with, and it's not the kind I will leave with either. If Jesus hadn't been brutally murdered by the repressive government in Jerusalem, perhaps I might have tried to believe in his way of thinking for the rest of my life. But surely no one — including Jesus — can expect us to believe in this type philosophy after all that has happened. I mean look what happened to his own cousin John. Even John ended up a victim of violence. And I can tell you, John was not nearly as nonviolent in his thinking as was Jesus. John's thinking was much closer to my own than to Jesus'. That's why I'm here. I don't know what Rome has in store for the rest of us, or if Romans will now be satisfied having killed Jesus. I mean, after all, there isn't much any of us can do now that the Master is gone. But I tell you what. If any of those Roman bastards come into Parthia looking for me, they better come ready for the fight of their life. Because there is no way I'm going to end up hanging from a tree. They're going to have to come after me with more than a warrant.'

[BJ]: 'Is there any way you would go back to Jerusalem?'

[SIMON]: 'I think Jesus would have to call me back personally, and somehow I think the likelihood of that is somewhat remote. Jesus himself would have to come up to me and say, "Simon, I want you to get your behind back to Israel and go out and preach to the people that what I said about universal brotherhood was stronger than those nails they put in my body." If Jesus calls me, I'll go. If Peter or John or James or anybody else calls me, I'll tell them, "Thanks but no thanks. Call me if you're going to pick up arms against the people who killed Jesus and who killed the hopes of our people." If they call me to come back and fight, I will be there in a heartbeat. Other than that, I am through with the whole business.'

[BJ]: 'Simon, what are your personal plans now that Jesus is dead?'

[SIMON]: 'I plan to work for change. I plan to work with all of those who wish to see a free Israel, no matter who they are or what their method of overthrowing the government is.'

[BJ]: 'Does that mean you will now endorse even terrorism?'

[SIMON]: 'I mean that we must be free by whatever means necessary.'

[BJ]: 'But wouldn't that dishonor the memory of Jesus, who seemed so intent on preaching a nonviolent doctrine to your people?'

[SIMON]: 'Perhaps, and I know that I have a responsibility to that memory, having been privileged to have been a member of the inner circle of Jesus. But I also know deep in my heart that the people of God must be free. We can no longer suffer under the yoke of the brutal regimes of Pilate and Herod. And unless the people rise up and overthrow these dictators, our people will suffer for countless more years to come. And we won't even be able to put our hope in the coming of the messiah, because the messiah already came, and they killed him. And now you must excuse me. I'm moving deeper into the interior, and I don't wish to delay my journey any longer. I wish you peace in the name of the man whose life gave new meaning to my own.'

"Well, there you have it. This interview was conducted less than an hour ago, and during it Simon seemed to suggest at times that he believed that Jesus' message was impracticable, while at the same time softening the impact of that statement by saying that perhaps Jesus was trying to teach by the lesson of his failure. He said that he believed Jesus was the messiah, and yet even the messiah could not seem to make nonviolence work as a method for bringing about social change. He also made it clear that he would work to bring about change by whatever means necessary. That certainly opened the possibility that he intends to become a part of one of the many terrorist organizations at loose in the Middle East. He also made it clear that if the authorities came into Parthia looking for him, they had better come with 'more than a warrant.' In all, Simon seemed to be at times angry, disappointed, and even confused. He spoke with great passion about Jesus the man but appeared not to be thrilled with the mission. But one thing is sure. Jesus' death at the hands of the Roman authorities, along with the complicity of the temple, clearly left him angry and bitter.

"We will have more on this story, including complete analyses by our Middle Eastern experts, on the six-thirty news. For now this is Blaine Jennings reporting live from somewhere near the Parthian border."

– CHAPTER ELEVEN –

M ARCUS'S HANDS were tight on the reins as he rode toward the palace of the governor. When he had stopped earlier to make an appointment, a secretary had told him that the governor would see him at his earliest convenience. "At my earliest convenience?" thought Marcus as he neared the palace. "Since when does the governor see a commander in the Roman army at the commander's convenience?" The hand of Sejanus was surely in this, and Marcus was not sure just how resentful Pilate would be over having to explain his actions to a mere soldier.

A palace guard met him at the gate, took his horse, and pointed him toward the inner chamber of the palace. Marcus had never formally met the governor and hoped that Pilate had not heard rumors about his contempt for him as a leader. He decided not to worry about it because he was there at the order of the emperor and must therefore do his job as best he could. All the same he had a mental picture of Pilate, Sejanus, and the emperor sitting around a year from now, drinking and laughing, while he did sentry duty in the Parthian desert. "All the result of just doing my job," he thought.

Pilate's assistant met him in the outer office of the governor. He was a thin man with a lean face and a sad look like a horse that has been ridden all day. When he looked up at Marcus, his eyes turned from sadness to animosity, like black coals set on fire. Political assistants were known for their fierce loyalty to their bosses. He obviously felt that Marcus's presence was a threat to Pilate, and it infuriated him to know there was nothing he could do to protect his boss from what might happen here.

"Please sit down, Mr. Marcus," he said. "I'm sure his excellency will be with you shortly."

Marcus took a seat and tried to conceal his emotions. There was contempt in the man's voice, and Marcus was not used to being spoken to in that manner. But he knew it would be a waste of time to say anything to this public servant because it would only make him more arrogant. He did make a mental note, however, of this man's behavior. "For future reference," he thought.

Considering how he was being treated thus far, Marcus began to worry and wondered if Pilate would treat him with disdain. Would he dress him down in front of the staff? Would he refuse to answer all questions? Only time would tell. Just then the assistant told Marcus to follow him into the governor's office. The office was a vast expanse of marble flooring with a single table and two chairs. Marcus frowned. The governor was nowhere in sight.

"Please wait, Mr. Marcus, the governor informed me that he will come soon." Marcus felt that if this man called him Mr. Marcus one more time, all bets would be off, and he would deck the guy right where he stood. He was about to sit down when the governor walked in. "This is it," he thought, "here goes nothing — and everything." Marcus saluted. "Hail Caesar, and greetings to your excellency," he said, a bit more loudly then he had intended to.

"Hail Caesar, and greetings to you, my friend," Pilate replied.

Marcus was caught off guard. Pilate seemed genuinely friendly toward him and up close seemed much brighter, and more congenial, than when he had seen him at official functions in the past. Pilate was a man of contrasting characteristics. On the one hand, he looked like an aristocratic foreign minister, tall, lean, and even a bit haughty. On the other hand, he also appeared as though he could take on any five common thugs in a street fight by himself and emerge victorious.

Pilate extended his hand. Marcus shook it and was again surprised by the warmth and confidence he felt.

"Marcus," said Pilate, "let's go upstairs to my personal quarters; there we can have a drink and talk undisturbed. I left orders for us not to be disturbed."

Marcus followed Pilate up the stairs to the governor's personal residence. He had never been here before and felt ill at ease. "Only the most important of dignitaries ever gets into this part of the palace," he thought.

As they reached the top of the stairs, they went through a small doorway guarded by two centurions and then through another door with two more guards posted outside. They all snapped at attention when Pilate walked by, but the governor never looked up or acknowledged them. Finally they entered a large sitting room decorated with all sorts of Roman works of art. Beautiful Persian carpets made the floor come alive with rainbow colors while magnificent candelabra glowed from each corner of the room. It was another world in here. It was like the home of a rich Roman politician, only this was not Rome; it was Judea. Marcus's opinion about Pilate began to change. The occupant of such a room had to possess some culture and refinement.

After bidding Marcus to take a seat, Pilate offered him a glass of wine, which he himself poured. He declined to pour one for himself. Then Pilate joined him on the low, long couch in the center of the room. This too surprised Marcus, for it seemed too informal for the occasion.

"So, commander, you have been sent by the dogs of war to investigate just what took place here over the last few days. The fact that someone of your rank and personality was sent here tells me one thing right away: you were given this assignment by someone rather high up the chain of command in Rome, and I bet you I can tell who it was. I smell the hand of my old friend and mentor, General Sejanus. Did he suddenly appear over your bed while you lay sleeping and in his best intimidating, haunting voice give you orders to investigate everything and everyone involved and then 'report back only to me'?"

When Pilate quoted Sejanus, he mocked, in an exaggerated way, Sejanus's deep and sardonic voice. This too amused Marcus, for no one had ever dared, to his knowledge, to poke fun at Sejanus. But for some reason, it also made him wonder, perhaps for the first time fully, just why he was put on this assignment. Was Demetrius right? Was he asked to do all of this so that he could be set up as a fall guy in case things didn't work out just right? After all, Sejanus knew Pilate. Why didn't he just speak to him directly? Why send a district commander to question, of all people, the governor?

"Well, your excellency, the general did make a somewhat dramatic appearance at my home and command me to initiate an investigation into what happened here. I have just come from the temple of the high priest, and now I am here..."

Pilate sensed his uneasiness: "Don't worry, commander, I will give you my complete cooperation. I promise. I know your record, and I know you are a good soldier and a loyal servant of Rome. It is important that you get all the information involving this whole affair so that you can report all of this back to the emperor. And let me calm your fears about something else. You probably have wondered why someone of your rank has been asked to conduct this investigation. The reason is that Rome would never officially investigate me, one of its provincial governors, over a matter like this, no matter how embarrassing this all turns out to be. Because, you see, if I screwed up something so badly that Rome had to conduct an official investigation, it would ultimately reflect on the judgment of the emperor in giving me this assignment in the first place. It would be as though an ambassador of some country after arriving there started a war due to his or her incompetence. Ultimately, that poor performance would reflect on the competency of the person who sent him or her there. So if Sejanus or the Roman ambassador conducted this investigation, it would take on a very official tone, and no one wants that. Even if they conducted one in secret, if it ever became known that it was done on such a high level, it would still be seen as an official investigation that reflects on their judgment.

"However, Rome would certainly want to know all that happened here, and they probably would not trust me to voluntarily tell them the whole truth, so they send you. You're bright, you're believed to be honest, and, most of all, you're vulnerable. You're vulnerable both to your own fear of us as well as to your own ambitions. I'm sure you see that the rewards as well as the perils could be great in something like this. Plus, in your case, the officials in Rome know they have a trump card, and that is your friend Antoni Demetrius. You see, despite all of Sejanus's rhetoric, they really are less interested in the truth than in finding a way to be absolved from all of this as quickly as possible. I've already received a communique from Rome on how they wish me to handle the press. The spin doctors are already working overtime. They know that now you too will have an interest in getting Rome out of this mess because it is the only way you can reap some personal benefits as well as save your friend's ass. It is typical empire politics, business as usual.

"But I want to assure you of this: I will not let them feed one of my commanders to the dogs. I did not ask for this assignment, and when I got it, everyone believed it was a dead-end job that would keep me out of Rome and out of trouble. But I am here now, and I am procurator. And part of my job here is to protect my soldiers from all enemies, whether from within or from without. So don't be afraid to ask me anything. I will tell you all that I know, and then we will face all of this together. Don't worry: I still have some influence with the powerbrokers, and it would not serve them well to try to ruin me. I have a pretty good idea where a lot of the skeletons are hidden around the palace. And I won't let them get to you without going through me."

Marcus could hardly believe all he was hearing. Was this the same Pilate who had seemed to have made so many early blunders in his administration? Was this sudden show of loyal support for one of his soldiers real, or was this part of some scheme the governor had devised to save his own skin? The only way to know more was to go straight to the questioning: "Your excellency, as I mentioned, I just came from the temple of the high priest, and if he was telling the truth, and I realize that could be a very big if, then I have a pretty good idea why they wanted Jesus out of the way. If you would, sir, please tell me just why you sentenced him to death under Roman law?"

"I did so because I absolutely, positively believed I had no choice in the matter. I did everything I could not to sentence him, but between the people's insistence that he die and Jesus' refusal to help in any way in his own defense, it was impossible for me to do anything else. If I had spared his life, it would have been because I, and I alone, wanted him to live. And that would have proven harder to justify in the long run than this will be in the short run."

Pilate took a deep breath, stood, and started to walk across the room. Suddenly, his ankle-length tunic seemed not to fit, and he shifted uneasily in it. He turned and walked back toward Marcus. "Do you know why Jesus is dead?" he said. "He is dead because he wanted to be. And that is why I worked so hard to save him. He wanted to die, and he wanted us to do him in. He wanted the Jews and the Romans to be the ones to put him to death. He was innocent of any crimes as far as I could see, and he certainly did not do anything to deserve dying on that cross. But as sure as I am standing here, commander, I tell you Jesus wanted to die. He wanted to die, and there was nothing I could do to stop it.

"When I first got the call I was told that they were bringing him here, demanding an emergency meeting right away, my first reaction was to tell them all to go to hell. But they had already arrested him, and I believed that if I didn't get involved right away things would get out of control and become really dangerous for Jesus. So I set up the meeting, and when they brought him in, all handcuffed and bloody, I was furious. I couldn't believe they'd had the nerve to treat someone of such stature in the Jewish community with such brutality. I asked what the meaning of all this was. They said that Jesus had been tried and convicted of a capital offense according to Jewish law and that the only reason they were here was for the formality of putting him to death. I said to them, 'If that was the case, why come to me? Why not put him to death yourselves?' They said that I knew they could not do it without my consent. I told them that they were damned right and that if they had, they too would become decorations for the crosses of Judea. I demanded to know just what he had done.

"They said at first that he had been convicted of blasphemy. I said, 'Against who?' And that's when they threw in an obviously made-up charge of sedition. I asked them what the evidence was. They said that he was seen preaching violent revolution and the overthrow of the Roman government. I asked them if they were all drunk or crazy, but they kept repeating the charges. I turned to Jesus and asked him if this was true, but he said nothing. I figured after the beating he had apparently taken at the hands of the temple people, he was somewhat afraid to speak, so I ordered them all to wait outside while I questioned Jesus alone. Once I had him alone I told him that he should not be afraid to speak to me and that I thought they were all full of crap. 'Just tell me what this is all about,' I said to him, 'and I will have you released and have their heads on a platter for this come morning.' But to my surprise, he still wouldn't say anything. He just stood there staring out into space.

"I told him that as governor I would have known if someone as famous as himself would have turned into an advocate of terrorism and that I did not believe for one second what I was hearing from the temple people. I told him we were both in a sticky situation and I wanted to help. I knew that it would not be good for our image to have him killed and that it would be better for us to put to death those who try to put us in this kind of situation. I told him that all he needed to do was to tell me if the charges against him were false, just as I knew they were. But he still would not answer me. He just kept staring off into space with a faraway look in his eyes. Not being a man of great patience and knowing I would have to allow the council members to return soon, I said to him that he should take heed because if he wouldn't help me out here, there was a possibility that his 'friends' outside could pull this off. That was the only time he ever said a word to me. Without turning once in my direction, he said in a very calm voice, 'You can't stop this you know. Nobody can. In a while this will all be over, and the winds of heaven will blow different forever.' That was it; that's all he said. I asked him what he meant and told him I could stop this in a moment. All he had to do was cooperate. But after he said those words, he never said another word to me. From that moment on I was determined to save him. What the hell was he talking about, the winds would blow different forever? What was that supposed to mean? I must confess I didn't much like the idea that he believed all of us gathered here were a part of some sort of destiny thing that none of us could do anything about. Nor did I care much for his attitude.

"I called for the council members to return to the room, and I said that I could find nothing to substantiate the charges they had leveled against him. I told them that I found him innocent and would not put him to death. At this they all started yelling, but I quickly silenced them. Yet I knew that because they had made a formal request and because the charges were as serious as they were, I could not ignore the charges altogether. It was then that I came up with what I thought was a brilliant idea.

"Somewhere I remembered reading that Jesus was originally a citizen of Galilee. I had received a courtesy call from Herod earlier that morning and agreed to have lunch with him after their Sabbath. I said to them that I had a counterproposal. I told the crowd to go to Herod, and if he agreed that these charges were serious, then I would consider their request. I told them to go and see Herod at once. I believed that Herod would do one of two things. He would agree that the charges were true, at which point I would have given him permission to put Jesus to death, or he would say that the charges were not true, at which point I would have told the council members that even their king did not agree with them, and if they had any further problems with Jesus, take it up with Herod. I figured either way it would absolve Rome from any of this. And if they decided to be the ones to ultimately carry out this act, they would be the ones who would have to deal with the worldwide political repercussions. I thought that might be something we could use to hold against them sometime in the future. The idea that the one time we left a really important decision in their hands they screwed it up so badly that they caused an international incident would be something that we could exploit quite handily. It would have shown the world that these people are surely not ready for any form of self-rule. However, Herod was too smart to fall for any of this. He sent Jesus back, excusing himself from the whole process. He said he did not wish to interfere with Rome's rightful authority to settle the matter. The ball was once again in our court."

"Sir," Marcus interjected. "Why did you not consult Rome on the matter once the king refused to get involved." Even before the words had left his lips, he knew the answer to his own question. He knew how Rome worked, especially when it involved high-ranking officers. Still he thought he had better ask the question, just to make sure he covered himself in his report.

Pilate too seemed to understand the need to have the question asked. "You know, when I first came to Judea, I marched in with quite a bit of fanfare. I didn't do that, as some thought, because I was an egomaniac. I did so because I thought it was important to show everyone in this town the strength of Rome. I still do not believe that most people here have any idea how powerful we are as an empire. I thought if I came into town in full-blown regalia, it would make a very powerful statement.

"But then, as you know, the people reacted in a way that surprised both me and my advisers. They believed so much in this idolatry business that they were ready to riot over the banners and statues with Caesar's image on them. Well, that didn't bother me because I knew that we could crush any revolt in a matter of minutes. But still, being new on the job and not wanting to embarrass either Rome or myself, I called Rome and asked for guidelines. Instead of guidelines, I received a lecture as though I was a common, first-year cadet at the academy. And over and over again I was told that I was sent there to be governor, and if I could not make decisions on my own, I would be hauled away and given something to do that was less of a strain on the brain. That was the phrase they used, 'a strain on the brain.' Imagine, we are talking here about decisions that could affect the lives of thousands of people, and I am given council as imbecilic as that. So I decided I would make two decisions that day.

"First, I would defuse the situation by removing the banners and everything that had Caesar's picture on it. I thought, 'The hell with them; I am not going to commit troops to a conflict in which even one soldier could get hurt over something...'" At this point Pilate stopped as though he caught himself saying perhaps a bit more than he felt was prudent considering the circumstances. He cleared his throat and then continued.

"And, second, I decided that I would never go to them with questions concerning how to handle things in this part of the world again.

I would make my own decisions, and if I was wrong, so be it. Commander, let's you and I level with one another. You and I are soldiers. We are not simply politicians; we are here to do what we think is correct and to follow orders. We must always do whatever it takes to serve the best interests of the empire. But we are also expected to take the heat for those decisions and take it with the attitude of the gladiators who fought and died in the days of old. When a problem as sticky as this Jesus affair takes place, Rome expects us to handle it, and if we mess up, we are expected to swallow the poison and pay for it ourselves. Rome must be protected at all costs. I had to make the decisions here. It was my responsibility and no one else's. You are here, my friend, to see if indeed I made the right choices. Calling Rome, which would have been the safe thing to do, I suppose, even though I was libel to receive the same stupid advice, was an option I felt was not available to me."

Pilate looked up at Marcus and gave him a wry smile. "Have I thoroughly confused you, my friend, or shall I continue?"

"I believe I am with you so far, your excellency, though I do have some questions. Please continue, and I'll try not to interrupt you unless I feel it is necessary."

Pilate sat down again, and Marcus asked: "What happened after Jesus returned from seeing Herod?"

"By that time it was morning, and Caiaphas and his crowd had gathered a group of supporters to return with them. They were all insisting that Jesus be put to death immediately. This time they began to say that he was guilty of setting himself up as a king and telling the people that they should not pay taxes. I told them I found nothing in any evidence presented to me, which to this point had been mostly just talk, that would justify these charges or warrant the death penalty. I told them that I did not understand why they were going to such lengths to convince me otherwise. They said he was a criminal and that under Jewish law he had to be executed. They said that it would be an offense to their rights as a people if I did not sentence him to death in accordance with their traditions. 'Rights,' I'm thinking to myself, 'what rights?' It was at this point that members of my staff dug out the old Cultural Noninterference Treaty, and I began to understand what the Jews were talking about. But I also knew that the treaty might give us a way out of this mess if we were pushed much further.

"Once again I brought him back inside, and this time I told him that I was not very sure that I could save him unless he really began to cooperate with me. I told him that as a technical matter of law, they could indeed force me to put him to death. I asked him about this business concerning taxes. He didn't answer me, but then he knew he didn't need to: it was very clear that Jesus was too smart a man to openly tell people not to pay their taxes. But you know something? Now that I think about it, he did say one other thing to me. I asked him if he believed himself to be a king. He said something to me like, 'If that's what you wish to call me' or something like that. I don't remember his exact words, but I remember his answer really pissed me off. I said to him, 'What the hell do you mean, if that's what *I* wish to call you? I'm not the one who has dragged you in here half-dead, calling for your blood. Those are your people out there.'

"After that I must tell you I was overcome with the strangest pathos. I wanted to save him while, at the same time, I too suddenly wanted to see him dead. I wanted to save him because, as I said, I did not like being forced and tricked into a situation I couldn't control. Jesus kept looking at me as if to say, 'Come on, let's get it over with. After all, you along with all the rest of these people are no more than pawns in this awful Fellini-like screenplay, so stop trying to run from your destiny.' He started looking at me in a way that suggested all of us gathered in this place were all born for the sole purpose of fulfilling his own private destiny. I thought, 'Who the hell do you think you are?'"

Once again Pilate seemed to catch himself drifting off in thought and proceeded to return to the narrative he had begun: "I decided I would not bother speaking to Jesus anymore, because I believed it to be futile. I took him back outside and told the crowd present that I would not execute him. I told them that he did need to be taught a lesson in humility and that perhaps a few minutes alone with the lash would make him more likable to everyone. They began to shout that it was not enough, but I silenced them. I called for the guard and ordered him to be put to the lash. I said that I wanted him beaten, not in the presence of the crowd, but in earshot of them. I thought perhaps a few good screams from Jesus would make them less blood-thirsty. When I ordered the guard to take him inside, I caught a look at Jesus' face."

Pilate grew quiet for a few moments. He looked blankly at a few statues in the room and then at the lion emblazoned on the carpet, which seemed to be mocking him. Marcus wanted to ask him what was the matter but felt it better to remain quiet until Pilate decided to either share what was troubling him or move on with the story. Then Pilate spoke: "I truly wish to hell I hadn't done that. I wish I had just put him to death right at that moment."

"Why?" asked Marcus. "After all, scourging is an old and honorable practice when dealing with prisoners."

"I wish I hadn't because it was an absolutely superfluous act that did nothing to help the predicament. It only added to the brutality and grandeur of the situation. It was a mistake, and I now believe crucifying him was a mistake. Anyway, if we had to put him to death, I should have ordered him to be taken into a jail cell and quietly knifed or something. But once I had him whipped, I became an unwilling actor in this gross play that was being directed by Jesus and whoever his God happens to be. By the gods, what a martyr's death we gave him. Death on the cross, crucifixion."

At that moment, Pilate walked over and picked up a newspaper. "Look at these headlines: 'Jesus Tortured and Executed by Jews and Romans.' Look at these stories on the inside: 'Jesus Beaten and Brutally Executed on Cross: Left to Die While Granting Forgiveness to All Who Took Part.' Look at this one: 'Jesus Dies Because of Beliefs.' Look at the drawings they made of him, head all bloodied because of that stupid crown of thorns. Look at the look on his face, those big, sad, suffering eyes, wounds in his hands and feet. He comes across looking like the martyr to end all martyrs. We come across looking like..."

Pilate stood for a minute staring at the papers, then he suddenly turned toward Marcus and spoke: "Do you know what they do in America?"

"Sir?" said Marcus, thoroughly caught off guard at this apparent sudden departure from the topic at hand.

"In America, people marked for execution are left in prison to contemplate their fate for years. They put them in prison for as long as ten years, maybe more. They give them years to think about how they will die and what it will feel like, making them live just a few yards from the room where their lives will be taken. They let them go through the process of getting their hopes up and then dashing them through a system they call appeals, each time sentencing them to death once again. Then one morning they come into their cells and walk them down a hall and strap them into chairs that shoot electricity through them until their heads catch on fire. Imagine, ten or fifteen years after you have been arrested, sitting in a prison waiting to die.

"Now, take a look at this story, commander," said Pilate. "I read this one this morning." Pilate opened another newspaper. "This one is from the *Washington Eagle,* the ultra right-wing, conservative newspaper in the States. There is virtually nothing Jesus said or did while he was alive that these people would have ever agreed with. Look what it says: 'Jesus Left on a Cross for Three Hours Bravely Waiting for Death.' He suffers three hours, and now to them he is a martyr, not so much for how he lived but for how he died. Meanwhile, in their country, those poor bastards suffer for ten years waiting to die, and we are the brutes of history while they are civilized. But I will tell you this much: none of the civilized countries seem to give a damn about all the other poor slobs who get executed in this country, you know the ones who have no international reputation. Most of the world never even heard of executions by crucifixion before it happened to Jesus. You know someday people will look upon this thing and talk about how brutal we were, not because we routinely executed people in this part of the world but for the way we executed Jesus."

Marcus felt a pain in the pit of his stomach. Again someone was speaking of this event as though it would live long beyond next month. Marcus did not want to believe this. Why would this event be of any great significance to anyone in the years to come? His thoughts were interrupted by the sound of Pilate's voice begging to be forgiven for once again straying from the narrative.

"Well, anyway," Pilate continued, "I had him beaten, and as you can imagine, he never cried out once for the guard to stop. Before they brought him back out, I went inside to see him, and he was looking like a first-class martyr for sure. I thought, 'If I were on this guy's payroll, I could not have served him better than I just did.' I was absolutely determined now at all cost to prevent him from dying at our hands. I wanted nothing to do at all with the death of this man. I did not want to become a player in this game. 'To hell with the treaty,' I thought to myself. 'To hell with the treaty, and to hell with all of you.'

"I brought him outside and said that I hoped everyone was satisfied and that I had other matters to take care of and wanted nothing more to do with this whole affair. I was turning to walk away when the high priest called out to me and asked if I was prepared to let someone go from the prisons because of the holiday tradition. I told them that I would and thought to myself that perhaps they were going to ask that Jesus be released. I thought so because I believed that they had decided they were going to get nowhere with me, and so they wanted him released with the idea that they might quietly assassinate him one dark night. Also, they could all protect themselves with the notion that they tried to do what was right and were prevented from doing so by me. Well, as you know, the way this prison Sabbath release thing is done is that you bring out two prisoners and ask the crowd to chose one or the other. Once they pick one, he is then pardoned and set free. The only prisoners exempt from this practice are political prisoners guilty of conspiring against Rome.

"They had indicated quite strongly that they preferred one of them to be the current prisoner, Jesus. As I said, I believed they wanted me to release him because it would be a way for them to back out with grace. Still, I wanted to stack the deck to make sure that Jesus would be released. So I told them that since they had picked one of the prisoners, I would pick the other.

"I asked the guard in charge of the garrison to get me the list of prisoners we had on hand. 'Who can I pick,' I thought, 'who these people would never have the nerve to ask me to free?' Since the list was in alphabetical order, it didn't take me long to come up with the perfect name: Barabbas."

Marcus was familiar with the name from the police files that came across his desk. Barabbas was an absolutely vicious killer. He had started out as a small-time drug dealer, but through sheer guts and a penchant for ruthlessness, he quickly grew to become one of the country's biggest crime lords. He headed a local cartel that dealt not only in narcotics but in such crimes as prostitution and child pornography. For a while, despite his numerous crimes of violence, many of the people looked upon him as a sort of folk hero. He presented himself as a Robin Hood–type bandit who would even give large amounts of money to charitable organizations. Sadly enough, as long as he kept enough money flowing, people seemed to make excuses for the "misunderstood" bandit. "He's just a businessman who the establishment doesn't like," they would often say when some example of his crimes would surface. Those who seemed to try to expose him for the vicious killer he was would ultimately end up "missing" and, sooner or later, show up dead. Still he was careful never to attack anyone connected with Rome. He made sure that if drugs were ever found in the hands of Romans, they could never be traced back to his organization.

All seemed to go well for Barabbas until the famous Rabbi Rosen case. Bernard Rosen was a young, energetic rabbi who was given his first congregation in one of the poorest sections of Jerusalem. Almost immediately, Rabbi Rosen began to effect change in the community. His youthful exuberance, combined with a nearly fanatical love for the people in his congregation, produced a spirit of hope in the neighborhood that soon began to spread beyond the confines of his parish. His work with both the youth and the elderly produced incredible results. In just six short months after his arrival, he had established a food kitchen in the neighborhood that fed hundreds of people a day. He organized many of the business leaders in East Jerusalem to help establish a home for runaway youth. He knew how to work with established temple leaders, as well as street toughs, to get things done. He labored at times twenty hours a day and, within a few short years, became practically a legend in and around Jerusalem.

One day he received an emergency call to the house of a parishioner, and when he arrived, he found a man holding his fourteen-year-old daughter in his arms. She was in great pain and convulsing violently. He called for a doctor, and when he returned, he saw the girl was slipping away fast. He said some prayers over the girl and held her hand. He knew what she was dying from because he recognized the signs. She was an addict, like hundreds of other young people in the community. As he prayed, he looked over at the pain and grief of the father, sobbing and begging his little girl not to die. In that moment he felt helpless for the first time in his life, and his prayers were only reaching as high as the ceiling. For a moment his mind drifted toward the cause of their pain, but he was suddenly brought back to the present by a cry of anguish from the father. The girl had died.

When he left that house he swore that as God was his witness, he would mount a campaign against the man who was mostly responsible for shipping so much poison into the community. The thief and vicious drug lord, Barabbas. Rabbi Rosen tackled going after Barabbas the same way he did everything else in life, with a vengeance. He organized rallies naming Barabbas in public as a villainous scourge on society. He organized neighborhood watches to alert the authorities whenever any of Barabbas's men tried to sell drugs in the community. He went to the newspapers and the television stations whenever possible to expose the corruption that he found in some of the local circles of government where politicians often seemed to "look the other way" as far as Barabbas was concerned. All of this of course did not go unnoticed by Barabbas, who at first tried to ignore the rabbi and later tried to bribe him. It seemed, however, that no amount of "reasoning" could get through to the rabbi, so Barabbas took what he believed was the only course of action left to him. He decided to have the rabbi killed.

It had always been Barabbas's intention to have the preacher assassinated one night in some dark alley somewhere. He could then say that while he and the rabbi did not always see eye to eye, still it was regrettable that such a young, energetic man of God was cut down in the prime of his life. But then one day when a particularly large shipment of drugs worth several hundred pounds of gold was being unloaded from a ship that had just docked at an abandoned pier in the city of Apollonia, the movers were surprised to find themselves surrounded by dozens of members of the rabbi's temple, all wielding sticks and clubs. How the rabbi had found out about the shipment remained a mystery — after all Apollonia is a bit of a distance from Jerusalem — but somehow he had learned of its location. They seized the shipment and the men, made what they called a "citizen's arrest," and dragged the smugglers and the shipment toward the center of town. They called the local police, but before the authorities could arrive, the rabbi and his men had put all the drugs into a large pile, poured gasoline all over it, and set fire to the drugs right there in the street in front of a large crowd who had gathered to see what was going on. By this time, someone had alerted the news media, and when they arrived, the rabbi and his men held an impromptu news conference.

Once again the young rabbi called Barabbas by name and yelled into the cameras that this was what would happen from now on. "Remember the words of Solomon, oh Barabbas, and repent, you drug-smuggling thief: 'A wise man makes his father proud of him; a foolish one brings his mother grief. Wealth you get by dishonesty will do you no good, but honesty will save your life. The Lord will not let good people go hungry, but will keep the wicked from getting what they want'" [Proverbs 10:1–4].

Then the rabbi and members of his congregation all danced around the fire chanting various psalms and hymns of victory while the blaze grew higher and higher.

Barabbas was livid. He was embarrassed not only in front of other fellow crime lords, including the head of the local cartel in Apollonia to whom he had promised a sizable cut, but also on television. He decided that not only must this rabbi be taught a lesson but so must his congregation and any other temple that would try to cross him. His lieutenants tried to dissuade him from doing anything rash, claiming that the rabbi was too hot to harm at this time, but Barabbas would hear none of it. "What's good for the drugs, is good for the rabbi," he yelled at his people. So one night during the Saturday evening services, several men came up to the rabbi's synagogue, and from outside they found a way to bolt the doors of the temple shut. They knew the windows of the temple were too high for anyone to climb out of, but low enough to toss something through. And with the full congregation present, right in the middle of the reading of the Torah, they threw several bottles filled with oil with burning rags tied to them through the window. In moments, the whole temple was aflame. That night, Rabbi Rosen, along with over a hundred members of his congregation, was killed in the fire.

When the news reached the public about the devastating fire, people were shocked beyond belief. That so many Jewish lives could be ruthlessly snuffed out was bad enough, but that someone would dare destroy those lives by setting fire to a temple was simply beyond comprehension. The only thing more incomprehensible to the community would have been the idea that this horror could have been perpetrated by another Jew. Surely, the people thought, Rome or some other outside group was responsible for this outrage.

Unfortunately for Barabbas, while the killers were making their getaway, they were spotted by a man who, upon seeing the blaze, whipped out his video camera and filmed the assassins fleeing. One of the men caught on film was the chief lieutenant of Barabbas, who within hours was arrested at his palatial home in the suburbs of Bethany. At first, of course, he vehemently denied any involvement with such a deed. The authorities then showed him the tape, but the man insisted that while the person on film perhaps looked a little like him, it was not, and no court would convict him on such evidence. At that point the officer in charge told him that perhaps he was correct and that if he insisted he was not the person on the video, they would release him. However, he said, they wouldn't release him back into the suburbs where he lived, but instead they would release him into the neighborhood of the temple burning, *after* showing the tape on the morning news. "Who knows," said the officer, "maybe what's left of the rabbi's congregation won't think the likeness is that close either." Upon hearing this, the man quickly did the prudent thing. He cut a deal for life in prison and rolled over on his boss by giving them the name of the one who had ordered the temple be torched. The next morning, the headline of every Jewish newspaper read: "BARABBAS ORDERED TEMPLE BLAZE."

A cry of outrage arose from the people, and a nationwide manhunt was called for. For the first time Rome knew that it had to get involved and began to put considerable manpower into the search, and so hundreds of military units were put on alert to find Barabbas. From Galilee to Idumaea, and from Joppa to Peraea, the call went out to find and capture Barabbas. While all the while claiming his innocence, Barabbas ran from town to town, always managing to stay one step ahead of the authorities. He also seemed to leave a trail of blood wherever he hid, often killing to hide his tracks. In what was perhaps the first time in history, Jews willingly collaborated with the Roman authorities in order to track down one of their own people. And when he was caught, a cry went out from all over the provinces that at last they had caught Barabbas.

What was interesting about this case was that Barabbas had been turned into a political figure as well. The longer he eluded the authorities, the more his name was used as a symbol of Roman indifference to the plight of the people. "If he were killing Romans," the Jewish politicians would all holler, "he would have been caught and convicted years ago." "Why can't the famous Roman justice system rid our streets of Barabbas?" the editorial writers would all ponder in print.

Pilate continued, "I knew at last I had them all, including Jesus. I told them that I believed the high priest had an excellent idea. I would release for them a prisoner. This would serve a number of purposes. It would allow them to have their traditions met; it would allow me the opportunity to act in accordance with the treaty we had signed with them; and it would allow me to rid myself of Jesus while at the same time teaching those people a lesson in Roman rule."

Pilate went on: "I told them I had chosen a second prisoner and would allow them to make the final decision about who would be released. I said that once this choice was made, that would be the end of the matter. I asked if everyone understood. They all agreed, and I told them to wait. I whispered to the guard to bring out Barabbas. The guard turned his head and looked at me as though I had just asked him to take the life of his firstborn. I repeated my order in such a way that he hurried off to obey. I then waited with joyful anticipation for the results. While I was waiting, I had visions of Rome reading my report and congratulating me on a job well done. I even had thoughts of the mighty Sejanus coming to Judea with praise on his lips. Of course, he would have found a way of taking credit for the way I handled things. He would have said it was all due to his tutelage.

"Well, within a short while they brought up the prisoner. I had ordered that his face be covered with a hood so that I could dramatically surprise the crowd present. I said to them, 'Well, here is my candidate for release.' I could hear grumbling in the crowd as they looked with suspicion on the man in chains with the hood over his face. I said, 'Who shall I release, Jesus or this man?' and at that point I reached over and pulled the hood from Barabbas's head. A gasp came from deep within the crowd. There before them stood the one man whom I knew they despised almost as much as they did me. I had given them a choice, while at the same time denying them one. Now it was time to see just what they were made of.

"For a moment there was silence. 'Well,' I said to them, 'I am waiting for your answer. Shall I release your king or shall I set Barabbas loose among you once again? I gave you my word as your governor, and as the representative of the Roman Empire, that I would release one of these two men. Whatever decision you make shall become law, and nothing anyone says here will ever reverse the decision. Make up your minds, and make it quick, for I grow tired of this foolishness.'

"I thought, 'It is done; he is free; it is over.' I must tell you, commander, that in all of my years as a soldier, and in all of my years dealing in the back rooms of imperial politics, I never saw anyone do what the people that day did in my courtyard. For you see, they saw this move on my part as trying to rob them of power, even though as an occupied people it's more like their illusion of power. And the idea of power had so corrupted them that they actually began to call out for Barabbas to be set free. When they called for Barabbas, I stood and shouted, 'Are you mad? You're telling me that you want me to kill Jesus, and set Barabbas free?' 'Yes,' they shouted, 'that is what we want.' I said to them that it would mean Barabbas would be free to roam the countryside again and kill their wives and children. I turned and pointed toward Jesus and said, 'This man has never killed any of you.' Caiaphas turned and yelled that Jesus would become the death of us all and then began to chant the name of Barabbas. Within a short time, many people in the crowd began to join in.

"I signaled for the guards, and when they arrived I ordered calm be restored. I then said that I would not and could not go back on my word, and if they demanded Barabbas's release, they should be aware that I would not go through the time and expense of ordering another massive search for him after he murdered their children and wives. 'Then their blood be on our hands,' they shouted back. 'Set free Barabbas.'

"What could I do?" Pilate said with a wistful look in his eyes. "I had already pledged I would let one of them go free and made that pledge in the name of myself and Rome. There was no way I could back out of it, no way on earth. I called for a bowl of water to be brought to me. In full view of everyone I said that I washed my hands of the mess. I knew that I would have to answer to Rome for my actions, commander, but there was simply no way I was going to back out of my pledge. I washed my hands and turned him over to the guards. The rest is, as they say, history."

For a moment they both sat in silence. Then all at once Pilate stood up, glanced around the room at the growing shadows, and began to beckon Marcus toward the door. "There you have it, commander. Report back to your superiors. I'm afraid I must go down and work on my statement for the press. I will of course get a copy of your report, either from you or from someone else, somewhere along the line. Please be accurate in what you report; to do otherwise will cause both of us in the end a lot of needless grief."

At first Marcus was surprised at how abruptly the meeting had come to an end and wanted to protest its termination without his having a chance to question Pilate further. But then he realized that he really had no more questions: Pilate's explanation of the events seemed to make perfect sense. If the story was true, Pilate's decisions were right and justifiable. He had gone about dealing with the situation in a logical, Roman manner. And while he had indeed acquired a new respect for his governor, he still did not believe he was smart enough to make this story up on such short notice.

Marcus thanked the governor for his time and promised him that his report would read favorably. He asked the governor if he would be available for more questions if the need should so arise.

"You know where to find me," was Pilate's reply. "Besides," he continued, "after all of this, I doubt I will be transferred back to Rome any time soon."

Marcus thanked him again and rode away to speak to the next person on his list: the Hebrew king Herod.

– CHAPTER TWELVE –

GERRY PICKED UP THE PHONE and put in a call to David Ben Leven. "I must talk to you right away," Gerry said. "It's very important." David protested the time and said that they were all due to meet at the king's press conference in a few hours anyway.

"This is very important," said Gerry. "Please meet me in an hour at your office."

Within the hour, both she and David were sitting in the front office of the *Judean*.

"OK Gerry, what's so important that you got an old man out of bed in the middle of the night?"

"Did you hear the news about the scribe who was murdered last night?"

"Yeah, Joseph of Arimathea. He was robbed or something. It happens all the time in Judea. It's a shame because he was a good man. But what has that got to do with you getting me up in the middle of the night? You weren't the one who robbed him were you?" David meant the remark as a joke, but it didn't draw much of a smile from Gerry. David decided to be quiet and simply listen to whatever tale he was about to be told.

At that point, Gerry began to tell him of the experience she had had with Alan and Joseph. She wasn't at first sure just how much she should reveal but then decided that since they had already shared so much, particularly with the Judas letter, she would tell the whole story.

After she had finished, she waited for David's reaction.

"Did Joseph understand that you were a TV reporter?" he asked.

"I explained that to him," said Gerry. "Why?"

"Because it sounds to me as though he was primarily concerned with establishing a printed record of the trial. I'm surprised he didn't go to a newspaper person."

Gerry found herself getting annoyed. "I really don't believe any of that matters at this point. This man came to me with a story that said basically that the trial was illegal and that he went to Pilate and claimed the body, and now he's dead. Who killed him? Did they do it because he spoke to me? And forgive me if this doesn't sound professional, but are they coming after me next? What does all of this mean?"

"Gerry, don't get paranoid on me. Remember where you are. I can't imagine anyone would kill him over what he told you. So what if the trial was illegal? We already heard rumors to that effect going around. I think what he told you was important for the record historically perhaps, but worth killing a Western reporter over? I don't think so. The poor man was probably killed by some fanatic or robbed for his purse, as the report indicated. Besides, what that fellow told you was quite correct. If anyone wanted you dead, you would be history by now."

Gerry began to feel the hairs rise on the back of her neck. Again with the "you could be dog meat if we wanted you to be" routine. "What is with these people all of a sudden?" she thought. "Why is everybody trying to make me feel like an extremely swatable mosquito?"

"I would suggest that if you're still worried about the whole matter, talk to your friend Marcus," David continued. "He after all represents the local law in this part of town, as much as there is any that is."

David could see the look of concern on his friend's face. It was concern that suggested she was hurt because David did not seem to take all of this more seriously.

"Look, Gerry. You are the adopted older sister of my children. Do you think I would tell you what I just did if I thought you were in any real danger? I tell you, there's nothing Joseph told you that in and of itself was worth killing him, let alone you, over. Maybe someone thought he had to die for what he knew, but killing you over it would simply not be worth the trouble. I'm sorry if that burst your bubble of importance, but what I have told you is true. Go back to your room and relax; get some sleep. I assure you that you have nothing to worry about. If it will make you feel any better, I'll make some calls just to double-check everything. I still have one or two connections with certain elements in this city who would know if anything was up. But please don't worry. I know this town, and I know how people think here. It will be all right. I promise you."

While Gerry did not feel totally convinced of all she had heard, she did trust David. No one knew the politics of the region better than he did. She also knew that David did genuinely care for her and would not expose her to danger. "Besides," she thought, "if anyone wants me dead, it's apparently as easy as getting a drink of water, remember? So I guess it doesn't pay to worry."

Gerry thought the best way to get her mind off of all of this was once again to concentrate on her work: "What do you think the king is going to say about all of this?" she asked David.

"Well, Herod is a strange bird, as you well know. But still he seems to come out of this one relatively clean, both from what you tell me Joseph told you and from what I've heard around town. The old boy did stand somewhat in judgment of Jesus, at least that's what the word on the street is, but apparently he was not the one who passed the final decree on him. Still it will be interesting, to say the least, to hear just what he has to say. If nothing else, it should prove to be quite entertaining."

A few hours later Gerry and David, along with scores of other reporters, were gathered at the local residence of the king. Gerry was covering the news conference live, with Gary Thomas again anchoring the broadcast back in New York. Gerry began: "Good morning, ladies and gentleman. This is Gerry Simmons reporting to you live from the Judean residence of the Hebrew king Herod. In a short time he is scheduled to begin a news conference to answer questions on what role he or his representatives played in the execution of Jesus of Nazareth. The reports we have gotten so far as we attempt to piece this bizarre story together are that apparently Jesus was brought before Herod to be judged by him, but he referred the whole matter back to Rome and refused to get personally involved in it. Some are saying it was a smart move on the part of the king, because even though there was probably no love lost between Jesus and the king, the king can claim absolute innocence in this matter."

"Gerry, Gary Thomas here in New York. Have there been any official statements made whatsoever regarding the king's role in all of this, either by Rome or the palace, or has everything been deferred to the news conference?"

"Well, Gary, those of us who know the king and how he operates are somewhat surprised at just how little the king has said publicly in all of this. As you know the king is known in these parts as somewhat of a character, rarely at a loss for words about anything. However, many believe that the king may have decided to remain quiet, particularly in light of the recent controversy surrounding his role in the execution of John."

"Gerry, I assume you're speaking about the man known as John the Baptist. Is that correct?"

"Right, Gary. As you and much of the world know, Herod was responsible for the death of perhaps the second most famous figure in this part of the world, the man known as John the Baptist, or Baptizer, as some referred to him. Herod had him arrested, and he was executed in his cell. The whole affair was shrouded somewhat in secrecy, and few were ever able to get to the bottom of what happened. Just what John had been arrested for was never fully explained to the press, and the mantle of national security was placed over the entire episode. However, many saw the whole incident as a sad commentary, not so much on Herod, as on the people in the region in general. John was after all one of the most popular figures ever to come out of this area, and when he was arrested and then put to death, many people thought there would be a full-scale revolt, a sort of people's revolution."

"Excuse me, Gerry, but did Herod himself think the people would rise up if he put John to death?"

"Gary, the king took the threat very seriously. In fact it was rumored that he even doubled the guard around the palace and put the police and the military on full alert. It was generally believed that John was so beloved and so popular that taking his life would cause at the least a public outcry of enormous proportions. But, as you know, very little was done or said on the part of the general public once the news of John's death got out. There were the usual editorials and the public protestations of various interest groups, but, in general, the public did absolutely nothing. Gary?"

"Gerry, I can see behind you that someone has come to the podium. It appears to be a representative of the king. It looks as though he's going to make a statement."

The camera focused on the man at the podium, who began to speak: "Ladies and gentleman, the king is on his way down to the auditorium. If you will please take your seats, we will be able to get started as soon as he arrives. The king has agreed to answer all of your questions regarding the episode surrounding Jesus. However, he will not answer any questions surrounding the recent occurrence dealing with John or any other issues involving national security. Thank you for your cooperation."

The cameras switched back to New York: "Gerry, I find it interesting that the king is seeking to set ground rules even before he arrives and that he should set them regarding the very topic we were just discussing. And speaking of this issue, is it the general feeling that because there was so little public reaction to John's death, the powers that be decided they could execute Jesus without fear of an uprising?"

"Absolutely, Gary. The talk from most of the insiders here is that once the Sanhedrin saw how little people reacted to the execution of John, they felt reasonably sure that they could seek to put Jesus to death as well. They probably convinced Rome that based on what took place regarding John's death, Rome could act without fear of reprisals from the people. As you know, Rome would prefer not to have a rebellion in this part of the world, even though it could crush it without much effort, given the considerable man power it has here. Still, revolutions are messy business, and Rome is trying to clean up its image as the iron-fisted government in the velvet glove these days."

"Gerry, I see the king is on his way toward the podium."

"Right, Gary. We'll get back to you at the conclusion of the conference."

Herod, in full regalia and accompanied by a brace of soldiers, moved slowly, in a cadenced step, smiling and waving at the cameras and his favorite reporters. At the podium, he began in his smoothest, calmest voice: "Ladies and gentleman, hello, shalom, welcome to the holy land. I will have a brief statement to make, and then I will answer your questions. However, I must tell you before we start that I don't really have a lot of answers for you. Most of the decisions that were made surrounding this whole affair were made by people other than myself. I suggest that if you have a lot of questions about this affair, address them to the Roman high council, or to the Sanhedrin, neither of which I am a member. But since you have all come such a long way, I know that you would feel cheated as reporters if you did not have a chance to question the king, so here we are.

"First and foremost let me state that I met Jesus once and once only. I happened to be here to celebrate Passover in Jerusalem. That was my only purpose for being in town during the time of Jesus' death. I had not long settled in when I received an urgent message from the Roman procurator, my friend the governor. I was told that he had had

Jesus arrested, and since Jesus was from one of my provinces, I was going to be extended the courtesy of being the one to pass judgment on him. I told the messenger to return to my friend the governor and to explain that while I was honored that he felt I should be consulted in this manner, I wanted nothing to do with any of this, and if he had arrested him, then he should deal with him. As I stated earlier, I had never met Jesus, and I didn't know Jesus, except by reputation. I had no personal bone to pick with him, and as far as I was concerned, this was between Rome and the local religious and civil authorities. I let the governor know that I would support whatever decisions they chose to make, but I also made it clear that just because he was from Nazareth cut no ice with me whatsoever. If he was guilty of breaking the law, then he was guilty, and that was that.

"Because I felt I had made it clear that there was absolutely no need to send Jesus to me, I naturally was rather surprised to find him and half of Jerusalem standing in my living quarters shortly thereafter. I told everyone present what I had communicated earlier to Pilate: I wanted nothing to do with this; this was between the local folks and Rome. I then sent everyone packing back to the procurator, and that was that. I played no official role in his death. Now, what do you want to ask me?"

"Your majesty, while you may have played no official role in all of this, did you at least render an opinion to Pilate as to what should be done with Jesus?"

"Yes, my opinion was this. I said to all those present, 'Look, if he is guilty of some capital offense, execute him. If he is not, let him go. Why on earth are you going through all of these stupid maneuvers?' Bringing him here, sitting him there, bringing him before this one and then that one...It was ridiculous. Jesus was an Israelite and as such was subject to the same laws as everybody else here. Next?"

"Your majesty, did you feel any need to find out the particulars of the indictment against him? After all, you must have known that his being put to death would garner worldwide attention. Were you at all concerned that if he were put to death, and was later found innocent of whatever charges were brought against him, that it might put your kingdom in a most unfavorable light?"

"No. Next?"

"Your majesty, you told us that you had never met Jesus before. Did you have any conversation with him the night he was brought before you, and if so, could you share with us what was said?"

"I told him, 'Son, it seems you're in a hell of a lot of trouble.' I told him that I had heard that he had supposedly performed miracles. I told him that if he were capable of doing any kind of magic, now seemed like a good time to pull some kind of rabbit out of his hat. I also told him that as his king, my best advice to him was to start trying to prove his innocence right here and now, and to keep on trying as hard as he could. I told him if he didn't, he would wind up on that cross as sure as I was in front of him, and that no amount of so-called notoriety would save his behind once those Roman brothers of his got their hands on him."

"Did he say anything when you told him this?"

"He said something about doing his father's will. I asked him if his father wasn't Joseph, a local carpenter who died a while back. I asked him if his father had left something in his will about him dying on a cross for no discernible reason. He just looked at me with that look that all these young preachers who believe they are superspecial and called by God give you, that look like they have some knowledge that the rest of us don't have. I told him that Pilate would have some surprise for him, and it wouldn't be particularity pleasant, unless he started trying to do something to save himself. But I knew it was hopeless. He already had the look, and I knew he wouldn't change and would wind up a self-proclaimed martyr — although self-proclaimed might not be exactly accurate, because I'm sure by the time this is all over, many of you will make him a martyr in your papers and on TV. Like I told you, I sent him back to Pilate and told the governor to deal with him himself. I did all I could. Next?"

"Your majesty, are you saying that you agreed with Rome's decision to put Jesus to death?"

"I'm saying this ain't about my agreeing or disagreeing. None of this was my decision to make. By the time I got here, Jesus was already arrested and in the hands of the Roman authorities. If I had arrested Jesus, I would not be particularly happy if Rome came into my palace and started telling me how to handle a local situation. By the same token, once he was in the hands of the local authorities, and once Rome had a hand in it, it became their situation, period, end of story."

"Your majesty, did you feel that if you had wanted to intervene, you would have had the authority to act in a way contrary to Rome's wishes?"

"I guess, considering that they were the ones who sent him to me in the first place, I could have had some say in the matter. I am not just a figurehead in this part of the world, you know, despite what some might suggest. Besides, I must possess some authority, considering I acted in a way contrary to their wishes anyway and sent him back to them rather than rule on this mess myself, now didn't I?"

"Your majesty, what did you think of the decision on the part of the people present to apparently call for the release of a known killer like Barabbas over Jesus?"

"I thought it was damn stupid. But it's the law, and the people had a right to call for his release. Like I said, if everyone agreed he was guilty, he should have been dealt with like he was, and that would be that. I think my friend the governor learned some valuable lessons about our people in this whole affair."

"Your majesty, before you began, a spokesperson came down and told us that we were not allowed to ask any questions about John the Baptist. I would like to ask a related question, however, only because I think it reflects a lot on what has happened. It seems there was a strong rumor going around that you yourself had threatened to kill Jesus and that he escaped from you only because he received a warning from your brother Philip. Would you care to comment on that?"

The king's face reddened; he grabbed the edge of the podium as if to splinter it; but he quickly recovered his composure and answered calmly: "Yeah, well, I heard that too, and that crap, if you'll pardon the expression, is precisely what you just called it, a rumor. I had no personal bone to pick with the man. As far as I was concerned, he could have preached about universal brotherhood, or whatever he was preaching about, until the cows came home. While I am a devoutly religious man, I am not a rabbi. Nor, as I said earlier, am I a member of the Sanhedrin. If he violated some religious law, it was up to them to deal with him. As long as he didn't violate any state law, I would not have been the one to go after him. However, apparently he did do some things that both the Sanhedrin and the empire agreed were capital offenses, because here we all are talking about it. And that is the last thing I will say about anything dealing with John."

"Your majesty, to what do you contribute the downfall of Jesus?"

"I believe, in part, he became too ambitious. All this talk about him being a king himself and all — I think it all just got to him. He forgot that, in many ways, all of our people are on the same side, and sometimes reason is more persuasive than confrontation. After all, we are all reasonable people here and..."

"Oooohhhh yes, *reason!*" In the back of the room, a man stood up and began to shout. At first the palace guards began to move toward him, but suddenly the media recognized him as one of the twelve men who were Jesus' frequent companions. At once, before the guards could get to him, he was surrounded by reporters. He swayed, gesticulated. Some thought he might be drunk; others thought that he was simply overcome with grief and had become irrational. He seemed to be a little of both, given that he had shown up at the palace of the king.

"Reasonable men, ambition, everyone just doing their job while the best hope for Israel lies in a borrowed tomb. And my, how Roman we Jews have all become! Let me speak to you in a language that Roman governors and now Jewish kings can understand. Let me, a noble Jew just like the rest of my fine colleagues now either in hiding or in denial, express my opinion in Roman language." At this the man, whom some believed was Thomas, stood on a chair. It was quite clear now that he had indeed had a bit too much to drink, but he seemed so overcome with grief that he apparently did not care how he looked or just what people might think of what he was about to do. He pointed toward the podium, lurched forward slightly, as if he were about to fall, righted himself, and then began to speak: "Friends, Romans, and countrymen, lend me your ears. I come to bury Jesus, not to praise him. The evil that men do lives after them, while the good is oft interred with their bones; so let it be with Jesus. The noble Herod hath told you Jesus was ambitious...." At this the man turned and pointed toward the front of the room where the king stared with a look of disbelief that was quickly turning into outrage. "If it were so, it was a grievous fault, and grievously hath Jesus answered it. Here, under leave of Herod and the rest — for Herod is an honorable man."

The man closed his eyes for a second, seemed to sober, and spoke then more quietly and calmly: "Come I to speak in Jesus' funeral. Jesus was my friend. He was faithful and just to me, faithful and just to the whole stinking bunch of hypocrites who now either sing his praises while he lies dead or point the finger of guilt to the most innocent of us all.

"But Herod says he was ambitious; and Herod is an honorable man. He hath brought many captives home to God, whose ransom did the general coffers fill. Did this in Jesus seem ambitious? When the poor have cried, Jesus hath wept. Ambition should be made of sterner stuff: yet Herod says he was ambitious, and Herod is an honorable man. I thrice presented Jesus a kingly crown, which thrice he did refuse: Was this ambitious?" The man opened his eyes and stared back at Herod.

The man lowered his voice again and said: "I would have given him my life, traded it away for his, but he would not hear of it. Even though he was so frightened that night in the garden, he still would not trade his life for my worthless and ignoble one. Yet Herod says Jesus was ambitious; and sure, he is an honorable man."

At this the man turned toward everyone in the room and began to shout in a mocking voice: "I speak not to disprove what Herod spoke, but here I am to speak what I do know."

He turned and spoke directly to the cameras, the words and alcohol intensifying his grief. He almost fell as he slurred out the next few sentences: "You all did love him once, not without cause: What cause withholds you then to mourn for him? O judgment! thou are fled to brutish beasts, and men have lost their reason. *The whole goddamn world has lost its reason.* Bear with me; my heart is in the coffin there with Jesus, and I must pause till it come back to me." His head drooped, and he began to weep.

At the front of the room, the king began to applaud, though he was both livid and strangely embarrassed by what had just taken place. He shouted: "Bravo! Wonderful! The only things missing were some masks and props and a chorus, you poor, pathetic, drunken fool. It's no wonder your master ended up dead with the likes of you as an adviser. I'm sure right now Jesus, wherever he is, is saying, 'With friends like that scum, who needed Romans?' Guards! Remove this drunk and take him to sleep it off somewhere. Don't hurt him. We must not give our friends from the media cause to write about us as though we are all barbarians in this part of the world."

At once the man was surrounded by guards and removed from the hall. Reporters tried to shout questions at the man, but the guards were efficient, and within seconds, the man was gone. Only the words "Jesus will return to judge us all" could be heard again and again coming from the man's mouth.

Once the man was removed, everyone in the room quickly turned toward the king, shouting questions at him, but instead of resuming the news conference, the king, who by now was visibly outraged, abruptly ended it: "Ladies and gentlemen, I have affairs of state that I must attend to. You all pretty well know the story and can see that I had very little involvement in the whole deal. I must go. I am sure that you will all have a great time writing about the little sideshow that took place here. I hope you enjoyed it. We do after all always try our best to make ourselves look like utter fools for your writing pleasure." At that he quickly turned toward the door and walked away.

The reporters rushed from the room, either to get to a phone or to find a corner where they could report live from the scene.

Gerry found her crew and moved them to an area of the hall where there was some quiet. She adjusted the mike pinned to her blouse and began to broadcast back to New York: "Well, ladies and gentlemen, as you can see there was a rather strange twist to the king's news conference: a man who many believe is one of the twelve so-called apostles of Jesus took over the news conference and assailed the king and many of the government officials whom he apparently felt were responsible for putting Jesus to death. The king became visibly agitated, had the man removed from the building, and then abruptly ended his news conference. Just another strange episode in this whole bizarre affair. Gary?"

"Gerry, has anyone positively identified the man as one of the twelve advisers of Jesus?"

"I believe some here in the room knew him, but more importantly, the king seemed to recognize him. You see, Gary, despite how close Jesus' advisers were, they always made it a point to stay somewhat in the background whenever Jesus made public appearances. So someone like myself, for instance, who had seen Jesus personally on only a couple of occasions but was never assigned to cover him directly, still would not know on sight who all of his inside people were or what they looked like. We all knew some of the more well known ones like Peter, who was visibly quite striking both in his stature and in his manner. I believe I heard the name Thomas mentioned by some of the reporters in the room, however, and I do know one of his advisers was named Thomas. Gary?"

"Gerry, we are checking into the identity of the man right now and should have an answer in a few moments. It looked from here as if the king was really quite upset at the man. Was he visibly angered by what took place?"

"Oh yes. You could see that the king was really steamed by the interruption, particularly on international TV. The king has always been sensitive to how his people come across to the rest of the world. The fact that his kingdom is occupied by Rome has always been a rather sensitive issue with him, and what he lacks in real power, many believe he tries to make up in appearance. To have a fellow Jew stand up on international TV and practically call him a coward and a traitor I'm sure sent Herod through the roof. You could tell toward the end he could barely contain himself."

"Gerry, one of our people here in the newsroom recognized the speech that the man was using to make his point as the one used by Marc Antony in the Shakespearean play *Julius Caesar*. Interestingly enough, Marc Antony uses that speech to point out the hypocrisy of those who had just assassinated Caesar, sarcastically using the phrase over and over that Brutus, one of the assassins and best friend to Caesar, was an 'honorable man.' Gerry, do you believe the man was trying to make a political statement as well as to protest what had happened?"

"Well, Gary, it is rare that things happen in this part of the world by accident. Now I must confess that I haven't read much Shakespeare since high school, so I can't really comment on the piece used by this man, but I can tell you that if what you say is true, and of course I don't doubt it if you say it is, then that parody, if you will, was used exactly in the manner you suggested."

"Gerry, I guess a question that begs to be asked at this point is: What do you think is going to happen to the man? I, along with millions of other people, saw that he was escorted out of the building. Was he being arrested?"

"Well, Gary, I really don't know. I do know that it is unlikely that anything serious is going to happen to him, at least not right away, because all of this took place on international TV. The king did make a point to tell the guards not to hurt him, and so I imagine he will be all right. Of course, once all of the media attention dies down and most of the international press corps leaves, then I would suspect that there could be a real chance that some serious harm could come to the man. Herod after all has the reputation of being quite ruthless to his enemies, along with having the memory of an elephant, so I'm sure that whoever that fellow was, he now has a powerful enemy in King Herod. Gary?"

"Gerry, how did you assess the man's condition. He appeared to us to be slightly inebriated."

"He seemed a bit more than slightly inebriated, Gary, but he also seemed at times to be quite overcome with grief. At moments you could see tears in the man's eyes when he talked particularly about Jesus aiding and walking with the poor and about his love for the man."

"Gerry, we have to go to a station break, and then we are going to go to our local news. We are still tying to identify exactly who the man was who interrupted the king's news conference and castigated both his king and his fellow countrymen for their lack of support for Jesus and for their alliance with Rome. For Gerry Simmons in Judea and the rest of the news team, this is Gary Thomas in New York."

When the cameras stopped rolling and the lights dimmed, Gerry went to find David. He was standing in a hallway alone, looking out over a courtyard full of flowers and statues of gods and warriors. Gerry tapped him on the shoulder. "David, what did you think of the day's events, my friend. I'll tell you one thing, you people are never dull."

David turned to face her. "It was what kept us alive all these years, the fact that you could never tell what was going to happen in the Middle East from one day to the next. It keeps our occupiers off guard," he said with a wry smile.

"Seriously," said Gerry, "do you think the king's conscience was bothered by that guy who stood up and condemned him on international TV? I can't imagine Herod having much of a conscience."

"I think the king was upstaged," said David, "and that bothered the hell out of him. This was supposed to be his show. How dare some lunatic get on the air and talk about things that would shame the heart of every Jewish bureaucrat in Israel? If you want to be prophetic, be prophetic on your own time, not on mine, is what Herod was probably thinking."

"Did you see what happened to the man?" Gerry asked.

"They whisked him away once they got him outside. I tell you one thing. That guy was either on something, was just plain nuts, or was some kind of saint. Because Herod is going to be after him like white on rice once everybody clears out of town. He has got to know that he has signed his own death warrant."

"I'm afraid you might be right. If Jesus was the messiah sent to do battle against Rome and this guy was one of his foot soldiers, I'm afraid the score is about to become two to nothing in favor of the empire."

David nodded and said, "Amen."

– CHAPTER THIRTEEN –

MARCUS WAS RIDING through the narrow, twisting streets toward the king's palace when he was suddenly surrounded by members of the Praetorian Guard.

"Commander Marcus, please come with us," said the captain of the guard as he pointed east of Marcus's original destination. Surrounded, Marcus rode off with them, not knowing exactly what was going on, assuming Sejanus wanted to be briefed about the investigation.

They came to a secluded house on the outskirts of town. The house was surrounded by security officers, members of the guard, and Roman secret police. Guards were everywhere, as if a summit conference involving the heads of every major country in the hemisphere was taking place inside. Marcus knew all this meant that Sejanus was inside, and this time their meeting was to be "official." "Still," he thought, "this seems like an awful lot of firepower even for Sejanus."

Marcus dismounted and was escorted to the door of the house. A dozen or more guards were posted by the door. Marcus moved through them and entered a large but bare room. Sejanus — his face dour but his uniform magnificent, adorned with gold — stood in the middle of the space.

Marcus spoke first: "I have done as you asked, sir, and have spoken to most of the key people who would have had something to do with the Jesus situation. I have not yet written a report but am prepared to give you my report orally if you wish."

"Hold your report, commander, and follow me," was Sejanus's only comment. Marcus followed Sejanus up a flight of stairs, past even more members of the Praetorian Guard and secret police. Sejanus knocked once and opened the door to the back room of the house where Marcus was given the shock of his life. Nothing had prepared him for what he now saw; for there, seated at the head of the table in this rather large room, sat the emperor himself.

He wore his crown and a pure white tunic with purple stripes at the hems. Marcus stared for a moment, trying to regain his composure, and then noticed other high-ranking members of the royal council were present. In fact, it seemed the emperor's entire council was present.

"Your highness," said Sejanus, "please permit me to introduce Commander Marcus, the officer put in charge of reviewing the empire's role in the execution of Jesus. Commander Marcus, your sovereign lord and majesty, the emperor of Rome."

Marcus had never met the emperor and had never — ambitious as he was — seriously believed he would ever meet him face-to-face except on some sort of reception line at the palace someday, along with hundreds of other guests.

He began to search his mind for the appropriate greeting for the emperor. Was he to say "Hail Caesar" to Caesar? He knew one said that to everyone else of importance in the empire. Was he to salute, or should he bow first? "What do I do?" he kept thinking. Finally he raised his right fist in the air, hit his chest (a little harder than he meant to), and said, "Greetings noble Caesar, and welcome to Judea."

The emperor smiled at Marcus, knowing what kind of effect his presence was having on this unsuspecting officer. The emperor then said, "Thank you, commander, I am pleased to be here."

The emperor made a gesture signaling Marcus to sit and spoke calmly: "I guess you are somewhat surprised to see your emperor here in your little part of the world. Well, commander, frankly, I'm a bit surprised to see me here as well. Let me tell you why we are here. General Sejanus phoned me yesterday and said he was about to come here and get an initial report from you concerning this little matter of Jesus' death. Many of my council members have developed quite a bit of concern over this matter, and when the general told me of his visit, one of my cabinet members said he wanted to go along and hear the information firsthand. I told him that I was sure the general would give us an accurate account of what took place here, but the council member insisted on going along. Well, before you knew it, more of my advisers were asking to come and hear from you firsthand just what took place. It appears you have become quite a celebrity among my councilors and cabinet members.

"Well, before you could say 'Great Caesar's Ghost,' fights started to break out as to who should come and speak with you personally and who should not. That is when I decided that maybe we all should come down and benefit firsthand from your keen investigative skills. Of course, my general here did not like the idea of any of us coming at all. He felt, and perhaps quite rightly, that he should be the one to come and question you himself, and then report back to us in Rome. I am sure that you have already experienced the, shall we say, quite persuasive personality of the general here. But I promised him that we would try not to encumber his powerful presence here. We simply wanted to hear firsthand for ourselves just what happened. When his lordship the general protested still further, I gently reminded him who was emperor of Rome."

Marcus could feel the tension in the room when the emperor made that last remark. He also believed that if any other person in the whole empire had made a remark like that in Sejanus's presence, Sejanus would have cut that person to shreds.

"So you see, commander, we are all interested in what you have found out."

Suddenly the emperor began to laugh, for he could see the apprehension still on Marcus's face.

"Well, commander, perhaps I should be a bit more candid with you. I don't want to put any undue pressure on you — I'm sure a soldier's getting a sudden visit from his emperor, especially in this part of the world, is a bit nerve-racking — but we wanted to get as close as possible to the source of information about what happened. I was a soldier once too, you know, so I have some idea what you are going through." He and everyone in the room began to laugh again — everyone, that is, except Sejanus, who looked as cold as ice.

"For a long time I had been promising King Herod that I would favor him with a visit in order to dedicate the city that he is graciously building in my honor. Pilate also has been after me to come here for a state visit, though he was never really able to articulate to my satisfaction just why. So we thought now would be a good time to come and visit this part of our realm, having never been here before."

The emperor pulled a handkerchief from beneath his tunic and began to wipe his brow, for it was truly hot now that it was midday.

"I called the governor personally last evening and told him of our visit here. I am seeing him some time later this afternoon. I first wanted to speak with you and hear your report. Now, commander, let us have your report. Just tell us in your own words how you would assess the whole situation from beginning to end. Please be honest to us in your report. I can tell you now that we believe you have done a very thorough and fine job, and you need not fear any recriminations from us based on what you tell us. Tell us who you spoke with and what your evaluation of each visit to each person was."

Marcus still did not feel comfortable, but he had just been ordered to tell all he knew. It was then that he realized he had not fully had the chance to digest all that he had learned from his visits to Pilate, Caiaphas, and, most of all, Demetrius. What was he going to tell the emperor about Demetrius? He knew that he had to say something about the experience Demetrius had had with Jesus, but he wasn't sure just what. He thought that he had settled this in his mind already but realized quite painfully that he still had not.

It was then that he also realized he had not spoken to one important person on the list: the young soldier at the execution site, the one who, when Jesus died, supposedly had some sort of "reaction" that did not seem to fit the behavior of a Roman soldier. He realized he had come to the conclusion that the young soldier's reaction would help explain what had happened to Demetrius. He also realized he had been putting off talking to the young officer because he was not sure he wanted to reach a conclusion about his close friend.

"Commander? Are you with us?"

Marcus knew he could stall no longer: "Your highness, I only had time to put together a preliminary report in my head, and as yet I have nothing in writing. I will of course give to your highness and your council members all of the information I do have, but..."

"Commander, just tell us what you have, and kindly skip the commentary." The voice was startlingly frank. It was the voice of Sejanus.

"Your highness, while I have as I said made only a preliminary investigation of the events leading up to the death of Jesus, it is my considered opinion that all that took place was not a part of any elaborate conspiracy to embarrass the empire. I believe that the Jewish priesthood acted in what they believed was their own best interest, and Pilate was backed into a corner due to a set of circumstances over which he had very little control."

"Interesting commander," said the emperor. "First tell me why you believe the Jewish priesthood acted in their own best interest in this matter, and why you believe that their interest was not in conflict with ours."

"I believe they did so because Jesus in their eyes had become a considerable threat to their stability. In a relatively short period of time, he became the most prolific speaker to come out of these parts in many years, and he apparently had a gift for making the common people lose their fear of both them and us. In short, he began convincingly posing as their divine protector from heaven. At least that is how they seem to have interpreted his ministry. And the priesthood believed that Jesus was sooner or later going to move the majority of the people from their side over to his. They saw that as potentially disastrous, because they knew that in the event that took place, they would become less useful to us.

"His Lordship Sejanus in our first meeting believed that that fear could be at the bottom of much of this, and I believe his original interpretation of the circumstances was indeed correct. I do not feel that they were either clever enough or motivated enough to use this as a way to affect some change in the status quo as regards their relationship with Rome."

"So you are telling us," said the emperor, "that you do not believe that their motives in getting us involved in this were in any way connected to a plot to embarrass the empire and to make us look like fools in the eyes of the world?"

"No, your highness, I do not, at least not from my preliminary investigation. I just don't believe from talking with the high priest that he was looking that far in the future. I believe that if they could have executed Jesus on their own, they would have done so without ever involving us. I base this on one simple premise: I do not believe Caiaphas has enough foresight and cleverness to pull off such a complex coup. I believe instead that his motives were based on his religious patriotism. He believes that extremism in the pursuit of Judaism is no vice. He has come to the conclusion that the only way his God's message is going to get out to the people is if the temple survives. Therefore, he will do anything to see that it survives, and I do mean anything. And that is why he will never be a threat to us. He has lost faith in his deity's ability to survive without the temple; therefore, he believes that nothing he does in defense of the temple can be wrong. As long as we threaten the temple, your highness, we will always have Caiaphas and people like him in our pocket."

At this point one of the council members broke in to speak: "I believe the commander has given us a very astute observation. I have seen this kind of superpatriotic fervor. It is very common throughout the empire."

"The empire?" said another member. "It is common throughout the world. I seem to remember an American president having to leave his job because he and a group of superpatriots believed that their republic would not survive unless their party was in power. They did all kinds of crazy things in the name of patriotism, including breaking into the other party's headquarters. I remember reading about one guy, one of the burglars, who used to put his hands over cigarette lighters to show those who worked for him that he was a leader capable of withstanding great pain. He did this so that his men would follow him anywhere. Of course it turned out he wanted them to follow him into the other side's campaign headquarters to steal some files or something."

A few of the councilors began to laugh, and another member took up the story: "There was another guy even more recently than that, a decorated war hero who got caught dealing in an arms-for-hostage scandal against the American laws. His own president was getting on TV and denying that such an operation would ever take place in America, and yet this guy was doing it right under their noses. Before you know it he was shredding papers late into the night, hiding stuff from many of his superior officers, all in the name of patriotism. When he got caught and was brought before his own governing board, he lied through his teeth. He obviously felt that even his own parliament or whatever they call it was not as patriotic as he was."

"Yes," said another member of the emperor's council, "but did you notice how he was received by the general public? They loved the guy. He was seen by many as a hero, the only one who had the guts to stand up for his country. Why they even..."

"Gentlemen, gentlemen please, cried the emperor. Can we get back to the commander's report. Save your discussions for the trip home."

The emperor turned to Marcus: "Do you see what I have to put up with, commander? Everyone wants to be an expert on everything. Please forgive them. They don't get out much as a group." The emperor smiled and resumed: "So you believe that Caiaphas is on the level because he is of the belief that the only way his religion is going to survive is if the temple is left standing, and, therefore, his protection of the temple is the same to him as protecting Judaism itself, is that correct?"

"Yes, your highness. I don't believe he would have risked our vengeance on the temple for any sort of political gain. He did what he did purely to get Jesus out of the way. He knew that if the people had followed Jesus to the point where the authorities lost control over them, they might have begun to revolt first against the priesthood and then perhaps against us. Caiaphas was fully aware that if that were to happen, we would have come in and crushed any such revolt and maybe the temple along with it. He saw that as the destruction of God among them, and he could never have lived with the idea that all of this took place while he was the high priest. I truly believe that that was his entire motivation."

"Was there any reason why the event took place when it did, commander?"

"I believe it had to do with several variables all culminating at once. Jesus had received a huge welcome into Jerusalem just prior to this taking place, and this time of year passions run high among the Jewish people. There was also a general belief that despite the big crowds on Sunday, Jesus' ministry was on the wane; therefore, if Jesus was going to make some kind of move, this would have been the time for him to do so. The temple authorities may have felt that if they were going to move against him, it was now or never. I also believe that the Sanhedrin may have been encouraged by the lack of response on the part of the people to the death of John the Baptist. They may have felt that they could use that fact — while it was still fresh in everyone's mind — to persuade the governor to their way of thinking."

"Speaking of whom, tell me, commander, how you would assess the performance of your governor here in Judea. Again, I advise you to be honest. You have my word as your emperor that everything you share with us will be kept strictly confidential. Are we agreed on that, gentlemen?" the emperor said looking around the room.

There was a general nod of agreement. The emperor, however, seemed to feel the need to emphasize the point even further: "Need I remind anyone here that this meeting is strictly classified under national security?"

There was a silence that signaled agreement throughout the room.

"Very well, commander, please continue."

"Your highness, after a rather lengthy interview with the governor, I came to the conclusion that he acted responsibly in most of the situations leading up to the death of Jesus."

"You said most, commander. What did you mean by most?" Once again the icy voice of Sejanus filled the room, as if a door had suddenly blown open on a wintry day and a blast of arctic air had invaded the premises.

"General, put away your sabre and please let the commander tell this in his own way," said the emperor. For the first time Sejanus showed signs of irritation. He got up from his chair and walked over toward an open window. One could not help feel sorry for the trees that had to endure Sejanus's gaze at that moment, for the stare was surely lethal.

One of the council members rose and whispered into the ear of the emperor. The two of them then rose, walked to where Sejanus stood, and began speaking in low voices. Marcus had a few moments to gather his thoughts, and it was then, during the curious little exchange between the emperor and Sejanus, that Marcus's mind took him on a little journey that would change his life forever. Something very disturbing was happening to him. He couldn't figure out why what just happened in the room zoomed him off in this direction.

He noticed for the first time just how uncomfortable he felt in the midst of all this intense power. Being ambitious, he had always hoped to one day belong to this inner circle of Roman power. Yet there was something about the way the emperor talked to Sejanus — in a manner that others would never dream of using — and about the way all of the senators and other council members really seemed to fit into this power elite that made him feel like an outsider. He had never before seen the corridors of real political power this close up but always had assumed he would naturally fit in if ever given the opportunity. Could this mean that he would never belong?

As he thought about it, he realized that wasn't quite it. Rather, his unease stemmed from his terrible feeling that these men — men of extraordinary power — did not see him as a real symbol of Roman authority in Judea. In fact, to them he was not much different from Caiaphas, Herod, Judas, Jesus, or anybody else in the region. He was simply a pawn. And men like the emperor or Sejanus didn't take pawns seriously because they were too small, too insignificant. Men of their caliber always dealt with issues of power, global stability, international economics, and so on. Pawns were the least of their concerns because pawns were always expendable.

He began to think back to some of the conversations he had had over the past few days with the men he had interrogated in the Jesus affair. He remembered Pilate proclaiming he would stick by Marcus no matter what, but he now knew that if it came to a choice between Marcus's life or career and the good of the empire, Pilate wouldn't hesitate for a moment to hand him over to Sejanus. If the men in this room determined that — no matter what the truth was — Marcus had to be purged, then the emperor or Sejanus would have him purged and not lose a moment's rest over it.

And what about Caiaphas, the superpatriot? How easily all the men in room understood his position in all of this. Of course they all understood it. Caiaphas put the temple above the people it was supposedly there to serve. To Caiaphas, it didn't matter how many of his people suffered as a result of actions taken in order to keep his temple standing. The temple must survive, and the kings and queens and bishops must be protected to carry out the grand mandates. Pawns, you sacrifice.

All the men sitting at the table would also have easily understood the decision to release Barabbas. After all, that only meant a few more people would die, but the institution would remain safe. People dying was always a small price to pay for the preservation of grand ideas and noble institutions. Did Pilate's lack of ability to foresee what choice the Sanhedrin would make, if given the opportunity to choose between a man and the temple, contribute toward these men's overall feeling of his incompetence? He should have known that an individual, even of Jesus' caliber, was far less important than the temple itself. The people were not Caiaphas's major concern. History, religion, and law came first for him.

And what did it matter to men like Sejanus that Antoni Demetrius was perhaps the most loyal soldier ever to have served in the Roman army? What would his personal service to the empire be worth in comparison to history, gods, and nations?

Marcus was at a loss as to what was happening to him. Why was he suddenly feeling all of this? Why had the emperor's seemingly simple castigation of Sejanus brought out such intensive soul searching?

It was then that he began to hear the voice of his old friend Demetrius saying over and over again, "Marcus, the man had no eyes," referring to the supposed miracle that Jesus had performed on the blind beggar Bartimeus. It was then that all he had ever heard or known about Jesus came rushing forward in his mind and filled him with anguish.

Demetrius had said that he knew Jesus possessed power, real power, of a kind not found here in this room where the most powerful people in the empire were gathered. Jesus "ordered" Demetrius's son to get well, and according to Demetrius, the entire heavens obeyed him. If this were true, then surely Jesus possessed a power far greater than anyone gathered here. Demetrius knew about the power gathered in this room even better than Marcus did, and yet he said that Jesus possessed real power, a power that was greater than anything found on this earth.

And yet there was a distinct difference between Jesus and the powerbrokers here before him. In the name of the empire, or the temple, or the Jewish kingdom, anything and everyone else was ultimately expendable. In the name of Jesus' power, the only one expendable was Jesus himself.

Marcus remembered reading once that Jesus had said, "Greater love has no man than he give up his life for his friends." Marcus had believed that whoever had made out the report containing that statement misunderstood what Jesus had said. He was sure that the report had to have read, "...give up his life for his kingdom, or his country, or his temple." That concept was indeed simple for someone like Marcus to understand. "We Romans," he thought, "understand this idea well. In fact we probably invented the saying." Now he understood for the first time that Jesus did indeed mean "his friends," because he was not willing to sacrifice anyone for an institution, not even his beloved so-called kingdom of God. That was how the whole rest of the world worked. People could always be sacrificed for countries or institutions. Yet Jesus was only willing to sacrifice himself. Everyone else he wanted to save. And yet this was a man who had power to make blind men see?

Marcus remembered watching an old black and white news report that played a tape of the Indian prophet Gandhi saying to his followers, "There are many things I am willing to die for, but nothing I am willing to kill for." Marcus reflected that because the British Empire did not put Gandhi to death, he went on to bring the empire to its knees, eventually forcing the British to give up a valuable piece of their kingdom. He remembered how the talk around the Roman Empire was that they not only should have locked him up but should have dispatched him to Allah. Then perhaps India would still belong to the British. Like Jesus, Gandhi claimed a closeness to God and would not take up arms, or sacrifice anyone's life but his own, not even to win independence. And yet, he still defeated the people of power.

Marcus didn't notice it, but the emperor, Sejanus, and the council members were beginning to walk back to their seats. "Commander, are you with us?"

Marcus felt like an actor who suddenly realizes he has forgotten his lines while on stage, knowing that any minute he is due to give a major speech. He kept hearing the emperor humiliate the most dangerous and powerful man in the empire in front of this roomful of people, including a lowly commander in the military. What would Sejanus do to get back at him? What people in the empire would be sacrificed to atone for this insult? Everything at this level was done at a cost to someone — that is the way the channels of real power work. Someone would pay; someone always does.

Marcus began to think back to how he had operated as a soldier, and he began to see how his rise in rank affected his outlook on people. He began to see how expendable people had become in his own life. Had he not treated the men under him with less and less compassion the higher he rose in rank? Had he not cared less and less for the feelings of individual people the more he felt responsible for the good of the empire? Marcus always believed that to be a sign he was becoming a better soldier. He remembered hearing someone say something quite similar regarding the death of Jesus: "Is it not better for one man to die than for the nation to suffer?"

Yes, he thought about how uncomfortable he felt in this room, but he was then reminded of how uncomfortable he had felt among superior officers when he was a rookie soldier, or when he had first met the company commander of his first post. But as he grew in rank and maturity, he always managed to get over his feelings. . . .

That is when a new and frightening revelation hit him: he need not fear never fitting into the halls of real power. He knew indeed he would be able to fit into this circle one day. All he had to do was give up a little more of himself as he rose up the ladder of success, just like he had been doing all along. If he gave up being Marcus the man and became simply Marcus the soldier, then before long he would indeed be ready to assume real command. After all, who was the most feared and loyal member of the empire? It was Lucius Sejanus, the man whom no one ever thought of today as a mere human. He was the epitome of Roman power, and everyone knew he would sacrifice anything, and anyone, to see that the empire survived. He rose so quickly in rank because he learned the lesson early. Even as a young captain in the Roman Secret Police he realized that ruthlessness was necessary to empire building, and in order to get truly ruthless, you first have to die to self and become a part of a machinery, a machinery that was designed for the good of the people who are so easily sacrificed to it.

Marcus remembered one of the earlier legends already circulating about Jesus, one about him supposedly meeting the devil. The devil said to him that he would give Jesus real power — the kind the Roman Empire understood — if Jesus would give up preaching and practicing another kind of power. According to the legend, the devil offered Jesus the devil's own empire, the kind that all in this room were not only prepared to die for (or so they might say) but prepared to have others die for as well. Jesus rejected it in favor of some other kind of power, one that he suggested is far greater. Greater than the power of Rome? It was because Jesus had supposedly made that kind of choice that Marcus knew the story was only a legend, dreamed up by fanatical followers no doubt.

"Commander? Do we have your attention?"

Marcus realized he was hearing the voice of the emperor. "How long have I been on this crazy flight of fancy?" he thought. "Have I been asked questions and not answered?" Marcus had never behaved this way before. What was happening to him and why?

"You were telling us that you believed the governor acted responsibly to the empire in most ways. You were about to explain when the general interrupted you."

"Please forgive me, your highness. Yes, I believed that Pilate did act with the best interests of the empire in mind because he never wanted to execute Jesus but was forced into in part by the treaty and in part by Jesus' unwillingness to defend himself against the charges. I believe..."

"Very good, commander, I am happy to hear that. Now tell me about your comrade Centurion Demetrius."

"That's it?" he thought. "That's all you want to hear about the governor? Don't you want to know the particulars? That is, after all, why you have come here, is it not? Why do you want to now hear about Demetrius? He had less to do with this than any of you."

And then like a door opening and closing in his mind, he suddenly realized something — the investigation was over. "This thing has been settled," Marcus thought to himself. "This is becoming old news already, and everyone in this room is ready to get back down to empire business. The only thing left in all of this is deciding who's going to pay the bill." Marcus considered who would be the scapegoat: the emperor, Sejanus, Herod, Pilate, the valuable territory of Israel, the temple whose motives everyone here understood so well? Was it the loyal commander who gathered the material, or would it be the person whom he was to report on next? Someone was going to pay.

Who would it be? He remembered Demetrius telling him to play it absolutely straight with "them" if he did not want to end up like Demetrius, and the suggestion now seemed ludicrous. They were both loyal soldiers, he had thought to himself at the time — surely nothing could ever happen to them as long as they both remained loyal to the empire.

And now suddenly there was a great interest in the centurion's behavior in all of this. Sure the emperor had come to Judea, but it was not to find out everything — somewhere in the last few days the realization had set in that nobody was going to care that much in the end what had happened to Jesus. Finding out the truth was less important now than finding someone to pay for all the trouble this had caused. Because as everyone knows, gods always demand a sacrifice for being troubled.

Marcus took a deep breath and began to speak very slowly: "Your highness, I believe that the centurion was profoundly moved by a personal encounter with Jesus that greatly affected his feelings toward the evangelist, but did not in any way compromise his loyalty to the empire."

"How were his feelings greatly affected toward this rebel?" asked one of the council members.

"Rebel?" thought Marcus. "Now we suddenly refer to him as this rebel? A short time ago everyone traveled here to find out who was responsible for putting this prophet to death, thus causing the empire embarrassment in the eyes of the world. Now he is a common rebel."

"According to the centurion, Jesus healed his son from a serious, and indeed life-threatening, illness. Just how it was done remains somewhat of a mystery, but the centurion swears that it is so."

"And tell me, commander, in your professional opinion as a soldier sworn to protect the vital interests of the empire, do you believe that this association with Jesus could in any way interfere with his duties as an officer in the imperial army of Rome?"

All eyes in the room turned toward Marcus. He knew he had to give an answer, and in his mind he knew exactly what that answer would be.

"Be careful how you answer this, commander," said Sejanus.

"You can use all of the force you can muster from hell, your lordship," Marcus thought. "There is no way I am going to sell my friend down the river. I know that Demetrius is the most loyal member of the empire, even more so than you or I. If Demetrius had thought for a moment that Jesus was a threat, he would have followed that through to its end, not just to the place where expediency becomes the catchword for the day. He would never decide that once public opinion died down, there was a need to do only what was right for politics. He would want to know if the empire was indeed in trouble and would pursue the truth, no matter where it led the investigation. There is no way I will ever tell this crowd before me that my friend was a threat, never."

"Commander, I am waiting for your answer. Do you believe that because of the centurion's encounter with Jesus, that he is either now, or could become, a threat to the empire?"

"I asked the centurion that exact question, and he has assured me that no matter what would happen in the future regarding Jesus, or his followers, he would always remain true to the empire."

"Commander," said the emperor, "I did not ask you what the centurion told you on his own behalf. We want to know what you believe. Do you believe that the centurion might become a threat some day, or do you believe that he will always, absolutely be loyal to whatever the empire orders him to do? The question is clear, is it not? Now answer it!"

As Marcus formed the words, "Yes, he will always be loyal," in his mind, he heard a stranger deep within his soul say out loud the words, *I do not know.* The words fell to the ground with the weight of a dead man, and he almost tried to physically grab them before they totally left his lips.

Marcus sat for what seemed like years in this now painful, wooden chair as he tried to assess what had just taken place. What had he done? Why had he said what he did? Did he just sell out his friend for the sake of the empire?

"Well, thank you, commander, for your fine work in investigating this matter. I have good news for you. It appears this whole affair turned out to be less of a public relations problem then we all had thought. It seems the world is already getting back to normal and that in a few short years, few people will even remember this Jesus fellow. From my earlier conversation with Pilate, I too believe he acted with the best interest of the empire in mind, what with the treaty and all. As you know, your governor hasn't always acted with the most prudence, but in this case, perhaps he is learning something about leadership. Anyway, the good news is I am hereby ordering a complete suspension of all investigations into the matter of Jesus' death in regard to its relation to the empire. I am returning you to your post where you may assume command of your old duties."

At that the emperor stood, signaling an end to the meeting. Everyone else stood as well and began to talk among themselves. In the midst of all of this, Sejanus walked over to Marcus, took him by the arm, and began to escort him toward the door. "No," Marcus thought to himself, "this is all happening too fast." He needed time to say something more about his friend. He needed to say that he did not mean his words to come out the way they did and that Demetrius was more loyal than anyone. He wanted to say something about patriotism not ever being worth sacrificing someone else's life for. Yet he could not get the words out in time, and before he could say much more of anything, he was out the door standing alone with Sejanus.

"Sir," said Marcus, "I am afraid I may have . . ."

Sejanus cut him off before he could continue. "The centurion is no longer your concern, commander. We will deal with him now."

For the first time, Sejanus did not seem larger than life to Marcus.

"Sir, I do not wish for my friend to die. He is a loyal soldier and will not be a threat to the empire. I know this to be true. I do not know what made me hesitate inside, but you must inform the emperor that Antoni Demetrius is truly loyal."

"It is a little late for that, don't you think, commander? Besides, you worry much too much over the welfare of your friend. When I came to see you in your home at the beginning of this, I told you never to let your loyalty to your friends interfere with you responsibilities to the empire. Inside you did not, and that has not gone unnoticed by the emperor and, of equal importance, by me. Now let me let you in on a little national security secret. The decision as to what to do with the centurion was made well before you arrived. Once we knew that this whole affair would not turn out as we had feared, we went to see the centurion ourselves."

"Sir, why? You had not yet received my report on what took place."

"Oh, we already knew what was said long before you came here today. We knew about every word, even when you took that little stroll in the garden. We knew the moment you left what our decision concerning Centurion Demetrius would be. What took place inside this room was an assessment of your own ability to serve in the imperial army of Rome. You did well, commander, and because you did, I will not mention to the emperor your little outburst here. Farewell, commander, your services will not go unnoticed by the empire."

Saying that Sejanus turned and walked back inside the room. Marcus was again surrounded by Praetorian Guard members who escorted him down the steps. Before they reached the bottom, he heard Sejanus say from the top of the stairs: "Do not try and contact your friend or his family ever again. They are alive and will remain so. They will no longer be located where you last saw them. They have been exiled." He then came down the steps toward Marcus and whispered, "Your extracting from him that oath of loyalty may have saved his life."

Sejanus put out his hand toward Marcus. Marcus, though quite confused, was about to shake Sejanus's hand when he heard from Sejanus the words, "The ring."

Marcus remembered the ring that was given to him by Sejanus and removed it from his breastplate pocket. Sejanus took it, turned, walked back up the stairs, and disappeared behind the door, slamming it shut.

A short time later Marcus sat in his study, still wondering what had happened. How in such a short amount of time could things have turned around so dramatically in his life? Who could have imagined that the execution of Jesus would ever have had such an impact on his world? And what had he done to Demetrius? Had he in fact saved his life or helped send him into exile?

Marcus knew he had to talk to someone about all that had taken place. But who? It was then that his phone rang. Marcus did not answer it because although he knew he needed to talk, he didn't feel like speaking to just anyone about trivial matters. After six rings, his answering machine picked up. Marcus waited for his own message to play and then listened to hear who was on the line. A familiar voice sounded: "Hi, Commander Marcus, this is Gerry Simmons. I was wondering if you wanted to get together for that drink soon. The strangest thing has happened. I'm being recalled to the States. It seems the Jesus story has lost the public's interest. A big multiple murder has just taken place in the Bronx, and a fire has burned down one of the city's oldest department stores. There's some speculation that it was due to a terrorist bombing. My editor thinks we have gotten just about all there is to get here, and even though I told him that we were uncovering some interesting new stuff, he has ordered me home, so if we're going to have that drink, we'd better do it soon. Give me a call. I'm still at the same place."

When the phone clicked, Marcus thought that seeing Gerry would be a good idea. He would send her a note after he pulled himself together. He shook his head in disbelief at the very notion of his having to struggle to get his emotions under control.

He walked across the room and looked in the mirror. His handsome, rugged face looked a little more worn than usual, and for the first time in his adult life, he felt tears, real tears, well up in his eyes.

"The man had no eyes," he kept hearing his best friend Demetrius say. And then he sat down again in his chair and stared into space. He wished he could be healed of this moment.

– CHAPTER FOURTEEN –

GERRY WAS IN HER HOTEL ROOM packing when a cable news station interrupted its regular broadcast: "Well, ladies and gentlemen, there is a new twist to the story of the death of the well-known evangelist and civil-rights worker Jesus. Early this morning when mourners went to his grave site, they found that his grave had been apparently broken into, and his body had been evidently removed from the grave. No one has yet claimed responsibility for this bizarre act, but as of late this morning, the body of Jesus has disappeared and is listed as missing. What is perhaps strangest of all is the fact that Rome had posted guards right outside of the tomb of Jesus, and yet when questioned they did not seem to have seen who the culprit or culprits were, or for what purpose the body was taken. . . . "

Marcus was livid. "Now what?" he thought. "Hasn't this thing gone on long enough and caused enough trouble without this happening? Jesus was far less trouble when he was alive than he is now that he is dead," was the only thought that went through his mind.

A few moments later he marched into headquarters, wearing civilian clothes since he was off duty and was soon to meet Gerry Simmons for a farewell drink.

"Who was in charge of guarding the tomb?" he yelled with real anger in his voice. I want them in here, *now!* A short time later, the two men who were in charge of guarding the tomb, along with their immediate supervisor, crowded into Marcus's office.

"Gentlemen, I have to tell you, before you say a word, that I'm really sick and tired of the general incompetence I'm seeing around here. So whatever you have to tell me better be damn good because I am in no mood to hear any nonsense."

The sergeant in charge turned to the two men and instructed them to tell Marcus everything they had told him earlier.

"Chief, it's like we told the sarge, we don't know exactly what happened. We were guarding the tomb, and except for some women visitors who we had just let pass, nothing much was going on. Suddenly, we feel something like an earthquake; I swear, that's what it felt like. We both started running around to see what was going on, like if any houses were falling down. What seemed so strange was that nothing seemed to be disturbed, no buildings were crumbling, nothing. We headed back to the tomb when suddenly we hear a scream. We run back toward the entrance of the tomb when first we see that the stone in front of it has been moved back. This surprised the crap out of us because, as you know, it took six of our guys including Captain Vergas to move that SOB rock, but we never saw anyone run past us. We figure the earthquake we felt moved it, but again, the rock seemed to be the only thing disturbed. No trees are knocked over, no other stones seem to be out of place, nothing. We run inside the entrance, and there we see the women we just let pass, standing inside the tomb. One of them turns to me and says, 'What have you done with our Master's body?' I say to her, 'What the hell are you talking about?' At that point, we both look around and, sure enough, the body is missing. It's gone. We search the place high and low, looking for the damn corpse. Nothing, it's gone."

At this point, the other guard continued the story: "Now we turn to the women inside and ask them what happened. They both say they came to say some prayers at the grave site; when they get here the stone has been moved away and the body is gone. Then they tell us that someone inside the tomb told them not to look in there because this place is for dead people, or something like that. I tell them that they must be drunk or something, because the only people up here are us and them. At first we thought they somehow snatched it."

"Yeah," said the other guard, "we thought they were acting, or putting us on in some way. But, chief, I tell you they were not acting. This one woman was almost hysterical. If they were acting, they both deserve Academy Awards because they were damn near frantic."

Marcus had long been known and admired as a soldier who went about his work, no matter what it was, in a thoroughly cool and professional manner. He was particularly admired for the calm he showed under fire. Now, though, he glared at his subordinates and spoke with real anger and passion: "Get to the point," he yelled. "What happened up there?"

"Well, chief, it's like we were saying: the women were hysterical and crying and accusing us of hiding the body. I told Julius here to stay inside and see that nobody leaves, and I went outside to have another look around. I looked around the grounds, behind every rock, and I swear, there was nothing. Nobody anywhere."

"Then," said Marcus, "someone must have come up, moved the body and taken it away. Did you men leave your post any time during the night?"

"Chief, Julius and I were there all night. And there is only one way up that hill toward the entrance to that cave. Plus, as I said, it would have had to have been at least five or six guys, because that stone is one heavy SOB. There isn't any way that many guys could have come up that path without one of us seeing them. And those women surely couldn't have budged that rock an inch."

"But even if a bunch of guys had somehow gotten past us," the other guard said, "there sure as hell isn't any way they could have moved that big rock without us hearing it. No way! Even if we had been asleep, the sound of that rock would have awakened even the dead. When those women came up the path, they were alone. Just when we let them past, we felt this thing like an earthquake. That's when we ran down the road and started looking around. About two minutes later is when we hear the screams. We ran back up the path, into the cave, and that's when we saw the women standing in the empty tomb crying about the body being missing and talking about some guy telling them that stuff about not looking in the tomb for the body."

Marcus interrupted them once again: "Didn't you see the stone move? Weren't you standing in front of the cave when this so-called earthquake struck? What about the women? Did they say anything about feeling this earthquake?"

"Every sixty minutes or so, we would walk down the path about a hundred yards just to look around and see if everything was quiet. We were just about halfway down the path when we saw the women coming up the road. We waved them through and walked about another fifty feet when we felt the rumbling. We turned and ran right back up the hill. We could not have been gone from the front of the tomb for more then five or six minutes. If some group did this, they would have had only that short amount of time to move that rock and take the body and escape. And when we started down the hill, that rock was solidly in place."

"What about this guy who spoke to these women, did you question them about him?" asked Marcus.

"Of course, we did, chief, but then they claim they can't find him either. That's when I thought they were making all of this up, but I tell you, chief, there is no way that in that short amount of time they could have taken the body out of the tomb, hid it somewhere, and run back into the tomb without either Julius or me seeing anything."

"So what the hell are you telling me?" Marcus yelled. "Are you telling me that the body of Jesus just got up and walked away? Are you saying he was perhaps transported out into goddamned space? Are you saying that Roman inefficiency runs so deep in my command that perhaps we never really killed him at all? We put holes in his hands and feet, stick a sword in his side, leave him on the cross for friggin' three hours, and still we didn't manage to kill him? He was able to just get up and walk away? Is that what I'm hearing?"

In his entire military life, Marcus had never raised his voice this much when speaking to the men under his command. He always believed that officers who had to yell at their men were not good commanding officers. He believed that the men had to be treated with quiet firmness. And yet, here he was yelling, almost at the top of his lungs, at these two soldiers.

For the first time, the men stopped calling him by the more familiar title of chief and began referring to him as sir.

"Sir, I can only tell you what I know, and what I know is that I have no idea how anybody could have gotten up that hill any time during the night with both of us on duty and somehow roll away that stone without either of us hearing a thing, snatch the body, and run off. That means, then, that the only time they could have done it was when we felt that earthquake, or whatever it was, because except for our six-minute walk down that small path every hour, that's the only time we left the front of that tomb. But that would have meant that the women would have had to know just when whatever happened there was going to happen. They would have had to have been calm enough, through the ground moving, to get the body, hide it in a damn good place, 'cause we sure couldn't find it, and then get back into the cave in a matter of a couple of minutes."

"I guess somebody managed to do exactly that," said the other guard, "because that body sure isn't anywhere to be found. We both went over every square inch of that tomb with a fine-tooth comb, and there wasn't any trace of the corpus delecti."

"Gentlemen," Marcus said, now restraining his anger, "I want you to sit down with the investigations officer and tell him in full detail everything that happened from the time you were born to this very minute. Is that clear? Then I want you to convey to him that I expect to have a report on my desk within the next couple of hours. And in that report there had better be some answers. This is the last straw. I will not have this kind of thing happening under my command. I'm going to have everybody from the governor to the press to the emperor himself breathing down my neck in a matter of hours, and I am not going to sit on the hot seat alone on this one. Is that understood? Dismissed."

The men headed toward the door when Marcus called out to them: "And by the way, gentlemen, consider yourselves on report until further notice, understood?"

"Yes, sir," they both replied and went through the door. The sergeant remained. He was a thirty-year veteran in the Roman army and had served in many parts of the empire. He was known as a real soldier's soldier and had seen many years of combat. He was due to retire in a few months. Everyone referred to him as either sergeant or J. R.

When the two soldiers left the office, Marcus turned to J. R. and, with a look of total desperation, said, "Whatever advice you might feel compelled to give, I don't want to hear it, is that clear?" Even though Marcus was half-serious, still he said it with warmth, because most of the men in his command reacted toward the sergeant that way, with genuine affection.

The sergeant playfully shrugged his solders and said, "Me? Not me, sir. I'm just standing here."

Marcus smiled for the first time in what seemed like hours, but he soon felt the smile fade from his face, and his mood once again turned sullen. "What do you think really happened up there?" he said to the older soldier.

"I have no idea, Marcus, I really don't. But I will tell you this. I know those two guys, and they are not the kind of soldiers who would either fall asleep on the job or just make something like this up to cover their tracks. If they say they don't know what happened up there, you can bet they truly don't. They're good soldiers. I know them both. I know their families; they're regular army, not like most of these mercenaries we hire in this part of the country. If it had been a couple of those mercenaries, I would think anything was possible, including the possibility of their snatching the body themselves in order to ransom it off later. But not these guys. That's why I gave them this assignment. I handpicked them myself, Marcus, and unless you no longer trust my judgment, you got to believe that whatever they are telling you is true to the best of their knowledge."

"So what do you think happened? Speculate, guess, lie, tell me something."

"Somebody got in there and took away the body of Jesus, pure and simple. And they did it in such a way that it completely pulled the wool over our eyes. They pulled it off while two veteran soldiers kept watch over the tomb. I don't know how they did it, but somehow they got it done."

"What do you mean?" Marcus asked the sergeant.

"Well, I've been in this business a long time, and I know human nature. Pilate was absolutely correct in his suspicions that someone would probably come along and try to steal the body of Jesus in order to make it seem like he mysteriously rose from the dead. It makes perfect sense if you're trying to build a movement around a mythical character like Jesus was. What better way to prove to these poor, backward people that everything they said about him when he was alive was true, than to have him rise from the dead after we put him into the hard, cold grave? Why they would have done it is very clear to me. What I don't know is how they did it."

"Well, they had to have done it sometime during the night, and the guards must have fallen asleep, or maybe they were drugged somehow and never knew they were asleep. Maybe while they were drugged, men came up the hill, took away the body, and put the stone back without our people ever knowing what happened to them. I want blood tests taken from both the guards and urine tests as well. Is that clear?"

"Yes, sir," said the sergeant. "But I doubt you'll find anything."

"Well, there has to be an answer to this, and I need to know what happened and soon. I believe that if I don't, Rome is going to come down on me with both feet. I can see Sejanus shipping me to the last outpost of the empire before the news of this even reaches the emperor. I'm still not sure that this whole Jesus affair, happening in my command, isn't going to end me up in a deep mess anyway. I got to see how the high command works, up close and personal. And I'm here to tell you, my old friend, there are a lot fewer things that are sacred in this man's empire than I ever thought before all this got started."

The sergeant looked inquiringly at Marcus and said: "It's why I never wanted a command position of my own, even though I was given the chance on more than one occasion to move up the ladder and become an officer. Besides, I believe men should work for a living. Unlike you guys, I never wanted the hassle of dealing with the higher ups. Let's face it, my boy, Rome did not get to where it is today without having people at the top who were willing to sacrifice a lot of people at the bottom. I wanted to stay low enough that I wouldn't be worth the effort if anything ever happened in my lifetime like this Jesus thing."

"I think I see what you mean," said Marcus. "Well, this thing was done with cunning and skill, I'll grant you that. But we'll learn how they did it, in the same way that we figured out about Judas and the rest." Marcus looked over at the sergeant and noticed he had his head down and had a slight smile on his face. He looked in that instant very wise.

"What are you grinning at, you old shark?" Marcus said with affection in his voice.

"Well, commander, there is one other possibility. A possibility that you, an officer, can never afford to seriously entertain I suppose, because you are ambitious and have your whole life and career ahead of you, while I am an old soldier who is about to fade away. Therefore, I can be forgiven for flights of fancy."

Marcus could not imagine what J. R. was getting at. "All right. What is the other possibility?" he asked.

"Maybe Jesus did rise from the dead."

Marcus was again caught off guard, just as he had been over and over again by the strange events that had taken place since Jesus was executed. He was almost getting used to the feeling. But he knew right from the moment the words left the sergeant's lips that he wanted no part in wherever this conversation was about to go. He was just beginning to rationalize his role in the exile of his dearest and closest friend. He was just starting to convince himself that Demetrius would not have been able to serve in the Roman army after they had put to death the man whom he believed had saved his son's life. He was talking himself into believing that he had really saved his friend's life, as Sejanus had suggested to him. Perhaps the enemy to their friendship was Jesus and whatever magic spell he had put on his friend. He therefore did not want to hear anything that would give the slightest credence to the notion that there was anything to his friend's crazy ideas about the man now missing in body. And yet he couldn't help asking: "What are you talking about, J. R.?" And this time there was far less affection in his voice than before. He felt his words had come out cruelly, so he tried to soften his tone: "What do you mean he could have risen from the dead? Are you telling me you now believe in ghosts?"

"Here is what I am telling you, my young and ambitious commander. There are two ways of looking at life. One is to say that what happens in this world, on this earth, is the be-all and end-all of existence: we live, we die, and everything about life and about death is found on the earth. That's what most of the high-level people in the empire believe. Even though we have our gods and the rest, they still only believe in what we can reach out and touch, or grab in our case. And you know I have a whole drawer full of medals to show that I was involved in much of the grabbing myself.

"But you know what? After thirty campaigns and six injuries and countless acts of violence on behalf of the empire, all of which I am still proud of, I think there may indeed be another point of view. And that is the idea that there is more to life and death than this [the sergeant tapped his foot against the floor]: that there is indeed a spiritual world, a heaven, another world beyond the limits of this empire or any empire, a world filled with mysteries that we can't even begin to comprehend. Maybe this thing with the body is one of those mysteries."

Marcus gave the old soldier a look of such puzzlement that it caused the old man to laugh. "If you're thinking of putting me up for a section eight a few months before I retire, commander, just hold on a bit and let me explain," he said with a chuckle.

Marcus smiled and said, "Go on, what are you driving at, sergeant?"

"I don't know myself really. I do know that in my old age, I'm questioning more things about the way I lived my life than I ever did before. When I was a young, gung-ho soldier, I believed in Rome, the empire, and duty to my emperor, period. Everything came second to my duty toward the empire. My grandfather was a soldier; my father was a soldier; my son is one now. Did I ever tell you that my great-grandfather served under Julius the First, the greatest Caesar of them all? We come from a long line of military people, and I am proud of having served the empire with distinction.

"But I also know that things are changing, and nothing can remain the same forever. And I believe that one thing that frightens many people, particularly of my generation in the empire, is the notion that perhaps there is more to life than this. Maybe there is more to everything than what we know, not only in the empire, but in the world. And maybe compared to what's out there [he spread his arms], or in here [he tapped his skull], the empire is not all that it's cracked up to be. Have you ever read Emerson, commander? He says that 'what lies behind us, and what lies before us are tiny matters compared to what lies within us.' That thought can be very frightening to people who have given up everything, including much that once lay within, for duty to a single higher cause, only to find out that maybe there really is something greater after all."

Marcus was flabbergasted at the way this old, hardened veteran was speaking. If he had said these things before another commander, the old soldier might have been brought up on charges of treason against the empire. Sejanus would hardly have stood for this kind of talk going on in his presence. After all, to a soldier, what could be greater than the sense of honor and duty to empire? Why was this crusty old man, who would still lop off the head of an enemy at a moment's notice, quoting people like Ralph Waldo Emerson? It did not add up.

The old man continued, "You know, the other day, I was reading my grandson's homework. He was doing a paper on the universe. Boy, I tell you, the things they teach these kids in school these days are amazing. He was writing about some galaxy known as M87, named after a Frenchman, Charles Messier, who counted comets from a tower in France in the 1700s. According to what the kid writes, M87 is approximately fifty million light-years away. I asked my grandson how far away that was and what a light-year is. Do you know what he told me? He said that they measure a light-year by the speed of light, which, according to what his teachers tell him, is 186,000 miles per second. Think about that, Marcus. Everything that we are doing in this case is by empire standards, which we believe is the greatest thing there is. And yet light can in one second be 186,000 miles away from you, me, the emperor, Jerusalem, everything.

"Well, anyway, according to this speed-of-light thing, if this M87 galaxy is fifty million light-years away, that means if you wanted to get to this galaxy, if you left overnight and traveled at 186,000 miles per second, it would take fifty million years to get there. And according to what he was taught, there are billions of galaxies way the hell out beyond that one. And you should hear what he says about things like black holes in spaces and other phenomena like that."

Marcus was hearing things that he did not like in the least. He hoped against hope that he wasn't getting it and tried desperately to make light of the old man's wisdom. "What does your grandson's high school paper on the universe have to do with any of this?" Marcus asked. "And when did you become a student of classic literature?" Marcus realized how snobbish he sounded, and hoped the old soldier would not take offense. He really did genuinely like the old man.

"Oh, you would be surprised how much I have read in my old age. Noncommissioned officers can read too you know. And what has my grandson's paper got to do with any of this? Only this, Marcus: I think there is stuff about life and death that we are only beginning to understand, and that stuff goes way beyond the confines of the empire or the material things of the world. But let's for now use standard empire procedures to look at what we do know. To begin, Jesus was supposed to have done things that no one could explain, but because we believe in our own powers of reason and deduction, we decided that if we couldn't explain it, it probably did not happen. And all of the witnesses that we questioned over the years who claimed to have either personally experienced some phenomenon or at least witnessed something, we automatically assumed were either lying or stupid.

"We know that something happened to one of our very own and finest officers, Antoni Demetrius, when he came in contact with the man. Yes, Marcus, I know about Demetrius. And you know that he was not a man who was given to flights of fancy, unlike an old about-to-retire war-horse like myself. We know that because what he said couldn't be disproved, the empire decided to ignore everything we know about him personally and declared him a threat to the empire who must be removed from the scene. He is now exiled. What else do we know? Well, we also know that Jesus was put to death, and having been around enough dead people in my time, I can tell you personally that he was as dead as a doorknob when they took him off of that cross.

"We know we put him in a tomb, covered the tomb with a rock that weighed almost a ton, and put two of our best men on the job guarding the entrance. They report feeling an earthquake that nobody else felt, that did no damage to anything in the immediate vicinity, but that, conveniently, moved away the stone. Some women went into the tomb, and the body of the dead man was gone. Let's examine it further, commander. The women reported talking to a stranger who, when the guards entered the tomb, was nowhere to be found. When questioned further the only thing they could remember about him was that his clothes seemed to shine very brightly. We know there is only one way up or down that mountain where the tomb is located, and within the short amount of time that all of this took place, there is no way that anyone on this earth could have physically snatched the body, hid it, and not been seen by anyone.

"Even if there were a bunch of people hiding around the perimeter of the grave site, how did they open the tomb without either one of the guards seeing or hearing a thing and manage to do it within minutes of the guards going to investigate the tremor they felt? I don't think any of it is possible, do you? So, once you eliminate the possible, you must begin to look at the impossible.

"And all I am saying is, considering that someone or something was able to make the sun and the moon and places in space that you and I or even the emperor couldn't get to in fifty million years traveling at 186,000 miles per second, who's to say what's really impossible? When you consider that with all the strength we boast about, we still can't make it rain one day, or stop one thunderstorm, even if we know it's coming, then who's to say what something or someone from another world could do in our puny little world if they decided to get involved? I'm not saying that I have any idea who or what that was. I don't know if I'm talking about gods or space creatures. But I am saying that maybe we're dealing with something we can't understand, a power that is bigger than we can comprehend. To deny that is to suggest that the empire is the ultimate power and glory, and we are the center of the universe. I know there are people in Rome who think like that, but I don't really know."

Marcus heard himself say under his breath, "the man had no eyes," and then looked up in hopes that J. R. didn't hear him.

"Excuse me, commander?" said the old soldier.

"Nothing J. R., I was just mumbling. Tell me," he continued, "why are you telling me all of this? Why are you talking all this supernatural, science fiction mumbo-jumbo?"

The old man paused for a while, and then, much to Marcus's surprise, he seemed to turn deadly serious. Marcus tried to remember if he had ever seen such a look on J. R.'s face. Even when he used to watch the old man bark out orders to the rest of the men, he always seemed to have a twinkle in his eye. Even though everybody knew that he was not a man to be trifled with, he still always seemed to have a look of affection in his eyes.

"I'll tell you, Marcus. I'm speaking like this because I'm wondering what's going to happen if we can't come up with some kind of logical explanation that will satisfy the politicians and the bureaucrats who believe that they are the ultimate power in the universe. What happens if we can't prove there was negligence on the part of our guards? You know what will happen? We will have to throw someone to the dogs so that we can prove that no other force could have played any role in this but the forces we control. And the best candidates for this sacrifice will be our two soldiers — men who have long careers in the army and who have never had a single blemish on their records. If they can chew up and spit out Demetrius, you know what they'll do to two enlisted men.

"Either you will be forced to give them our boys, or they will be forced to come after you. Because neither the emperor, Sejanus, the official council, nor anyone of the Roman brass can afford to believe for a moment that there is a greater power in the universe than themselves. Even though to be politically correct, they must say they believe in gods, there is not a one of them who could bear to believe that there is a power great enough to undo what the empire dared set in motion. None of those guys can afford to believe in some ultimate divine power, because even if they did, they, like Lucifer in *Paradise Lost,* would still believe it is better to reign in hell than to serve in heaven."

Marcus felt a twinge of pain at hearing the sound of Milton being used in this manner. He remembered how much comfort he himself had taken in the epic poem when traveling to see Demetrius that fateful evening.

"That's the real reason your friend had to be gotten out of the way," J. R. continued. "He was a threat to the empire all right, but not because he might not arrest some lawbreaker who claimed to be a follower of Jesus many years from now. He was much too dedicated to the empire to let that happen. He would have resigned first. It was because he might have dared suggest to someone that he was witness to a power greater than Rome's. He might let it slip to someone someday that he experienced something that would suggest that you can do things differently from the way we do them and, as a result, tap into a power greater than what we are all about. In short, maybe Jesus knew more about who he was than we do. I mean, Marcus, the man disappeared out of his tomb, and we have no way of explaining where he went."

Marcus felt he had been cursed by the gods for some transgression he could not remember. The whole thing started to take on a sense of the absurd that almost caused him to laugh out loud. In front of him was one of the oldest, toughest veterans in the army. Before now, he never would have thought that J. R. ever entertained thoughts of the supernatural, but now a stream of surprising, even revolutionary, notions was pouring from him. And J. R. was telling him this in order to explain that perhaps Jesus' body wasn't stolen — that perhaps, because of unknown forces in the heavens, it got up and walked away. Here is a cigar-smoking, whisky-drinking, thirty-year, battle-hardened veteran, who had more citations, medals, and commendations than anyone in the unit, telling him that perhaps the Jewish writings Marcus had once read about the "one who is to come" just might have been correct, and maybe Jesus was the guy they wrote about.

Marcus had just about all he could stand and was glad when he remembered that he was already late for his appointment with Gerry, who was waiting for him at the airport for their drink.

He got up rather slowly, and with a voice now empty of the anger and emotion that were there a little while ago, he spoke to the sergeant: "J. R., I want you to send the best people you have down to the tomb, and give it the works. I want prints, photos, the whole nine yards. Who knows: maybe you're right; maybe the only thing we'll find is a note from the heavens thanking us for starting a legend alongside another piece of paper that will be from the emperor. It will be my court-martial. Maybe you'll also find a note telling E.T. to phone home. Who the hell knows? Just go down there and find out what you can."

The warmth had returned to the old man's eyes, and he walked over to Marcus and held his arm: "We'll turn the place upside-down. I'll form a patrol and go over there myself. I'll get the kid from investigations to go over there as well. And listen, don't mind me. I don't know what the hell I'm talking about. Maybe I ought to move the date of my retirement up a few months. I think I'm just getting tired. Or maybe because I'm getting old, I need to believe in more of this mumbo-jumbo than I used to when I was a kid just starting out in the army. Funny, back then I felt invincible, even in the middle of all of those battles. Now that I'm getting old, I feel far more vulnerable just looking at the clock than when I was fighting the Parthians. You're a good soldier, Marcus, and I have always been proud of the way you've handled your command. I just don't want to see anything happen to either you or our two boys who guarded the tomb. Just remember one thing: if you have to look for answers, and you can't find them in the narrow halls of the empire, look elsewhere. That's all I'm telling you. Once the possible becomes impossible, then the impossible just might be the possible. After thirty years and a bad heart from all this smoking and drinking and killing, I can tell you this: there is more out there than what you see around you either in Judea or Rome or anywhere else. Call it religion, call it science, call it Fred, I don't care. But one day soldiering will end for you, just as it has for me, and just as it has for Antoni Demetrius. Don't wait until then to discover that there is more to life, and death, than what they teach you kids at the academy." Saying that, he smiled and left Marcus's office. Marcus could hear the old man barking orders as he gathered the detail that would march to the tomb and start the investigation into the mysterious disappearance of the body of Jesus. He knew, even before they left the building, what the report would say: they would find nothing.

When Marcus reached the airport he looked around for Gerry Simmons. He found her sitting at the bar: "Hi, Gerry, sorry I'm late."

"Marcus, I was beginning to think you weren't going to make it. Boy, am I sorry I'm being called back to the States so soon. It seems like this story just keeps popping up new surprises."

"That's true, Gerry; that indeed is the truth."

Gerry noticed that Marcus looked extremely tired. In the past he had always looked so bright and alert. He had always looked well suited to the title of commander. And yet today, he looked tired and worn. He didn't seem to have that imperial spark in his eye, that is, the spark of the conqueror, rather than the conquered.

For what seemed like a long time Marcus just sat there, looking out into space. This too did not seem like the Marcus that Gerry had known. It was true that Gerry never really knew Marcus well, but they had run into each other on more than one occasion, and when they did, they usually engaged each other in a lively conversation. They even had dinner together once or twice just so they could talk. Gerry was not sure why Marcus sat so quietly before her now.

"Marcus, are you all right?" Gerry finally asked.

"Pardon me? Oh, I'm sorry," Marcus replied. "This has been a long few days. It seems like months since this whole Jesus thing happened. Forgive me, I'm just tired. So, are you ready to get back to New York?"

"I guess so. I'm a little surprised that this story in the eyes of my editor seems to have already run its course. I would have thought that a story like the death of Jesus would have been on the front pages for weeks. I spoke to my editor earlier today, and he tells me that according to the latest polls, people are losing interest in this story rather quickly. It seems that stories surrounding the economy, and who committed the latest crime of the week, are what people are interested in. The execution of a man of character and greatness under suspicious circumstances, no offense, just isn't enough to stay on the people's minds that long. Jesus is fast becoming just another memory to a public whose attention span is getting smaller and smaller each day. I guess people are also becoming almost immune to death these days. They see so much of it. I suppose our industry has played a major role in death becoming a fact of life. Anyway, it will probably make a hell of a made-for-TV docudrama some day, but other than that it's fast becoming a footnote in history..."

Marcus still seemed far away. It was a look that totally perplexed Gerry. She had always found him so bright, so energetic. She also found him extremely attractive but never admitted to those feelings out loud, at least around him.

Finally Gerry asked, "So, Marcus, is there anymore news on the whereabouts of Jesus' body? Any clues on who took it? Boy, that's a bizarre twist. I'd sure like to cover that one."

"Nope, we're baffled by it. But I know we had better come up with some answers soon, or I might be on the next plane out of here right along with you. Do you think your editor can find me a job in New York?"

It was the first time Marcus had smiled since he arrived at the airport bar.

"I'm sure if we can't, the New York City Police Department could always use a capable investigator like yourself."

They both smiled, and it seemed to break the tension a little. Finally Marcus turned to Gerry and once again with a serious look asked, "Tell me, what do you think about what happened here?"

Gerry wasn't sure she understood the question. It seemed straightforward enough, but coming from Commander Marcus, it seemed to possess some hidden meaning. After all, here was the prefect of police asking a reporter what she thought had happened in his own town.

The Commander Marcus she knew was not in the habit of asking reporters for opinions. He after all worked for the empire, and empire folks seldom, if ever, admitted that there was anything they did not know.

"Well, Marcus, I'm sure you know more about what happened here than I do. It seems as though you guys were used by the Sanhedrin to do their dirty work. I believe they wanted Jesus out of the way, permanently. They felt they needed him eliminated, and according to my sources, they used illegal means to do it. I'm sure I'm not telling you anything you don't already know. I know you well enough to know that you must have conducted a thorough investigation. I believe..."

"Do you think he rose from the dead?" asked Marcus.

"Excuse me?"

I said, "Do you think he rose from the dead?"

"Marcus, did you get a head start on the drinking before you got here? What do you mean do I think he rose from the dead? That doesn't sound like the empire's finest soldier in the region talking. Why did you ask that?"

"Because I'm tired, and I don't have a clue as to where his body went. Gerry, I want to ask you some questions strictly off the record. I feel somewhat free to ask you this stuff because I know that you are about to get on a plane and go off to another world, a world you have assured me is already turning this into old news. I want you to be honest with me. It's important."

Gerry was again surprised at Marcus's seriousness. She had envisioned this little get together as a farewell drink, and perhaps indulging in a little intellectual tête-à-tête about Jesus and the empire. She was not prepared for his serious tone.

"Sure, Marcus, you know me. If it's off the record, then it is truly off the record."

"Tell me what you thought of the so-called miracles Jesus performed."

"I don't know," answered Gerry. "I always reported them as being rumors. I never saw any performed in my presence, and I never interviewed anyone who claimed to have been cured by him. So they were precisely that to me, just rumors."

"Did you believe Jesus was ever anymore than just a man?"

"Marcus, are you feeling all right? Why on earth would you ask me something like that? He's dead isn't he? No matter what you or anyone else said about him, when it came to the ultimate test, he failed just like everyone else. When you killed him, he died."

Marcus felt himself at a crossroad of sorts. He could admit to himself for the first time that he had some real questions, raised in part by Demetrius's repeated claims that "the man had no eyes," or he could deny what he was feeling and push it all down deep somewhere and pray to the gods that all would somehow be well again.

He wanted desperately to say to Gerry, "Yeah? When we killed him he died? Then where the hell is the body? We had men covering that tomb, and no one could get either in or out. And yet Jesus managed to escape. What did he do, come back as Houdini?"

He wanted to grab Gerry and say to her, "His healings were all rumors? Yeah? Well, let me tell you something. My closest friend in the whole goddamned world, who, by the way, I just happen to have stabbed in the back in the name of 'duty,' claims that Jesus not only cured a man whom he knew was blind but then went and cured his own dying son as well. And I have to believe him because he has never lied to me. He was a man absolutely committed to his word. So explain that to me."

He wanted to say that his governor told him that Jesus wanted to die and that no one — even members of the Roman upper echelon — could seem to prevent it, that everyone seemed to play right into the hands of something or someone beyond their control.

He wanted to grab Gerry and weep, literally weep, and tell her not only that had he lost his best friend but also that he had lost a huge part of his reason for existing. Because along with his friend, something else had been snatched away from him — his belief in the absolute authoritative power and virtue of the state. He couldn't fully sort out just what was happening to his "values," but for the first time he admitted to himself that his fundamental belief in the omnipotence of Rome was shaken.

He felt that once again he was about to be inflicted with some strange malady that sickened his spirit and will. Yet he felt he dared not admit out loud to a crack in the once unquestionable imperial code of duty and honor. Even as those powerful words, "duty and honor," went through his mind, they were translated into thoughts of duty without reason or dying without honor. With all that was happening inside of him, to Gerry he still felt compelled to choose another road, the road again of self-denial. This emotional conflict over duty versus conscience had nothing to do with simple patriotic duty to one's country in and of itself. In his heart he knew that. This feeling that was arousing such pathos within him had more to do with what he now saw as blind duty and honor paid for by someone else's blood. Yet just as he had in that room with his emperor, the day he felt as though he had betrayed Demetrius, he was about to say one thing even though his mind and heart screamed for him to say something else. He was about to tell Gerry that he was only joking, that these questions he was struggling with were only in his mind because he hadn't had enough sleep. He was going to say anything but the truth of his feelings. It was as if something inside kept telling him that as long as he did not mention his fears out loud, they would still remain only musings. But if he dared say what was in his heart, all of his worst nightmares would come true.

He was about to speak when he heard himself paged on the intercom: "Commander Marcus, please pick up the nearest white courtesy phone for an urgent message."

Marcus excused himself and walked over to the nearest phone and identified himself. He did not recognize the voice on the other end, but the voice told him to report back immediately to the garrison.

"I have to go," Marcus told Gerry when he returned. "Oh, and listen, I was only pulling your leg about all that stuff regarding Jesus. Have a safe trip back to the States."

Before Gerry could say much in response, Marcus embraced her, turned, and headed for the door.

Gerry stood, staring dumbfoundedly as the retreating figure. In all the years she had known him, Marcus had never shown this much emotion about anything in public. Something had happened, and it undoubtedly had to do with Jesus' death and the subsequent investigation. And she believed that anything that could have this kind of effect on the coolest professional soldier she had ever met must surely have one hell of a news story behind it.

Even though she had told Jim Pratt about the missing body, he had still ordered her home. "Mary Beth can handle things from this point," he told her. "Besides, like I said, this story is winding down, and your tour of the Middle East has ended, remember?"

She considered calling Jim and trying to convince him to let her stay. She thought of what she'd say: "That cool, aloof, unflappable Marcus, who barely ever shook my hand in the past, just embraced me in the airport bar in front of everyone and looked to me like he was on the verge of fighting back tears. I'm telling you, something really intense has happened here that goes way beyond the normal news that we cover. This is the story behind the story that I want to stay and investigate."

Yet she knew that a few weird questions and an embrace from Marcus were not exactly hard evidence that something big was brewing, and she figured it would sound to Jim like she was just looking for an excuse to stay in Judea longer than the story she was sent to cover warranted. So she turned and headed for her gate. She had the feeling she would never really know just what almost happened here, for in a short while she would be on a plane heading home.

She knew that in less than a day she would be back in her New York apartment where once again she would lie on her bed looking at the ceiling. There she would continue to marvel at the wild and wonderful Middle East as she prepared for her life back in the States. "What a country," she would say again with a sigh. "I wonder if we will ever know what happened to Jesus' body."

Meanwhile, Marcus headed back toward the garrison. He refused to think of what might be waiting for him when he got back. He decided to just go and see what was there.

When he walked in, he was met with cheers from a few of the soldiers. A stranger walked up to him, a soldier whom he did not recognize, but who held the same rank as himself.

Marcus asked what was going on.

When the soldier spoke, Marcus recognized the voice he had heard on the phone: "Commander, congratulations. I am your replacement. You, sir, have been promoted to the rank of legion commander and are to report to Rome immediately."

Once again Marcus was surprised. He wasn't quite sure just what to make of what he had just heard. He was being promoted and sent to Rome? "Why?" he wondered. He had of course dreamed of this moment, but he never dreamed that when he did get promoted his first reaction would be to question it.

Marcus turned to the soldiers in the room and said, "Thank you, gentleman, now kindly return to your post." He then turned to the commander and said, "Would you please step into my, pardon me, your, office, commander?"

They went inside the small office that until a few hours ago had belonged to Marcus. He did not have a lot of personal mementos, but he was astonished to see the few he had already put into a box, and a few of the new man's personal effects up on the walls and on the desk.

"Why am I being promoted? What about the missing body of Jesus? Doesn't Rome want me to start a detailed investigation into what happened?"

"You are not to concern yourself with any of this Jesus investigation any longer, Legion Commander Marcus. You have done your bit for the empire here in Judea. You are headed for bigger and better things. It is rumored that your call for promotion came from the highest levels of government. You are in line for great things, sir. My guess is that you will be a general in a matter of a year or so."

"And what is my assignment going to be in Rome, do you have any idea, commander?"

"No sir. I was just told to report here for duty and to hand deliver your orders to report back to Rome. You are to report there at 0800 hours Wednesday."

"Wednesday, that's the day after tomorrow! Why the rush?"

"I don't know, sir. But you know what they say, 'Ours is not to reason why. . . .' "

"Ours is but to do or die," finished Marcus. Marcus knew the slogan well, but for the first time the definition of dying took on a whole new meaning for him. He had always understood the "dying" in that slogan to be a sword through the chest for the sake of the empire, and for that he was always willing to sacrifice his life. But he felt another kind of death happening inside of him now, and he wasn't sure the empire or anything else was truly worth this kind of death.

He managed to thank the commander and assured him that he would be out of his command as soon as possible. He gathered his things and slipped out the backdoor. He was not in the mood for long good-byes, plus he felt strange about this "promotion." He could not figure it out, but for some reason he felt it was a promotion without honor. He never believed until now that it was possible to get a promotion without honor in the empire — unless you were someone like Pilate, who got where he was because of who he knew. "Is this now happening to me?" he asked himself. "Am I now getting promoted because of 'connections'? And what is this a promotion to?" His orders said only that he was to report to the division headquarters in Rome and that he was now a legion commander.

He looked back to headquarters, and for the first time since arriving in Judea, he wished he wasn't leaving. "Now there's a thought," he said to himself. From the moment he had set foot in Judea, he had looked forward to the day when he would be promoted and assigned somewhere else. Now he was promoted and heading for glorious Rome, and yet he was more empty inside than he had ever felt. He thought of something he had once seen scribbled on a wall. He had always thought that it must have been written by someone going through a hard time. Somehow, it had both attracted and confused him. It read:

I *wish* I was,
what I was,
when I *wished* I was,
what I am *now.*

As Marcus prepared to go home and pack his few remaining things, he thought of the first man he ever talked to who claimed to have had an encounter with Jesus. The man was brought in for questioning on some minor charge, but while he was in the garrison, someone said that he had been seen in the company of this hot new preacher from Galilee they had been alerted about, the Hebrew called Jesus. When questioned about this, the man said that he was not himself a follower of Jesus but that he fancied himself a student of human behavior. He claimed to have followed Jesus one day mainly to study the people who came to see him. (It was guessed by those in the garrison that he really followed the crowds to pick pockets.) He said that he was very impressed by one consistent factor when people came into Jesus' presence. He said people either adored him or despised him. They either fell on their knees in adoration or stomped away calling him everything but a gentleman. But one thing was for sure: everyone who met him face-to-face was in some way changed by the experience.

Marcus knew this was true of Demetrius, Pilate, Caiaphas, and Herod: all had been changed by their encounters with Jesus. The difference, however, was that as he rode off into a future now filled with questions about a life he had never questioned before, he realized that he too had been changed by this man. And he had never even met him face-to-face.